ERLE STANLEY GARDNER

- Cited by the *Guinness Book of World Records* as the #1 bestselling writer of all time!

- Author of more than 150 clever, authentic, and sophisticated mystery novels!

- Creator of the amazing Perry Mason, the savvy Della Street, and dynamite detective Paul Drake!

- THE ONLY AUTHOR WHO OUTSELLS AGATHA CHRISTIE, HAROLD ROBBINS, BARBARA CARTLAND, AND LOUIS L'AMOUR *COMBINED*!

Why?

Because he writes the best, most fascinating whodunits of all!

You'll want to read every one of them, from **BALLANTINE BOOKS**

The Case of the
Half-Wakened Wife

Erle Stanley Gardner

BALLANTINE BOOKS • NEW YORK

ISBN 0-345-37147-X

This edition published by arrangement with William Morrow and
Company.

Manufactured in the United States of America

First Ballantine Books Edition: April 1991

Cast of Characters

Chapter 1

At five minutes before three in the afternoon Jane Keller entered the bank and took her place at the end of the line in front of the window marked PAYING AND RECEIVING J-M.

As though her entrance had been an anticipated signal, the man in the dark blue pin stripe, single breasted suit took from his breast pocket a leather wallet, worn shiny from much use. Slowly he walked toward the line where Jane was standing.

Jane Keller frowned abstractedly at the clock on the far wall. It was easier for her pinched face to adjust itself to an expression of worried futility than into a smile. The line before the teller's window shuffled slowly forward. Jane Keller kept pace with it, from time to time looking up at the clock in the manner of one who must necessarily devote an increasing amount of mental energy to rearranging the pattern of life, and finds the responsibility too great a strain.

The man in the blue pin stripe moved up.

He was a shrewd-faced chap in his early forties, nervously wide-awake. A keen student of character would have classified the man as a savage, vicious little fighter who would never stand up in an aggressive, toe-to-toe slugging match, but would wait for the opportunity he wanted, then be quick to seize the advantage. If his opponent went down, the man would ruthlessly exterminate him. If he didn't, the man would run for cover—a crooked little opportunist who gave himself every advantage, specializing in gouging and kicking below the belt.

He moved up to stand beside Jane Keller in the line. The stubby fingers of his left hand suddenly shoved five one-hundred-dollar bills into Jane Keller's hand. "Here you are, Mrs. Keller."

1

Jane Keller's fingers automatically closed on the money. Then she looked down at it with the bewildered expression of one emerging from a sleep that has been troubled by some annoying dream. She turned her eyes to the face of the man in the dark suit.

The man behind Jane Keller growled, "You can't double up this way. Get back behind me at the end of the line."

Jane Keller's voice had once been well modulated; now it was getting slightly harsh as she found it necessary to cope with more and more annoying factors in life. "What's this?" she asked. "Who are you?"

The man was obviously reciting by rote. "I'm the agent for Scott Shelby. This is five months' deferred drilling payments under our oil lease on your property. Sign this receipt. Right here on the dotted line. Here's a pen."

He whipped a receipt book from his pocket, snapped back the cover and held the blanks where Jane Keller could see them.

"But . . . Why! . . . Mr. Shelby doesn't have any interest. . . . He has abandoned the property."

"Oh, no."

"He certainly has! He hasn't done anything with it for months."

"I'm making the payment covering deferred drilling. A hundred dollars a month. Isn't that right?"

"Why, yes. That's the rate. But . . . he had to pay it *every month* if he wanted to hold the property."

"Oh, no." The man was smiling now and his voice was almost patronizing as he recited glibly, "The lease provided that he must pay at that rate every month to keep his drilling rights. But another paragraph provided that any covenant of *any* sort in which either party has been in default can be fully performed by the party obligated, at any time within six months, unless in the meantime the lease has been terminated by written notice. You'd better read your lease."

The line moved forward. Automatically Jane Keller moved forward with it. The man behind Jane Keller said to Jane, "Don't take it."

2

The man in the blue pin stripe suit said, "I want a receipt."

"But I can't . . . I haven't . . . I don't own it anymore; I've sold it."

"*Sold* it?"

"Yes."

"When?"

"Why, the papers were signed two weeks ago."

"Who bought it?"

"Parker Benton."

"Well, Mr. Shelby doesn't know anything about that and he doesn't care. This is five months' back rent at one hundred dollars a month—deferred drilling payments. Our lease is with *you*. You can square things with the other people."

"I won't accept it."

"Why?"

"I've told you why. Because I've sold the property."

"Who did you say had bought it?"

"Mr. Parker Benton."

"What's his address?"

"The Knickerbocker Building."

Almost reluctantly the man in the blue pin stripe suit took back the five hundred dollars, said to the man standing in line just behind Jane Keller, "Would you mind giving me your card—I may need a witness."

The man scowled, said, "It's none of *my* business. Quit picking on a woman."

The line moved up, paused, moved again.

"Just a card," the man insisted. "All I want is your name and address."

The last man in the line hesitated a moment then produced a card.

The woman in front of Jane Keller picked up the money which the assistant cashier shoved through the wicket. Jane moved into position before the window. An officer of the bank appeared, summoned by the guard, and, sizing up the faces of the three people who clustered about the window, asked, "What's the trouble?"

3

Jane Keller said, "I wanted to make a deposit. This gentleman has just given me five hundred dollars."

"And you want to deposit it?"

"No, I gave it back to him. I don't want to deposit that money. This is money of my own."

"What's the trouble?"

The man in the blue suit said affably, "No trouble at all. I just want to . . ."

"Let Mrs. Keller tell it," the banker said sharply.

Jane Keller cleared her throat nervously. "I sold the island to Mr. Parker Benton and . . ."

"I know," the banker said. "The deal went through the bank. What about it?"

"My brother-in-law and I thought the oil lease was all finished."

"It was."

"But this gentleman claims it isn't."

The cold blue eyes of the banker shifted to the face of the stocky man, a face that was now hiding behind the mask of an affable grin.

"I'm representing Mr. Shelby," the man said, cheerfully. "I'm supposed to make a payment of five hundred dollars covering five months' payment for deferred drilling. The lease has a clause that any default doesn't invalidate the lease provided performance is made within six months, unless the lease has been canceled by written notice in the meantime."

"Where's the five hundred dollars?" the banker asked.

"I gave it back to him," Jane Keller said.

With the manner of one showing a bank's customer the protection afforded by the institution's impregnable righteousness, the official said, "Then that seems to terminate the matter. Get out."

"You know this lady?" the man asked.

"Certainly I know Mrs. Keller."

"And the gentleman here behind her?"

"Certainly."

The grin broadened into a smirk. "Thank you. I guess that's all. Remember about the five hundred bucks—all of you."

He melted away into the closing-hour crowd of the bank. Jane Keller's hand was shaking so that the tremor was noticeable as she held her money through the counter. "Oh dear, I'm so nervous."

"You needn't be," the banker smiled at her. "Those oil people are always trying to pull fast ones."

"But do you suppose there *is* such a clause in the lease?"

The smile was reassuring. "I wouldn't pay too much attention to it; but if you're worried, you might consult an attorney. . . . The bank can recommend one in case you'd like a lawyer. . . . Let's see, this deposit is three hundred and ninety-six dollars and fifty cents." He pushed it through the wicket to the teller. "There you are, Mrs. Keller. Thank you ever so much. Do you want us to see about a lawyer?"

"No thank you. I . . . I'll call my brother-in-law. He'll know what to do."

She snapped her purse shut and moved away from the window.

Chapter 2

Lawton Keller answered the telephone and Jane was relieved to hear his voice on the wire. There was something about Lawton's voice that always reassured her, probably its ringing note of confidence.

During his lifetime, Jane's husband, Gregory, had never cared greatly for Lawton; but Jane had put it down to brotherly jealousy. Lawton was the older; he had a smooth, easy assurance, a graceful, extemporaneous charm of manner. Gregory, on the other hand, had been reticent, inarticulate, sensitive, a man who modestly refrained from tooting his own horn and didn't like to hear others talk about themselves.

After Gregory's death, Lawton had taken Jane under his wing, advising her what to do with the insurance money, always offering alibis for their losses, which were invariably due to "conditions," and taking great credit to himself for their profits.

When Lawton answered the phone, Jane exclaimed with relief, "Oh Lawton, I'm so glad you're there!"

"What's the matter, Jane? You sound worried."

"I am."

"Where are you?"

"At the bank—in the phone booth."

"The bank's closed, isn't it? It's after three—or is it?"

"Yes. They're just closing it, the outer doors."

"Make your deposit all right?"

"Yes."

"What's the matter?"

"Lawton, you remember that oil lease on the island?"

"It wasn't exactly a lease," Lawton said judicially. "I consider it more an option for a lease. However, it's all over now."

"No, it isn't. A man who is the representative of Mr. Shelby caught me at the bank."

"At the bank?"

"Yes."

"How did he know you were going to be there?"

"I don't know."

"What did he want?"

"He wanted to pay me five hundred dollars."

"For what?"

"To keep the lease alive."

Lawton Keller's voice showed excitement. "Don't take it, Jane. Don't touch a . . ."

"I didn't, Lawton. I gave it right back to him."

"Gave it *back* to him," Lawton all but shouted. "You mean you *took* it?"

"Well I just sort of held it. He shoved the money into my hands, of course, well naturally . . . But I handed it right back."

"You shouldn't have ever touched it in the first place. What did you tell him?"

"I told him I couldn't take it, that the lease had expired."

"That's right. Don't tell him anything about the sale."

"Oh, but I did."

Lawton Keller's voice showed irritated impatience. "Don't tell *all* you know."

"Well, I thought . . . I thought he was entitled to an explanation."

"You didn't tell him the name of the person who is buying it, did you?"

"Why . . . why, yes. Shouldn't I have done it, Lawton?"

Lawton groaned over the telephone. "Jane, *why* didn't you call me?"

"There wasn't time. I'm calling you now."

"Well there's nothing you can do now. Come and see me right away. I'll wait here."

"All right. I have to go by and see Martha first."

"What does Martha want now?" Lawton Keller's voice was cold.

"Why, she doesn't want anything, Lawton, except—well,

7

you know, after all, she's my sister. I want to see how Margie is getting along."

"Well, cut it short and then get in touch with me. Jane, here's something you'd better do."

"What?"

"While you're there at the bank draw out every cent in your account."

"But why should I do that?"

"It's just a hunch. They might try to tie up your bank account."

"Who?"

"Shelby."

"But I don't see how he could."

"Never mind about that. You go over and draw out all your money."

"But the bank's closed."

"Just the front door. You're in there, and you can find someone to wait on you. Draw out every cent you've got. How much is it?"

"I don't know. Something over two thousand dollars."

"All right. Draw it out, every penny of it. Get it in the form of cash and carry it with you."

"Well . . . all right, if you say so, Lawton . . . if you think it's best."

"I think it's best, Jane, and don't talk with anyone else. Don't tell anyone about it."

"All right, Lawton."

"And then get in touch with me just as soon as you can get away from Martha."

"Yes, Lawton."

"Don't let Martha know you've got any money with you," he warned, and hung up.

Chapter 3

Jane Keller took a streetcar to South Omena Avenue, walked two blocks to a three story brick apartment house and pressed the bell marked "Manager."

After some five seconds the electric buzzer threw back the latch and Jane Keller entered an ornamental lobby which was as stiff as a nurse's starched uniform. She climbed half a dozen stairs to a corridor and stopped in front of the first door on the left, which was marked MANAGER, and below that in a little container a card bearing the words *Mrs. Martha Stanhope*.

Jane Keller tapped nervously on the door and Martha opened it.

Martha was Jane Keller's older sister. In her early forties, she was inclined to put on weight but still had enough pride in her personal appearance to combat the tendency. Her husband had died fifteen years earlier and she had never remarried. The necessity of making a living for herself and her daughter Marjorie had kept her watchfully eager to grasp every opportunity which might come her way. This eager, objective selfishness had become a dominant trait in her character. Her eyes were bright, alert, and greedy. Even when she smiled, her eyes remained watchful.

"Oh, hello, Jane. I didn't know it was you. I was dressing and thought it was someone looking for an apartment. You can put up a sign NO VACANCIES and still they come, asking questions about whether someone isn't going to leave, or if you don't know of some place . . . Come in and sit down. Margie will be in in a minute."

Jane followed Martha into the over-furnished apartment, sank down in a chair, placed her hands on her lap and smiled a wan, vague smile.

"What's the matter? You look all in," Martha said.

"Well, I . . . I've just had a jolt."

Martha Stanhope's eyes were hard and probing. "What sort of a jolt?" she asked, running the words together in a quick staccato of inquiry.

"I was at the bank."

"Yes, go on."

"A man tried to give me five hundred dollars."

"Oh," Martha said, and smiled. Relief relaxed the tension of her manner. She ceased to stand rigidly poised in front of her sister and moved easily over to a little locker, brought out a bottle of brandy and two glasses. "A little drink will do you good."

"Yes, I . . . I suppose so . . . not much, Martha."

Martha Stanhope poured out two stiff slugs of the brandy. "So you're upset because someone paid you five hundred dollars?"

"It was on that oil lease."

"What oil lease?"

"On the island."

"Oh, that," her sister said scornfully. "That was one of those deals Lawton promoted . . . I thought it was all over."

"I thought so too but I guess it isn't. The lease had some funny provision in it . . . that's what the man told me."

"Jane Keller, *will* you tell me what you're talking about?"

"Well, Mr. Shelby seems to think he can reinstate the lease by paying five hundred dollars."

"Go on," Martha snapped. "What would happen then?"

"Well, that's what I don't know."

Martha had been carrying the two glasses of brandy over toward Jane's chair. Now she stopped, her alert eyes wide with apprehension. "You mean something may happen to the sale?"

"I don't know."

Martha inhaled audibly, walked over to hand Jane one of the glasses of brandy. "Drink that," she said, and without waiting to sit down tossed off her own glass of brandy at a single gesture.

Jane Keller sipped the brandy, coughed, wiped her lips

with the handkerchief she was holding in her left hand, and once more smiled that vague somewhat wan smile.

Martha rattled out swiftly indignant words. "Now you listen to me, Jane Keller. Don't depend on Lawton Keller. He isn't worth a fig when it comes to real business. He's just a glib talker, who could never get to first base with a *man*. He makes his living out of impressing women. You know Gregory never had any use for him."

"Oh, I wouldn't say that."

"Well, *I* would. Two years ago you had forty thousand dollars in insurance money. How much of it have you got left?"

"Well, you can't blame the things that happened on Lawton. Good heavens, Martha, he isn't running the world!"

"You'd think he was to hear him talk. I'll bet he's lost *all* of that money for you. The island's all you have left."

"I should have sold the island earlier," Jane said. "The trouble with Lawton was he didn't have enough capital to really back his judgment. We had to play things on kind of a shoestring basis . . ."

"A shoestring basis of forty thousand dollars!" Martha Stanhope snorted. "If he'd had more capital, he'd have been just that much farther in the red . . . Now I don't know how Margie's going to take this. You told her she could count on five thousand dollars when that sale went through. She's marrying that discharged soldier and they're going to buy that grocery business. The papers on that are all signed and . . ."

"I know," Jane said wearily, "but don't worry about it now, Martha. It won't stop the sale."

"What makes you think it won't?"

"Lawton tells me they're just about ready to close the escrow. He wouldn't doubt but what the deal might go through tomorrow."

Metal clicked against metal as a latchkey was fitted to the door of the apartment.

Martha Stanhope said hastily, "That's Margie now."

"We won't say a word," Jane warned.

"Yes we will. You've got to tell her," Martha said.

11

"Well," Jane observed, taking a hasty sip of her brandy, "I don't know what there is to tell."

The door opened. Marjorie Stanhope included her mother and her aunt in her greeting, said, "What isn't there to tell?"

She was twenty-one and not particularly good-looking. Her figure had never curved out. There was a sallow appearance about her skin, and her black hair became stringy whenever she neglected weekly finger waves. Her eyes, wide and dark, could have made the face beautiful if there had been any animation in the girl's manner. There was none. The face seldom had expression, and when it did change there was an utter lack of spontaneity about it. As Martha had complained on occasion, "She sits and looks at you and just looks and looks, and you haven't the faintest idea of what she's thinking."

"Well," Marjorie asked, walking with characteristic, loose-jointed ease toward the closet, "what isn't there to tell?"

She let her soft tweed coat slide back down her arms, sniffed, and said, "Who has the alcoholic halitosis?"

"We both have, dear," her mother said. "There's the brandy over there on the sideboard. Have a drink."

Margie took off her hat, ran her fingers around the edges of her hair, poured herself a drink, and said, "What gives?"

"Your Aunt Jane's in trouble, dear."

"Lawton?" Margie asked, raising the brandy glass to the light.

"No, dear. It's trouble over an oil lease. It may affect the sale of the island property."

Margie had started to drink. Abruptly her hand became motionless. Then she lowered the glass, but looked neither at her mother nor at her Aunt Jane.

After a moment of strained silence she said, "All right, go on."

It was Jane Keller who started speaking rapidly. "It won't make any difference, Margie. Things are going to be all right; it's just a technicality that's bobbed up. I don't even know there's going to be any trouble about the sale. Lawton thinks the deal will go through escrow within the next day or two."

12

Margie paid no attention to the rapid words of reassurance. She said over her shoulder, "I suppose that means the loan's off. I'll tell Frank."

Both her mother and Aunt Jane started talking at once. "Don't do anything like that," Jane said almost sharply.

"It isn't that serious, dear," Martha Stanhope soothed.

Margie turned then to look at her mother. "Not that serious? Here's Frank Bomar, one leg shot away. He's not looking for charity, but wanting to build up a business. He's proud. He wouldn't marry me unless he had some way of making a living. We've signed the papers on this grocery store and put up our money. The rest was promised for next week. We're going to get married Saturday. Everything is contingent on this loan from Aunt Jane. I didn't ask for it; she volunteered it. Okay, suppose something happens to it. We lose the store. We lose Frank's two thousand. What does it do to Frank? I guess you people don't know what it means to be changed overnight from a perfect specimen of physical manhood to a cripple. I guess you don't know what it means to come back to a country that you've been fighting for that takes it all as matter-of-course where . . ."

She broke off abruptly, twisted her somewhat thin shoulders, raised the brandy glass to her lips, tilted her head back, and took the brandy neat in one swift gulp, put the empty glass down on the table, said to her mother, "Okay, where do we go from here?" and walked out of the room.

There was nothing sulky, nothing dramatic in her manner; she walked with calm, loose-jointed deliberation, closed the door softly behind her.

Jane glanced helplessly at her sister. "I'm sorry."

Martha said nothing.

"I presume she's gone to her bedroom to have a good cry," Jane said.

Martha Stanhope said, "She won't be crying. She'll sit down in a chair, fasten her eyes on the wall and simply sit there."

"Thinking?" Jane asked.

"I suppose so. . . . But you'll never know what she's thinking about. Speak to her and she'll answer just as calmly

13

and patiently as though there wasn't a thing wrong. Honestly, Jane, I just don't know what goes on in that girl's mind. I wish she'd cry or scream or have a tantrum or get angry or something. But she just shuts herself up inside of herself and you don't have the faintest idea what she's thinking.''

''Well, Lawton wants me to get over there right away. He . . .''

Martha Stanhope walked over to the coat closet, took out her hat and coat.

''Where are you going, Martha?''

''I'm going with you.''

''To Lawton? He . . .''

''Lawton nothing,'' Martha Stanhope said sarcastically, ''he's the one who got you into this, signing that oil lease. . . . That's when you *should* have seen a lawyer, before you signed it. I'm going to tell Margie where we're going.''

''Where *are* we going?'' Jane asked.

Martha said, ''We're going to see Perry Mason. . . . Wait a second. I'll tell Margie.''

She tapped at the door of Marjorie's bedroom, hesitated a moment, stepped inside, then softly closed the door.

It was nearly a minute later that she emerged, closed the door and said, ''All right, Jane, let's go.''

''What was she doing?'' Jane Keller asked.

''Sitting in a chair, looking out the window,'' Martha Stanhope said in a flat, expressionless voice.

Chapter 4

Martha Stanhope determinedly pushed open the door marked PERRY MASON, *Attorney at Law*, ENTRANCE, then held the door for Jane Keller, who was lagging somewhat dubiously behind.

The receptionist looked up from the switchboard, smiled, said, "Good afternoon."

"Is Mr. Mason in?"

The receptionist said, "Mr. Mason has left for the evening."

"Oh dear . . . Isn't there some way I could see him?"

"I'll let you talk with his secretary, Della Street."

"Please do."

The receptionist plugged in a line, said, "Miss Street, there are two women here who seem very anxious to see Mr. Mason. Could you . . . Thanks."

She pulled out the plug, smiled once more at the women, said, "Please be seated. Mr. Mason's personal secretary will be here in a moment."

The women sat down, exchanged glances. Jane Keller seemed definitely apprehensive as to whether what she was doing would meet with Lawton Keller's approval.

Martha Stanhope, her chin up, lips tight, met her sister's eyes with a glance that was almost hypnotic in its firm determination.

"Don't you think, Martha, that while we're waiting I could call Lawton and . . ."

"No."

Jane sighed, said dubiously, "Well . . . of course . . ."

The door that was marked PRIVATE opened and Della Street, trim, efficient, was smiling at them. "I'm sorry. Mr. Mason has left for the evening. But, if you'll give me your

15

names and tell me generally what you wanted to see him about . . ."

Martha Stanhope did the talking and Della Street made notes, getting the names, the addresses and the nature of their business.

When Martha had finished speaking, Della frowned down at her shorthand notes, said, "Mr. Mason won't be in any more this evening but Mr. Jackson is here."

"Who's Mr. Jackson?"

"He's an assistant to Mr. Mason . . . Frankly, Mr. Mason doesn't do very much except important cases in court and . . ."

"I know," Jane Keller said. "I didn't *think* he'd be interested."

"But," Della Street went on, "he's always interested in cases where there is an apparent injustice. I think you'd better talk with Mr. Jackson. It's after five now and you won't find any other lawyers in their offices, I'm afraid."

"We'll talk with him," Martha Stanhope said grimly.

"This way please," Della Street said.

Jackson was a legally erudite man who was never so happy as when his nose was buried in a law book, searching for some precedent which would give him a case that was "on all fours."

He seldom left the office before six or six-thirty, and then tore himself away from his law books with obvious reluctance, a man with a vast memory, studious habits and a meticulously formal type of mind. His eyes seemed more at home resting on the printed pages of his books than on the human faces of his clients.

Jackson at one time confessed to Perry Mason, "My greatest trouble is translating the problems of my clients into the proper legal category. Once I get them definitely fixed, however, I never have any trouble. I just keep on searching until I find a precedent. But it's hard for me to translate life into law."

The lower part of Jackson's face showed a certain nervous tension. His nose was long and thin. The taut mouth turned down slightly at the corners, and there were deep calipers stretching down from the nostrils. There was no tension, however, about the upper part of his head where the high forehead was placid in its tranquillity, the calm of absolute knowledge.

Jackson was, in his patient way, a genius at uncovering the exact needle he wanted from the haystack of legal decisions.

Naturally a cautious individual on his own account, he never ventured to pilot his clients through uncharted paths in the legal domain. Once Jackson had translated the problem of a client into its proper legal category, he delved into the books until he found where a similar case had gone to a court of last resort. Thereafter, unless the client impatiently took the bit in his teeth, he was never permitted to make a move which had not previously been made by some other litigant, duly taken to court, and thereafter adjudicated by some appellate tribunal.

So long as Jackson was following in the footsteps of some previous litigant he was crisp, decisive, and sure of himself. But if it ever became necessary for his feet to leave the charted legal paths and explore new realms, the man froze to a standstill.

When Jackson had married, he had proposed to an attractive widow some five years his senior, but quite definitely a widow. As Perry Mason had pointed out to Della Street, even in matrimonial affairs, Jackson was afraid to blaze a trail on his own initiative.

Jackson sat thoughtfully silent as he listened to Jane Keller's story, interspersed from time to time with comments from Martha Stanhope.

"Do you have a copy of this printed oil lease?" he asked.

"No, I haven't," Jane said. "My brother-in-law, Lawton, has it."

"I am very much interested in the exact wording of that provision," Jackson said.

Martha Stanhope said, "It wouldn't take her over half an hour or three quarters of an hour at the most to go out and get it."

Jackson looked at his watch. "I'm afraid that would be

17

pretty late. There's nothing that can be done tonight, in any event. However," he added somewhat wistfully, "I *would* like to get the facts clear in my own mind so that I could make a quick search and see if a similar provision hasn't been adjudicated somewhere. A printed contract indicates a definite possibility that an exactly identical provision has been construed by some court in some state."

"How would you go about finding that?" Martha asked.

Jackson waved his hand towards the law library. "The cases decided by courts of last resort in all of the states are printed and bound," he said. "We have them."

"And you can find a case like that?"

"Oh yes," Jackson said smiling reassuringly, "I can find it . . . I can nearly always find a case in point. It's just a question of knowing *where* to look and *how* to look, and then staying with it long enough."

"Well, Jane could go out. We might be able to get a cab. . . ."

"I could telephone Lawton," Jane said, "and get him to read that to me over the telephone and we could write it down."

Jackson said, "That's an idea." He pushed back his chair abruptly and said, "Wait there please," and after a perfunctory knock on the door of Mason's private office, said to Della Street, "Mr. Mason won't be back any more tonight I suppose?"

"I don't think so."

"There's a clause in this oil lease that I'd like to work on. Would you mind taking it down in shorthand for me if we can get someone to read it to us over the telephone?"

"Certainly not," Della Street said picking up her notebook. "I'll be glad to."

Jackson's smile was apologetic. "The stenographers have all left for the evening," he said. "I guess we're holding down the office."

"It's all right with me," Della said. "I'll write it out for you."

They entered Jackson's office. Gertie, the receptionist and telephone operator, had gone home, so Jackson's line was connected with the outside line through the switchboard. He dialed the number Jane Keller gave him, listened while Jane Keller carried on a conversation with her brother-in-law, a conversation which got down to the point at issue only after several minutes of voluble explanation as to the reason for the call and the necessity of consulting a lawyer.

Lawton said angrily, "Those lawyers will get *their* grub hooks into the deal and mess it all up. You'll wind up paying out all your dough. I can read and I know that lease like a book. No lawyer can . . ."

"I know, dear, but Martha felt we should see Mr. Mason, and it means so much to her—on account of Margie, you know."

"Margie!" Lawton exclaimed bitterly. "Sure, it means a lot to Martha. All those buzzard relations of yours, standing in line every time you put across a business deal . . . I can't keep enough operating capital to make investments if you're going to keep dissipating it with loans to your relatives."

"I know, Lawton dear, but please read me the provision in the lease over the telephone. . . . There's a girl coming to the phone to take it down."

Della Street's voice came over the wire, "I'm on an extension line, Mrs. Keller. If this gentleman will go ahead and read, I'll take it down in shorthand."

Lawton Keller, realizing there was another listener on the line, promptly modified his tone, said efficiently, "Just a moment," and then started reading the provision in the lease.

A few minutes later Della Street handed a neatly typed copy of the six months clause to Jackson.

Jackson became utterly oblivious of his clients as he perused the provision in question.

At length he looked up. "It looks like a joker," he said. "Now I am wondering about what's in the other part of the lease. I'm afraid I'm going to need the whole document. . . . Look here, why don't you get the lease and put it through the mail slot in the door of the office here. In that way I'll get it first thing in the morning and will be able to reach a decision more promptly."

"You can let us know right away, as soon as you see it?"

"It may take a little time," Jackson said. "I wouldn't want to limit myself on that."

Martha nodded to Jane Keller. "All right, Jane, we'll go out and get the lease."

Chapter 5

Perry Mason, hat pushed jauntily back on his head, came swinging down the corridor just as Della Street was leaving by the exit door of the private office.

"Well, for heaven's sakes, what brings *you* back?" she asked.

Mason grinned, "Been having a session with the district attorney."

"That's something."

"Uh huh, thought I'd drop in at the office to see if there was anything new. Everyone gone?"

"Jackson's in the law library."

Mason grinned. "Looking for a case that's on all fours?"

"Absolutely."

Mason said, "Jackson is never satisfied. If he had a replevin case involving a brown horse with a white right hind leg, he doesn't want a precedent that establishes a rule of law about just any old horse. He wants to keep looking until he finds one with a white right hind leg."

Della Street smiled, "*One* white right hind leg," she amended. "That's Jackson."

"What is it this time?" Mason asked.

"An oil lease . . . A couple of sisters, a vague dreamy little woman whom you'd like and a grim faced chiseler whom you wouldn't . . . Looks to me as though the chiseler might wind up with the money in the long run."

"They always do," Mason said. "What about the oil lease?"

"Some joker that provided any default could be straightened up within six months."

Mason said, "I suppose there's some new activity and the sharper wants to chisel in on it."

"No, something different. It's an island in the middle of the river about thirty miles up from the bay. Apparently just a beautiful place for a millionaire to have an island empire of his own. It isn't much good for ranching but it would be swell for a millionaire's estate."

Mason grinned, "The problem these days is to first find your millionaire."

"They've found one, Parker Benton."

Mason whistled.

"The deal's already in escrow," Della said. "This oil thing will kill it."

"How long's Jackson been working on it?"

"Only about an hour. I think he's waiting for the women to return and bring him the oil lease. He doesn't want them to know he's going to be in the office. He told them to drop it through the mail chute in the door, but I know he rang up his wife and told her he wouldn't be home for dinner."

"Again?"

"Again and again and again. If I were his wife I'd want to have him wear an identification tag with his photograph on it so I'd know who he was when he did come back to the house. Honestly, it seems to me she doesn't get to look at him often enough to remember what he looks like. He's always up here in the office with his nose stuck in some law book."

Mason said, "Let's take a look, Della," and opened the door of the law library.

Jackson was seated at the table. Already an imposing array of open books had been erected in a semi-circular barricade around him, and he was so deeply engrossed in the volume he was reading, that he didn't hear them enter.

For a moment Mason stood watching.

The expression on Jackson's face was similar to that of a fisherman who has just received a strike in a deep pool and then, after a couple of fruitless casts, is looking through his fly book, trying to find something else the trout will take.

"Hello, Jackson," Mason said, "you're working late."

Jackson looked up and blinked his eyes into focus. "A *most* interesting problem, Mr. Mason. It involves a potential

22

conflict between provisions in a lease, one of them providing specifically that in the event a certain sum of money is not paid by a certain time, the lessee shall lose all rights; and the other one, a blanket provision, to the effect that any breach can be cured within six months, unless the lessor has given a specific notice of termination."

Mason sat down on the corner of the law library table, tapped a cigarette, snapped a match into flame and asked, "Getting anywhere?"

"Well, yes and no."

"What's your theory?" Mason asked.

Jackson placed the open law book on the table, shoved it slightly to one side, then, swinging around in the chair, pressed the tips of his fingers together.

"The first big hurdle to get over is the question of a forfeiture. The law doesn't like forfeiture provisions in a document, and anything providing for a forfeiture is to be strictly construed. *That* would seem to subordinate the clause about payment of rental to the general clause providing that there can be performance at any time within six months unless a forfeiture has been sooner declared."

Mason said, "Remember that this is an oil and gas lease, Jackson."

"Well, what about it? It's still a lease, isn't it?"

Mason slid down from the corner of the library table, walked over to the shelf, ran his hand along the row of books, pulled down a red backed book, riffled through the pages, said, "Here's a line of decisions for you to look up, Jackson, taking a view that forfeiture clauses are a necessary part of an oil lease and that the statutory provisions requiring a forfeiture to be strictly interpreted against the party for whose benefit it is created, doesn't apply to oil leases."

Jackson jerked upright in the chair. "What's that?" he asked.

"Uh huh," Mason said lazily. "See the case of John versus Elberta Oil Company, 124 Cal. App. 744; Slater versus Boyd, 120 Cal. App. 457; Hall versus Augur, 82 Cal. App. 594."

Jackson said, somewhat querulously, "That phase of it

23

hadn't occurred to me. I don't know how it is you can walk into a law library and pick what you want out of thin air. *I* have to do a lot of plodding to even get the proper legal theory on which to work."

Mason said, "The theory on which *you* want to work is always the theory on which the other man *doesn't* want to work. How long will it be before you can give these women an opinion, Jackson?"

"Well, I'm hoping to have something by day after tomorrow, if it isn't too complicated, and I have luck."

Mason went back to perch on the edge of the table. He kept his right foot on the floor, swung his left foot in lazy swings. "Suppose that may be too late, Jackson?"

"I can't help it. It's the best I can do."

"As I understand it, there's a deal in escrow."

"That's right."

Mason said, "A lot depends on how anxious Parker Benton is for this property."

"Well, he certainly doesn't want to buy a lawsuit," Jackson said. "And yet, I don't see any other way out. There certainly *is* a clause in that oil lease which gives the lessee a leg to stand on, for a prima-facie case and there's nothing to prevent him filing suit."

"Is the document recorded?"

"No, apparently it contained a provision to the effect that drilling operations had to start immediately if the document was recorded. That was by way of insurance that the lessor wouldn't have his title all clouded up."

Mason said, "I don't think I'd go about it this way, Jackson."

"How else *can* you go about it?"

"Who's the man who has the oil lease?"

"A Scott Shelby."

"In the telephone book?"

"I haven't looked."

Mason said to Della Street, "Take a look, Della."

Della Street ran through the pages of the telephone book.

Mason said, almost musingly, "With a certain class of people, you have to be rough, Jackson."

"Yes, I suppose so. However, the law is a very exact science. There is always a remedy, if one knows where to hunt for it."

"And is smart enough to find it," Mason supplemented. "And isn't in a hurry. For my part, I have a different way of handling a chiseler."

"What's that?" Jackson asked.

"I kick his teeth in."

Jackson winced. "That expression always makes me shiver," he said. "I detest violence—of all forms."

Mason said, "I love it."

Della Street looked up, caught Mason's eye, nodded.

Mason gave her a signal and Della Street's nimble fingers whirred the dial of the telephone.

After a moment, she said into the telephone, "Mr. Scott Shelby, please, Mr. Mason's office is calling."

She held the line for a moment, the looked up and nodded to Mason.

Mason came over to stand beside her, waited while she said, "Is this Mr. Shelby? . . . Just a moment Mr. Shelby. This is Mr. Mason's office. Mr. Mason wants to talk with you."

She handed the telephone to Mason and moved to one side.

Mason said, "Hello, Mr. Shelby."

The voice which came over the wire was appraising, "Is this Mr. *Perry Mason*?"

"That's right."

"Was there something you wished?"

"Got a lawyer?" Mason asked.

"No. Why?"

"You're going to need one."

"I don't think so."

"I do."

"May I ask why?"

Mason said, "I have something to say. It's going to hurt. I'd prefer to deal with your lawyers."

"If it involves oil matters," Shelby said positively, "I

25

don't need any lawyer. I know more about oil leases than any lawyer I've ever talked with yet. What's on your mind?"

"The Jane Keller lease."

"What about it?"

"Suppose *you* tell *me*."

Shelby said, "There's nothing much to it, Mr. Mason. The lease is very simple and very plain. One of those straightforward documents that is put in ordinary business language and says what it means."

"In fine print," Mason commented.

"Well, of course, it's printed. It makes it a lot easier that way."

"Sure it does—for you."

"Now in this lease," Shelby went on, "I was to pay a hundred dollars a month until I started drilling. Any time I didn't pay, they could consider the lease at an end. That's fair enough, isn't it?"

"It would seem so."

"But," Shelby went on, "there was also a provision that if they didn't terminate by notice, I could come back at any time within six months and reinstate myself. Apparently they overlooked that."

"That your private joker, or did you borrow it?" Mason asked.

Shelby said suavely, "There's no use you and me arguing over the telephone, Mr. Mason. I understand there's a sale on. I don't want to be shortchanged. I won't have that property sold out from under me; but on the other hand, I don't want to interfere with a good sale. Look here, Mr. Mason, why don't you run over and have a chat with me?"

"Come on over here," Mason invited. "I'll wait."

"No, I'd prefer to talk in my office if we're going to talk. You know how those things are. . . . Now in this case, I understand the deal is just about ready to go through escrow. I don't want to do anything to rock the boat unless I have to. Why don't you come over . . ."

"I'll be over," Mason said.

"How soon?"

"Ten minutes."

"That'll be fine."

Mason hung up the telephone, said "Close up your law books and go home, Jackson."

Jackson was watching Mason with shocked eyes. "Good heavens, Mr. Mason! You're seeing this man, and you don't even know what's in the lease yet."

"I'll damn soon find out," Mason said. "Come on, Della. I'll want a witness."

"Can I be of help in that respect?" Jackson asked dubiously.

"Hell no," Mason told him cheerfully. "This guy's a chiseler. The party's going to be rough. You'd have a nervous breakdown. Let's go, Della."

"Coming," she said.

Jackson's stricken pale eyes rebuked them out of the office.

Chapter 6

The door of Scott Shelby's office was locked. Mason knocked. Almost immediately they could hear the sound of steps. A chunky man with pale complexion, slightly stooped shoulders and a high forehead opened the door and regarded his visitors with dark, restless eyes. Those eyes seemed hot with emotion. The face itself was that of a man who is cool, collected and thoroughly master of himself. Only his eyes belied the placid features.

"Mr. Mason?"

Mason nodded, said, "Shelby, I presume?"

The two men shook hands.

"Miss Street, my secretary."

"Come in," Shelby invited.

Shelby escorted them through an outer office into his private office, said "I want you folks to meet Miss Ellen Cushing. She has a real estate agency in the building and I knew she'd be working late. I asked her to come in." He laughed apologetically and then added, "Frankly, I wanted a witness and I see that Mr. Mason had the same idea. I *had* intended to try and palm Miss Cushing off as my secretary and then thought I couldn't get away with it so I decided to be frank. She's a witness."

"All right," Mason said, "Miss Street is a witness, too. We're two against two. I guess however, we don't need to bother about that angle of it."

"No, I guess not," Shelby admitted.

Mason said, "All right. What's your proposition?"

"Well, of course, Mr. Mason, I don't want to stand in the way and . . ."

"Never mind the preliminaries," Mason said. "They don't

mean anything to either of us. We're businessmen. Why not get down to brass tacks?''

"How high will your client go?" Shelby asked.

"I haven't the slightest idea."

"She'd be guided by your recommendations?"

"I don't know."

"Well, how high would you go?"

"Not very high," Mason said, sitting down and crossing his legs. "Anyone want a cigarette?"

Shelby said, "I smoke cigars myself."

Della Street and Ellen Cushing took cigarettes. While he was holding a match to Ellen Cushing's cigarette, Mason sized her up.

She was a woman who might have been either in the late twenties or the early thirties, a blonde with impudent grayish-green eyes, a supple, well curved figure, although her waist was slender and her stomach was flat. She sat very erect in her chair, her knees crossed, the toe of her well shod foot carefully pointed downward.

She was conscious of Mason's appraisal and her eyes raised from the flame of the match to regard the lawyer with quiet humor. It was as though she had said in words, "I knew I'd catch you doing that."

Mason grinned, turned his attention back to Shelby, said, "If you thought this was going to be easy, you're barking up the wrong tree."

"I knew that as soon as you phoned."

"Just so we understand each other," Mason said.

"However," Shelby said, "I don't want you to think this is a shake-down. I really had no idea a sale was being made until Mrs. Keller told my agent at the bank."

Mason's silence could have shown either that he felt that point was now unimportant or that he thought the man was a liar.

Shelby watched him in thoughtful brooding silence.

"It's your move," Mason said.

"I intend to give written notice to the title company and serve a copy on Parker Benton that I have a lease on the property. In fact, I have already prepared such notice and will attach to it a copy of the lease. I don't like to do it because the escrow is, I understand, about ready to be closed. Benton won't want oil wells on his island. He is, of course, acting on the assumption he's getting a clear title. They must have told him the place was free of clouds. My notice will make him take it subject to whatever rights I have.''

"You haven't any."

"The lease says I have."

"A joker."

"I don't so regard it. After all, it doesn't make any difference. Parker Benton isn't going to pay thirty thousand for a lawsuit."

"And you aren't going to sue," Mason said.

"I intend to, if I have to do it—to protect my rights. I hope I don't have to."

"It'll cost you ten thousand dollars to find out if you have any rights" Mason said.

"And take five years," Shelby observed.

"At a hundred a month."

"It'll cost your client something, too."

"Naturally," Mason admitted.

"And the sale will be off the minute I serve this notice."

"That won't help *you* any."

"It will hurt your client."

"We might bond against your claim."

"Benton wouldn't stand for it. But let's be reasonable, Mr. Mason. I don't want to block that sale. I only wanted to keep the lease alive. I didn't even know there was a sale pending until . . ."

"Yes, go on."

"Until Mrs. Keller told my agent when he tendered her the five hundred dollars at the bank."

"How did you know who was buying the property?"

"She told my agent."

"Told him Parker Benton was buying it?"

"Yes."

"How did you know that the escrow was just about ready to be closed and the deal concluded?"

Shelby's eyes suddenly shifted. "I . . . I think she told him."

"And I note that you know the amount of the purchase price. How did you get that?"

Shelby said abruptly, "I don't think you're doing yourself or your client any good by cross-examining me this way, Mr. Mason."

"How much?" Mason asked.

Shelby looked him in the eye. "All right. Since you want the figure, it's ten thousand dollars."

Mason got to his feet, nodded to Della Street, said, "I guess that's all."

"You'd better think it over," Shelby warned. "Benton is paying a great deal more for that island than it's worth, a lot more than any other person would pay. It's a *most* advantageous deal."

Mason started for the door, turned, said, "I guess it's only fair to tell you that when I start fighting I fight rather rough."

"Go ahead," Shelby said. "When you come right down to it, I am no gilded lily myself."

"That makes it perfectly fine," Mason said. "Just so we don't misunderstand each other."

"We don't. Only get this straight, Mr. Mason. The minute you leave this office, I'm going to mail a notice to the escrow company."

"All right," Mason said. "And the minute you do that, I'm going to sue to set aside the lease on the ground of fraud. I'm going to sue you for slander of title. I'm going to look into the question of whether the lease was signed on the strength of false representations."

"You go right ahead," Shelby said. "And by the time you get done with all that stuff, Benton will have bought and sold half a dozen other country homes. Your client will be left with an island on her hands, and the island will be subject to my oil lease."

Mason hesitated. "You think this offer of Benton's is more than she'd get from anyone else?"

"Considerably more."

"How much more?"

Shelby said, "The deal is for thirty thousand dollars. I consider that fifteen thousand dollars is a big price for the island. However, I'm willing to sell my interest in it for the ten thousand and that will still leave your client five thousand more than she could get from anyone else."

"In other words, you think the island is worth only about fifteen thousand dollars?"

"That's right."

"And you want ten thousand dollars in order to step back and let this sale go through?"

"Put it that way if you want to."

"But the figure is right? The amount is ten thousand?"

"Yes."

"That's bedrock?"

"Yes."

Mason said, "All right. Remember that you yourself have adopted the position that the deal with Benton is a good many thousand dollars more than the island is really worth."

"What's the object in remembering that?"

Mason grinned. "It affects the measure of damages in case I go after you for slander of title. You interfere with this sale and I'll stick you for damages."

"You couldn't get 'em if you did."

"I'll remember that, too."

Shelby said, "I was hoping we could have settled this thing amicably, Mr. Mason."

"Naturally, at that price."

"I *might* come down a little."

"How much?"

"Not over one thousand—or two thousand at the most."

"That's your final figure?"

"Absolutely."

"Good night," Mason said, and held the door open for Della Street.

Shelby hurriedly got up, walked around his desk. "After all, Mr. Mason, there's a great deal of money involved and . . ."

Mason stepped out into the corridor, pulled the door shut behind him, cutting off Shelby in midsentence.

They marched across to the elevators and pushed the button marked DOWN.

"Don't you think he'd have made more concessions?" Della Street asked curiously in a low voice.

"Sure."

"Then why not wait?"

"Because he'd have only come down to five thousand. The way things are now, he'll get in a panic and start letting his hair down. There's lots of time. Let him feel we're tough and not too eager and he'll get down to brass tacks."

"You were pretty rough with him."

"Uh huh."

"Because you think he's a chiseler?"

"Right."

"And that witness?"

Mason laughed, "Quote witness unquote. She's got her finger in the middle of the pie."

"You think she . . . Yes, I guess so. She did seem pretty—possessive, just her manner."

Mason said, "Remember, she's in the real estate business. Remember that Shelby has found out all about this deal, all about the escrow, all about the fact that the escrow is about ready to be closed, and knows the amount of the purchase price. Put one two together with the other two and tell me what the total is."

Della Street smiled at him. "Four."

"Four," Mason said, "is right."

The elevator came gliding up the shaft, stopped at the floor, the door slid back. A man got out, started across toward the door of Shelby's office, then abruptly whirled to regard Mason with surprise.

"Well, well," Mason said. "Sergeant Dorset of Homicide. What brings *you* here, Sergeant? Looking for a body?"

Dorset abruptly wheeled, walked back to the elevators, said to the operator, "Go on down. You can pick him up in a minute or two. Mason, I want to talk to you."

Mason smiled affably. "Go right ahead. I just had a very interesting visit with the district attorney this afternoon. Anything you can add will be in the nature of an anticlimax."

33

Dorset paid no attention to Mason's statement. "Who're you calling on up here?" he asked.

Mason smiled, and said nothing.

"All right, all right," Dorset said. "Go ahead. Be smart if you want to, but I was just wondering."

"I gathered you were."

Dorset jerked his thumb toward Shelby's office. "Know anything about that poison angle?"

Mason's foot pressed against Della's shoe. He said, "What do *you* suppose I'm up here for?"

"That's what bothers me," Dorset said. "I'll tell you one thing, Mason. If you're representing the person that poisoned him and are trying to get the thing all hushed up, you're out on a limb, because the doctor saved the stomach contents and had them analyzed. There was enough arsenic to have killed a horse. That's why *I'm* here. Now why are you here?"

Mason said, "Let's say that any resemblance between the reason I'm here and the reason *you're* here is purely coincidental."

Dorset frowned. "All right. Be smart. Remember, I've warned you. *Good* evening."

"Good-by," Mason said, and jabbed the elevator button once more as Sergeant Dorset pounded his aggressive way toward Scott Shelby's office.

"Do you gather that Mr. Scott Shelby has been on the receiving end of an attempted murder?" Della asked.

Mason was frowning as the red elevator light came on. "I'm darned if I know," he said, and then as he entered the elevator muttered almost musingly to himself, "Poison, huh? Now isn't *that* something?"

Chapter 7

Promptly at eight-forty the next morning Mason entered his office, met the surprised eyes of Della Street, said, "I know I'm early, but I want to talk with that Mrs. Keller when she comes in. I'm going to see if I can't find some grounds for going after that crook."

Della Street said, "I haven't even got your desk all dusted yet."

"That's all right. I'm going out to the law library and prowl around a bit. I'm getting as bad as Jackson. Looking for precedents. I wonder if those women left the oil lease last night?"

"I haven't looked in the outer office. I just got here myself."

"Take a look," Mason said.

Della Street went to the outer office and returned carrying an envelope. "They left it all right."

Mason opened the envelope, took out the lease, walked over to his desk, pushed back the swivel chair, sat down, and tilted back to put his feet up on the desk, all without taking his eyes from the printed contract.

"What time does Jackson come in, Della?" he asked.

"Right on the dot at nine o'clock. You can set your watch by it. I presume he catches a certain car, and has established a precedent which he can't break. Sometimes he'll stay at the office until ten or eleven o'clock at night, but he always comes to work at that same time every morning."

Mason said, "See if Gertie is in. I want to be certain that I see Mrs. Keller as soon as she comes to the office."

Della Street picked up the telephone. She waited a moment then said, "Oh, hello, Gertie. I was just wondering if you were here. Mr. Mason is in the office and he's going to

35

see Mrs. Keller when she comes in. You might tell Jackson and . . . What's that? . . . Just a minute.''

Della Street turned to Mason, said, ''Gertie didn't know you were in. There was a man in the office to see you. Gertie told him that you didn't ever get in before nine-thirty and he says he's coming back.''

''What's his name?'' Mason asked.

''Just a minute, I'll ask her.''

''What's his name, Gertie?''

Della Street turned to Perry Mason, said, ''It was Parker Benton.''

''He's in the office now?''

''He just left. He started for the elevator.''

''Catch him,'' Mason ordered.

Della Street dropped the telephone receiver into its cradle, dashed across the office, jerked open the door, and sprinted down the corridor.

The door from the outer office opened. The receptionist and switchboard operator said contritely, ''I'm so sorry, Mr. Mason. I didn't know you were in the office. I didn't even know Miss Street was here. I . . .''

''That's all right, Gertie,'' Mason said. ''It just happens I'm anxious to see this man, that's all.''

A moment later Della Street tapped on the door of Mason's office. Mason opened the door and looked over Della's shoulder to meet steely-gray eyes which probed out from under bushy eyebrows.

Mason said, ''I'm sorry, Mr. Benton. My receptionist didn't know I was in. I'm a little early this morning. Won't you come in?''

Benton shook hands.

He was a muscular, broad shouldered, well fed individual somewhere around fifty-five. Dark hair flecked with gray was combed straight back from his forehead. He wore no hat and the deep even tan of his face indicated that he spent much of his time out of doors. He was, perhaps, some twenty pounds overweight but he carried it well and the grip of his hand was muscular and cordial.

''As a matter of fact,'' he said, ''I heard that a Mr. Jackson

36

in your office was handling the matter I'm interested in. But it's quite important to me, and I wanted to talk to you personally about it."

"Sit down," Mason invited. "Who told you about Mr. Jackson?"

"Jane Keller."

"You've seen her?"

"Talked with her over the telephone."

"Would you mind telling me just what happened?"

"Well, I think you know the general background."

Mason said with a smile, "I prefer that *you* tell *me*."

Benton laughed. "There's no need beating around the bush, Mr. Mason, and no need to be cautious. The cat's out of the bag."

Mason offered his visitor a cigarette. "But under the circumstances it will help if you describe the cat so we'll be perfectly certain we're talking about the same animal."

Benton laughed outright, said, "Last night a man by the name of Shelby got in touch with me, said that he understood I was buying an island from Jane Keller, that if I wanted to get a good title to the land I'd have to make some arrangements with him because he had an oil lease and was intending to start drilling. He said he took it for granted that I wouldn't care to buy an island for residential purposes and then have him put some oil derricks in my front yard."

"What," Mason asked, "did you tell him?"

"Well, I asked him a few questions in order to get the picture."

"And then?" Mason asked.

Benton laughed and said, "And then I told him to go to hell. I hate being blackmailed."

Mason nodded.

"Now then, what can you tell me about the legal angles?"

"I don't think he has a leg to stand on legally. His contract lapsed five months ago. I think there's been an abandonment of the premises. I think there's been a termination of the lease by a mutual implied consent. I don't think the particular lease in question permits him to cure his default in the payment of rent, even if there hasn't been any abandonment or mutual termination by implied consent.''

''And suppose we take the thing to court?''

''We can lick him.''

''How long?''

Mason ran his hand over his wavy hair.

''Go ahead,'' Benton said. ''I'm a businessman, Mr. Mason. I have my own lawyers. I can find out about these things. I'm simply trying to save time.''

''Well, of course,'' Mason said, ''it depends somewhat on the amount of opposition we meet, whether Shelby is simply running a naked bluff or whether he's willing to spend some money to try and hold us up.''

''He'll spend some money to try and hold us up.''

''You know him?''

''I didn't, but I do.''

Mason raised his eyebrows.

Benton said, ''I keep a firm of confidential investigators under retainer. Whenever a thing of this sort crops up, I try to find out something of the nature of the man I'm dealing with.''

Mason's silence was an invitation to proceed.

After a moment Parker Benton said, ''I don't know why not. After all, we're jointly interested in this thing. I don't mind telling you, Mr. Mason, that I'm rather anxious to get that property if it can be worked out. But I certainly don't want to have someone punching oil wells in my front yard or turning my swimming pool into an oil sump.''

Mason nodded.

''Scott Shelby,'' Benton said, ''is a promoter. He's shrewd and he's probably crooked. He's something of a playboy, been married twice before. He now has a third wife considerably younger than he is. No one knows anything about his financial status because he keeps juggling his bank accounts around and is reputed to carry most of his money in the form of cash in a money belt. His credit is nil.''

''Beating the income tax?'' Mason asked.

Benton made a little gesture with his hands. ''You draw

38

your conclusions, I draw mine. In that way we don't run any risk of being sued for defamation of character."

Mason looked across at the other man. "Why did you come here?"

"I wanted to find out about the legal aspects of the situation."

"You have your own lawyers."

"I thought you might be more familiar with the situation."

"Why did you come here?"

Abruptly Parker Benton laughed and said, "All right, Mason, you win."

"Go ahead," Mason invited.

"All right," Benton said. "I'll put my cards on the table. That property is worth probably from fifteen to twenty thousand dollars. I'm paying thirty dollars for it. And I'm anxious to get it."

"How anxious?" Mason asked.

"*Very* anxious."

"You mean you'd pay Shelby some blackmail in order to buy him out?"

Benton said, "As far as the money is concerned, it doesn't make much difference. The principle of the thing does. I don't like to be held up. I definitely don't want to get the reputation of being an easy mark. I do want that property. If it costs money to get rid of Shelby, *you'll* pay the money. Get me?"

Mason nodded.

"Now then," Benton went on, "Shelby is running a bluff. He'll back it up if we start to call him. He'll have to. But he doesn't want a lawsuit any more than anyone else."

"You have something in mind?" Mason asked.

Benton looked at Mason, studying the lawyer, "You didn't have someone call me up early this morning?"

Mason silently shook his head.

"Very early this morning," Benton went on, "my telephone rang. A woman who seemed to know a great deal about the matter said that she was going to give me a friendly tip, that if I'd get Scott Shelby *and his wife* to accompany me sometime tonight on a cruise to the island aboard my yacht,

I could get a settlement of the case. This person, a woman whose voice sounded very attractive, by the way, said Shelby really wanted to settle, but that Shelby was hotheaded. His wife, Marion, was the real balance wheel, a very sensible, charming woman.''

Benton stopped talking, waiting for Mason to say something, but the lawyer merely kept quiet.

''What do you think of it?'' Benton asked at length.

''You don't know who called you?''

''No.''

''She was particular to suggest the conference be aboard your yacht?''

''Yes.''

''The destination the island?''

''Yes.''

''For all you know then,'' Mason said, smiling, ''the voice was that of Mrs. Shelby, herself. She was quite probably coached by her husband to say what she did.''

Benton nodded. ''I think that's the real explanation.''

''Well?'' Mason asked.

Benton said smiling, ''I'm going to ring up Shelby. I'm going to invite him and his wife to come out to my yacht for a little cruise. I want you to come also. I'll have Mrs. Keller there, all the interested parties. We'll have a get-together. If Shelby makes a reasonable price, we'll arrange a pool, pay him off and take a quitclaim.''

Mason said, ''If you'd like a suggestion, I'll give you one.''

''What?''

''The thing that will bother Shelby the most is that you might tell the title company to issue a certificate subject to that oil lease. Then the title company takes no responsibility for the oil lease and you go ahead and take the property. Then you tell Shelby to start suing *you.*''

''I'd still have a lawsuit on my hands,'' Benton said.

Mason said, ''I'm telling you that that would bother Shelby the most.''

Benton nodded. ''I get your point, thanks.''

Mason said, ''Engaging in litigation with you would be rather an expensive pastime.''

40

"Quite expensive," Benton said.

Mason said, "In one way we'd be suing Shelby to quit title so we could close the deal. He'd spar for time and run us crazy. This way I've suggested, you'd have the property and he'd have to sue you. It isn't a position he'd like to be in."

Benton pursed his lips, then asked abruptly, "You're not married, Mr. Mason?"

"No."

"I'm very anxious to have you come along on that yachting trip this afternoon. We leave here about four o'clock. There's lots of room. Is there someone you'd like to bring along?"

Mason glanced at Della Street. Almost imperceptibly she nodded. Mason said, "I'll bring my secretary."

"That will be fine. And if there's anyone else you want to bring, just bring them along. Anyone that would contribute to the life of the party. I want to make it something of a social success and then after we've all got acquainted we can sit down and talk business. And thank you very much, Mr. Mason, for giving me that lead about the angle to take in talking with Shelby."

"Where do I meet you?" Mason asked.

"I'll send a car about three-thirty. Now how about this Mr. Jackson? Do you think he'd like to go?"

Mason laughed. "I'm afraid that Jackson can't find anything in the law books which establishes a legal precedent for settling a lawsuit aboard a yacht."

"You mean he doesn't do anything without a precedent?"

"Nothing," Mason said.

Benton said definitely, "We don't want him then."

"I thought not."

"We'll be back late this evening?" Mason asked.

Benton pursed his lips, then smiled. "Frankly, Mr. Mason, I don't think we will. But the others won't know that. We're going up to the island. At this season, whenever there's a hot day, a fog usually drifts in at night. We can't come back in a fog. Get me?"

"I get you," Mason said.

"That's fine, then. Bring a bag with overnight things—and don't be surprised if you meet a strange assortment of people."

Chapter 8

The yacht glided smoothly up the bay, a hundred and thirty feet of sleek luxury. The throb of the big Diesel motors and the thrust of the twin propellers gave a sense of power underneath. The teakwood decks, mahogany trim, and comfortable deck chairs gave the passengers a sense of luxury, a quiet enjoyment of the good things of life.

As Mason let Parker Benton pilot him around to meet the various guests, the lawyer realized that the millionaire could hardly have selected a more propitious occasion for compromising a potential lawsuit. Not only did the environment make for friendly good feeling, but in the background there was always a suggestion of financial power on the part of the host.

Mason acknowledged the introduction to Jane Keller and to Lawton Keller, caught in Lawton Keller's eyes a glimpse of latent hostility. The brother-in-law didn't relish the idea of having lawyers checking up on him.

Benton had gone the limit to have everyone aboard who was at all interested, even to Martha Stanhope and her daughter.

Scott Shelby, definitely ill at ease, tried to cover his feelings by trying to be popular and friendly. His effort was just a little too obvious.

It was with agreeable surprise that Mason met Marion Shelby, a woman about twenty-five with dark brown, almost black, hair, gray-blue eyes and a friendly unspoiled manner. Her manner gave the impression that she knew nothing of the business background which made the trip so significant. To her mind an influential business acquaintance of her husband's was being nice and she was enjoying it immensely.

Parker Benton saw that cocktails were served. "No business of any kind, please," he warned. "Not until after dinner. Then we'll sit down at the big table in the cabin and talk. In the meantime let's relax and enjoy life."

Following which he took his guests around on a tour of the yacht, showing them the various staterooms, mechanical gadgets and lounging rooms.

Some time later, Mason moved over to stand at the rail, letting the brisk breeze tingle him into a feeling of physical well-being.

They had left the bay behind and were now within the confines of the river. The banks were less than a mile apart and the pilot was guiding the boat between spar buoys which marked a rather treacherous channel. The yacht was moving forward at half-speed skimming through the water as smoothly as a game fish in a cool pool.

The day had been hot, dry, cloudless, but now there was just a suggestion of fog drifting in from the bay, although the sky above remained a clear, deep blue.

Mason heard motion behind, then Scott Shelby's voice said, "I wanted to talk with you, Mr. Mason . . . alone."

"I'm afraid not."

"What do you mean?"

"I think that Benton's plan is for us to talk everything over all at once after dinner, not piecemeal."

"This is about something else."

"What?"

"Your friend Sergeant Dorset. He put in quite a bit of time asking me about what your business had been."

"He's an inquisitive chap."

"Rather a peculiar thing happened."

"Don't tell me about it unless you want to."

"I want to."

"I'm representing Jane Keller. I can't represent you."

"I understand that."

"Why talk to me then?"

"I just wanted to talk about Sergeant Dorset. I don't like him."

"Lots of people don't."

"I think he's trying to cook up something—to frame something on somebody."

"What and on whom?"

"I don't know. I wish I did."

"I'm not a mind reader."

"I was poisoned a few days ago."

"Indeed."

"I thought it was a simple case of food poisoning, but apparently it wasn't. Anyway that's what Dorset says. He wants to make a lot of trouble."

There was a moment of silence while the sound of water slipping past the sides of the boat was plainly audible, then Mason said, "I'm listening. That's all."

"My wife and I had dinner in this place. We didn't both eat the same thing. I had red wine; she had white wine. I had prime ribs of beef cooked rare and French fried potatoes; she had fried oysters and vegetables. We both had the same dessert. We both became ill about half an hour after eating. She was only slightly ill. I was quite ill—a typical case of food poisoning, wouldn't you say?"

"That's right."

"You mean it was?"

Mason grinned. "I mean I wouldn't say."

Shelby looked at the lawyer with manifest irritation in his restless dark eyes, then abruptly averted his glance.

Mason stood with his elbows over the rail looking down at the rippling water which curled up against the sides of the vessel, splashed over into little foam-crested ripples and then fell rapidly astern.

There was silence for several seconds, then Mason said abruptly, "Apparently we're headed for the island."

"I suppose so," Shelby said, and then after a moment added, "I was talking about this poisoning."

"So you were."

"I was pretty sick. I called a physician. This same physician treated my wife. I explained to him that it was food poisoning, probably something that had been canned because there was a burning metallic taste in my throat."

"I see," Mason commented.

"And do you know what happened?"

"No."

"Your friend Sergeant Dorset shows up yesterday afternoon and tells me that I had been poisoned by arsenic—and apparently wants to make something of it."

"Such as what?"

"Well, he asked me a lot of questions about what enemies I had and all that sort of tripe. Good Lord, I don't want the newspaper notoriety of anything like that, particularly right at this time. I'm putting across several important business deals."

"How did Sergeant Dorset think the arsenic got in the food?"

"That's just the point. He wanted *me* to tell *him*. Why doesn't he go to the restaurant? It must have been the cook at the restaurant."

"Anyone else poisoned?"

"Dorset said that there had been no other complaints."

Mason raised his eyes. The sun was setting and a thin moist haze seemed to be rising from the water.

Carlotta Benton came along the deck, said cheerily, "Oh, there you are. My, you look serious. I hope you haven't been spoiling your appetite by talking business."

Mason said, "On the contrary, Mr. Shelby was telling me about an illness."

Shelby kicked Mason on the ankle.

"Food poisoning," Shelby interposed. "Something I ate in a restaurant."

"One can't be too careful these days. I hope you're all right now?" Carlotta Benton said.

"Fit as a fiddle," Shelby told her.

"You look rather pale."

"I'm always that way."

"Well, I'm rounding up the guests for cocktails. Dinner will be served in about thirty minutes and Parker says he wants to give the cocktails time to take hold."

"Do you," Mason asked casually and with no intimation he already possessed information not shared by the others,

46

"know whether we're headed for some fixed destination, or are we just cruising?"

She laughed. "I'm not talking. Sealed orders."

"He's probably going to the island," Scott Shelby said.

She laughed. "I don't want to seem impolite, but I've been married twenty years. During that time I've learned to let my husband do the talking. About some things," she added hastily.

They all laughed politely and followed her down to the canopied after-deck where a radio had been tuned in to dance music.

Della Street had been dancing with Parker Benton and from the sparkle of animation in her eyes Mason saw that she had been enjoying herself immensely. Marion Shelby had been dancing with Lawton Keller, and from the somewhat amused tolerance mingled with a slightly watchful glint in the woman's eyes, Mason felt that Keller had probably been making passes at her, passes which had not been serious enough to call for definite action, yet which had left the woman slightly amused and slightly wary.

Scott Shelby seemed nervously restless. He said in an undertone to Mason, "I wish he'd get all this social stuff over and get down to brass tacks."

"Got some proposition?" Mason asked.

"I may have."

A steward in a white mess coat brought in cocktails and the conversation and drinking became general. Once or twice Shelby tried to bring the subject around to business but Parker Benton always headed him off.

With darkness, the faint mist which had been forming on the water thickened into fog, and as they sat down to dinner the hoarse fog whistle boomed out its eerie warning. Thereafter at regular intervals through the meal the fog whistle served to remind them that they were on the water and that a fog was settling down.

"Doesn't look as though we'll get back tonight," Parker Benton said.

"Wouldn't you tackle it in a fog?" Della Street inquired.

"Not unless I have to. It's dangerous in the channel."

"A collision?" Jane Keller asked anxiously. "Would the boat sink?"

"Not so much danger of a collision as danger of missing the channel and running aground on a mud flat and staying there for a lot longer than we'd like to," Benton said.

"Oh, but I couldn't stay all night," Mrs. Stanhope objected and then glanced at her sister.

"I'm afraid you may not have much choice in the matter. I've plenty of room and we can put everybody up nicely, but . . ."

"Look here," Scott Shelby interrupted, "what's the idea behind this thing? You know as well as I do that at this season of the year there's *always* fog that forms at night on this part of the river."

"Not always," Benton said.

"Well, nearly always."

Parker Benton was very suave. "I can get out the motorboat and put you ashore at a little town about ten miles upstream. There's an electric line which will get you back to the city."

"That would be deuced uncomfortable," Shelby said, "and I'm just recovering from a severe case of stomach trouble."

"Food poisoning," Marion Shelby hastened to explain.

"Well," Parker Benton announced, "I'm not going to risk the safety of the boat and the convenience of the other passengers. You can get in the launch and get an interurban if you want to."

"I don't want to."

"Well, all right," Benton laughed. "Sit here and enjoy life then. Let's see, I believe I have some champagne on ice."

"And I don't talk business when I've been drinking," Shelby declared.

At the close of the dinner as coffee and liqueurs were being served, the yacht suddenly throbbed and quivered as the engines were thrown into reverse. A moment later there was the rattle of the chain through the hawse pipes and a few minutes later the engines ceased running.

48

Parker Benton passed cigars, cigarettes, said, "Ladies and gentlemen, the island."

For a moment no one said anything.

Then Benton turned to Scott Shelby. "All right," he said. "What's your proposition?"

Shelby was terse. "I haven't any."

"Going to sit tight?" Benton asked.

"Perhaps."

Benton turned to Jane Keller, said, "You have thirty thousand dollars at stake, Mrs. Keller. Sometimes half a loaf is better than no bread. I have the island at stake. Sometimes a poor compromise is better than a good lawsuit. Now then, Shelby, what's your proposition?"

Shelby said, "Give me ten thousand dollars in cash and I'll make a quitclaim deed."

Benton said instantly, "That's too much."

"To me, it is ridiculously small. I think there's oil on the island."

Benton studied the smoke which was curling up in a thin, blue wisp from the end of his cigar. "To be perfectly frank with you, Shelby, I had felt that if Mrs. Keller wanted to shave the price she was getting by two thousand dollars, I would add two thousand dollars to what the island was costing me. That would make four thousand dollars that you could have for a quitclaim deed and you could then step out of the picture."

Shelby stiffly shook his head.

"Otherwise," Benton said, "I will either back out of the deal entirely, or," and here he glanced swiftly at Mason, and then slowed his delivery somewhat so that he spoke with calm deliberation, "I will instruct the escrow holder to accept a certificate of title, subject to the provisions of an outstanding oil lease. I feel that you don't have a leg to stand on and that I can get an injunction prohibiting you from setting foot on the island."

"You may get the injunction but it won't become final until after it has gone through the Supreme Court," Shelby said.

"And that also I am prepared to take into consideration,"

Benton went on, smiling. "I don't think it will make such a great deal of difference to me, Mr. Shelby. I am not buying this island for speculation. I am buying it for a home and since I don't intend to sell it, I don't care how long the litigation takes. Just so I keep you off the island."

"Suppose I win it?"

Parker Benton said, "My legal department is preparing an opinion on that. If their opinion coincides with that of Mr. Mason, I will be very much inclined to go ahead and complete the deal and then let you take any legal steps you see fit."

Shelby shifted his position. "That means no one would make any money out of it except the lawyers."

"And I'd have the island," Benton said.

"I don't think I'd like that idea," Shelby blurted.

"You don't have to take that way out," Parker Benton told him. "You can take four thousand dollars in cold hard cash and forget about it. Otherwise you'll have a lawsuit and a continuing expense."

"Are you making that four thousand dollars in the form of a definite offer?"

Parker Benton glanced at Jane Keller, then at Mason, said, "As far as my two thousand of it is concerned, it's an offer."

Martha Stanhope spoke up quickly. "Jane, you understand what Mr. Benton wants."

Lawton Keller said, "The way it looks to me, if Mr. Benton wants to buy that island, he should put up the entire four thousand dollars. After all, the price my sister-in-law is getting is low enough."

Benton looked at Lawton Keller with cold dislike. He said, "As far as I am concerned, my offer is final. I consider the two thousand dollars I am willing to donate as a very material concession on my part. Usually, it's up to the seller to convey a clear title."

Keller said, "You want this island."

"Of course, I want it."

"Well, go ahead and pay for it then."

"You mean you people won't put up two thousand dollars?"

Martha Stanhope said, "Lawton, I wish you'd shut up. Don't be so greedy. After all, Jane is the one that has the say and I think it's a very reasonable settlement myself."

"How about it, Mrs. Keller?" Benton asked. "Is it a definite offer?"

"What does Mr. Mason think?" Jane Keller asked.

Mason turned to Shelby. "If that is made as a definite offer, will you give us a definite acceptance?"

"No," Shelby said.

"As far as I'm concerned then, it's not a definite offer," Mason said. "If and when you tell us that an offer of four thousand dollars will be accepted, I think something might be worked out at that figure but I'm not going to make any offers in advance of some commitment on your part."

"Why not?"

"Because it weakens our position and leads to trading. We make an offer. Then you make an offer. Then someone wants to 'split the difference.' I don't do business that way. Make an offer of four thousand and I think it can be worked out. Wait for *my* clients to make an offer and you'll be waiting all winter."

"And that's that," Shelby said.

"Now then," Mason went on, "do you own that oil lease?"

"What do you mean?"

"Is it all yours or have you assigned it to some company?"

Shelby swiftly placed his hand to his chin, stroked the angle of his jaw, holding his hand so that his palm concealed his mouth. His eyes avoided those of Mason and those of his wife. He said, "I don't see that that makes any difference."

"It makes quite a bit of difference," Mason told him, "particularly whether the lease has been assigned and whether you're in a position to negotiate a settlement."

"If I negotiate a settlement, it will be all right. But I'm not going to settle on any such basis as you people have outlined."

Mason said, "I'm asking you definitely, do you own that oil lease?"

"I represent all parties concerned."

51

"Have you assigned part of it?"

"I don't see what that has to do with it."

"It has a lot to do with it," Parker Benton said. "I'm not going to conduct any negotiations except with the real owners and all of the owners."

"Well," Shelby blurted, "I have a partner. Someone who owns a half interest but she . . . that associate is perfectly willing to accept any settlement that is okayed by me."

"The name of your associate?" Parker Benton asked.

"Ellen Cushing," Shelby said.

Marion Shelby caught Mason's eyes, then swiftly averted hers.

"And you two own that lease?" Parker Benton asked. "You have the whole thing?"

"The whole thing."

"There have been no other assignments?"

"No."

"Just this partnership?"

"That's right."

"Will you accept four thousand dollars?" Benton asked.

"Definitely, finally and absolutely no."

"What's your minimum offer?"

"Ten thousand dollars."

Benton smiled. "Well, shall we go up to where we can have some dancing? I guess we're getting no place."

"That's a good lease," Shelby said. "I can force the lessor to accept the back rental."

"I don't care to discuss the legal aspects of the problem," Parker Benton said. "As far as I'm concerned, tomorrow afternoon I'll either drop the whole business or notify the title company that I'll accept a limited certificate. I don't know which."

Lawton Keller said somewhat anxiously, "Of course, if it comes to a showdown, I don't want you to think that we're . . ."

"You've already given me *your* position," Parker Benton interrupted, angrily.

"Well, it may not be final."

"It's final as far as you and I are concerned," Benton told

him. "If there are any more negotiations, they will be with Mason. But, as far as I'm concerned, I'm beginning to think I can find some property that will be equally satisfactory."

Abruptly Scott Shelby said, "If that's the way you feel about it, sit tight. It suits me."

"And now," Benton said, "to preserve that atmosphere of well-bred gentility which I had hoped would clothe our discussions, I think it will be well for us all to know where our staterooms are. Whether you prefer to stay in your rooms or to return for a little dancing is up to you. But, if you do return, please bear definitely in mind that we won't discuss any business and we will be friendly. There are seven staterooms aboard this yacht. You'll find in your staterooms a telephone system with a series of call buttons which will connect you with the steward, or with any one of the other rooms."

Parker Benton turned to the steward. "Please show our guests to their rooms," he said.

Lawton Keller said, "On second thought, I think it would be a good plan for Jane to sacrifice something in order to get out of a lawsuit. I'd be willing to go as high as two thousand . . ."

"Not interested," Scott Shelby snapped. "I'm not going to be pushed around either. I'm no cur to be ordered in and ordered out. The hell with all of you. Where's my room? I'll stay tonight on your damned yacht simply because it happens to be more convenient for me to stay aboard than go paddling around in a launch. But I'll get off first thing in the morning, and as far as I'm concerned you have my personal assurance that the minute you try to build anything on this island, I'll punch an oil well down in your front yard, whether I think there's any oil there or not."

Parker Benton said coldly, "That remains to be seen. I don't know how much money you have, but before you punch any wells in my front yard you'll wish you'd never seen an oil lease. Good night, everyone. As far as I'm concerned, I am going to my room and read. There'll be some confusion over the staterooms, I suppose, but the steward will get you

53

bedded down—all those who wish to stay. The launch will take any of you ashore if you want to catch the eleven o'clock interurban. And now, once more, good night.''

Chapter 9

Perry Mason, propped up on snowy pillows in a comfortable bed, adjusted the reading light and settled himself with a book. He had read the first chapter when the telephone tinkled a somewhat tentative summons, far different from the strident mechanical ring of the telephone bells in the city.

Mason picked up the receiver, said, "Hello," and heard Della Street's voice. "My gosh, Chief, isn't it ghastly?"

"Quite a difference all right in the social temperature from what it was before dinner."

"What do you suppose went wrong?"

"I don't know," Mason said. "I think Parker Benton resented Lawton Keller and then, of course, there's always the chance that the two thousand dollars *was* the top limit that he intended to place on a compromise. . . . It's quite possible he has some alternate piece of property, you know. He might feel there wasn't more than two thousand dollars difference between the two properties."

"I suppose so, but somehow he doesn't impress me as being that type. When he wants something, he wants it."

Mason laughed and said, "After all, we're talking about our host, and it's quite possible that others can tune in on the conversation."

"I don't care . . . I'm trying to settle down with a book I got from the ship's library."

"How is it?"

"It's supposed to be exciting but it can't hold my interest. I keep thinking about the people aboard this ship. There are so many people on it who hate some of the other people, and this fog makes them stay all night. . . . Have you been on deck?"

"I took a turn around before I rolled in . . ."

"Isn't that a thick and nasty fog?"

"It has settled down all right. How are you, Della, restless?"

"I was. I'm getting calmed down now."

Mason said, "We can go up and turn on the radio, get some dance music and . . ."

"Not unless you particularly want to, Chief. It's cold and foggy and . . . I just wanted to hear the sound of your voice. I'm just a little frightened tonight."

"Frightened?"

"Yes."

"Of what?"

"Darned if I know . . . I just don't like to be closeted with all this hatred . . ."

"Now," Mason said, "I'm beginning to get you. You have worked too long for a trial lawyer who specializes in murder cases. . . . Better go back to your book, Della, and then get a good night's sleep. It will probably be clear in the morning."

She laughed lightly, said, "After all, I guess I *am* getting susceptible to the creepy element in life. But, you do have to admit that it's spooky out here, with all this hate and greed bundled up in a thick fog and with the cold river underneath us."

"You'll feel better in the morning, Della. Night."

"Night," she said and hung up.

Mason returned to his book but suddenly found that the printed page could not hold his interest. He turned out the light, deliberately tried to compose himself to sleep. It was no use. The boat was shrouded now with a strange, oppressive silence, broken only now and again with little gurgling noises made by the water swirling past the hull. And from somewhere, a steady drip of fog-borne moisture, which had been almost inaudible as Mason had started to read, became now, with the increasing silence, a steady interminable *"pink"* . . . *"pink"* . . . *"pink"* . . . *"pink"* . . . *"pink."*

Mason twisted and turned restlessly, at length hunched the pillows into a back rest again and switched on the light and started reading.

56

It was nearing midnight when Mason impatiently closed the book and put on his clothes.

Out on deck, he found that the fog had thickened until it was impossible to see more than a few feet in any direction.

The boat had its trim bow facing upstream. Standing up there near the bow of the boat, Mason could hear the sullen gurgle of cold water as the current swirled around the anchor chain.

Slowly, thoughtfully, Mason moved aft, reached the stern of the vessel and saw a member of the crew, bundled up in a heavy mackinaw, standing motionless . . . a night watchman, caring nothing for the guests, simply waiting the night out, standing there as still as a statue.

Mason walked back to the bow again. He stumbled over a piece of rope, kicked it to one side, walked back to a position amidships on the starboard side and stood for some ten minutes lost in thought. He was aroused by hearing from the vicinity of the bow, the sudden stabbing sound of a woman's shrill scream, a sharp report followed almost instantly by a peculiar series of muffled splashes.

Mason looked to the stern. The man who had been on duty as watchman was no longer there. He had, perhaps, run toward the bow, keeping to the port side.

Mason turned to dash back toward the bow. He heard the soft patter of hurrying feet and then, almost without warning, a figure running rapidly down the deck collided with him.

Mason felt the soft touch of damp silk. His nostrils caught the faint scent of perfume.

The lawyer realized the woman he was holding in his arms was in a panic. He could feel the pumping of her heart, the tension of her muscles. Then as her hand moved and he caught the glint of faintly reflected light from some metallic object, he realized she was carrying a gun.

From up near the bow of the boat came that cry which is so ominous to seamen the world over.

"Man overboard! M A N O V E R R R - B O A R D ! !"

From the river there came a series of thumping noises against the side of the yacht, as some struggling kicking object was swept past by the current on the side of the ship opposite to that where Mason was standing.

There followed an instant of silence. There was no more splashing, no more banging against the side of the yacht. Then there was the noise of confusion as doors opened and closed. There was the sound of tense voices, hurrying feet.

"Please," the woman said, in a voice that was husky with emotion, "*please*, let me go."

Mason saw then that he was holding Marion Shelby in his arms.

"What happened?"

"No, no, please, please!"

Mason reached for the gun. "What's this?" he asked.

Abruptly he felt the muscles tighten. With a swift convulsive motion which involved her entire body, she squirmed around, pressed herself tight against him.

Abruptly she let her knees sag, dropped almost to the deck of the yacht. The lawyer clutched at her but the smooth silk of the nightdress slid along her skin. Before he could get a firmer hold, she had slipped her head under his arm. His fingers clutched the silk of the nightdress. He heard the sound of tearing cloth and then she was running down the deck.

A few moments later the deck was flooded with illumination. Someone threw over a life preserver with a carbide canister attached and a brilliant white light spread out over the surface of the water, illuminating the life preserver, the water around the yacht, and throwing against the heavy wall of fog a strange, distorted shadow of the yacht.

The current bore the life preserver smoothly, gently downstream.

Mason felt Parker Benton's hand on his arm, turned to see the yachtsman, dressed in pajamas and slippers, bundling a robe around him.

"What happened?" Benton asked.

Mason said, "I heard someone shout 'Man Overboard' and a splash."

"Did you hear a shot?"

"I heard an explosion of some sort."

Benton called out, "Rig up that searchlight."

A man from the top of the pilothouse said, "I'm getting it, sir."

The canvas cover was ripped off the searchlight. A moment later the arc sputtered into brilliance and then a long shaft of light pushed itself against the opalescent fog to be swallowed up in milky nothingness.

"Try the stern, a little back of that life preserver," Benton said.

The searchlight swung out to play on the water around the flare that was attached to the life preserver. A small boat splashed into the water. There was the sound of oars and a boat rowed rapidly down the stream, then turned and came back against the current. A man standing in the bow bent down, searching the water by the aid of a beam from a five cell hand flashlight.

Benton said, "Let's get everyone on deck. Find out if anyone's missing." Then turning to Mason, "You were up and fully dressed . . . hadn't gone to bed?"

Mason said, "I'd gone to bed but hadn't been able to sleep so I came up on deck for a breath of air."

"How long had you been here before you heard the commotion?"

"I don't know. Twenty minutes, perhaps."

"See anyone?"

"A man standing in the stern. I take it he was one of the crew."

"See anything else?"

"I saw a woman running down the deck, clad in her night clothes."

"Who was she?"

Mason met his eyes. "I'm sorry but I can't tell you that."

Benton regarded Mason thoughtfully. "Let's get one thing straight, Mason. I'm running this ship." Then he turned on his heel and strode away.

The night was filled with sounds of hectic activity now. Opening and closing doors and frightened feet sounded in the passageways and on the companionways. The swift babble of voices kept up an incessant chatter; and cutting through all of the sounds of confusion, a crisp, authoritative voice

59

was giving orders. The motorboat had been lowered to the water and the engines started. It cruised in a series of questing circles around the yacht.

Some ten minutes later, Mason was up near the bow standing by himself when Della Street quietly joined him, her elbows sliding along the rail.

"What is it, Chief?"

Mason kept his eyes fastened on the dark surface of the water, said in a low voice, "I don't know, Della. Take it easy."

She said, "Scott Shelby is missing."

"I thought he might be."

She said, "His wife was on deck. She says that . . ."

"Here comes some man. It's Parker Benton. He seems to be filled with grim purpose."

"I wonder if . . ."

Mason said, "Beat it, Della. Circulate around and pick up the gossip."

Parker Benton walked with purposeful bearing to where Mason was standing. "Mason," he said, "Scott Shelby is missing."

"So I hear."

"His wife was on deck. She's the woman you saw."

"Is she?"

"And couldn't identify," Benton said.

Mason remained silent.

"She says that her husband telephoned her. He seemed excited. He asked her to take the gun from the top of the dresser and bring it up to him on the deck, that he was telephoning from the bow of the ship and to come at once, that it was a matter of life or death."

"And what did Mrs. Shelby do?" Mason asked.

"She jumped out of bed, grabbed the gun, and didn't even wait to put a robe on. She came flying up the companionway and was just approaching the bow when she saw a vague figure swaying this way and that, apparently engaged in a struggle of some sort, but she saw only the one figure. The other must have been below the deck."

Benton stopped, studied Mason's face.

"Go on," the lawyer said.

"Just before she got there, the man lurched and fell overboard. She screamed as she heard the splash. Then there was the sound of an explosion and a series of splashing noises. By that time she had reached the bow, and could hear her name being called. She bent over the rail and could see the figure of a man in the water, a figure that was floundering around aimlessly as though badly wounded and trying to swim. Then the figure moved into the oval of light which came from a porthole in the forecastle and she could see the man's face. It was the face of her husband. He seemed partially paralyzed. He called her name, tried to call out some message. She couldn't hear what he said. His voice was almost inaudible. Then he abruptly ceased to struggle and was swept down by the current under the overhang of the bow. She thought he was coming down the starboard side and ran that way, but apparently he drifted down the port side.—She says that you stopped her. She was too excited to be coherent."

Mason said, "That story conforms substantially to the facts as I understand them."

"But," Parker Benton went on, "it doesn't conform to the facts as they must have happened."

"No?" Mason asked, with a rising inflection of surprise.

"No," Benton said, positively. "For one thing, he couldn't have been telephoning from the bow of the yacht."

"Why not?" Mason asked. "There's a telephone in a little waterproof box up there. When you were showing us around the yacht, you pointed that telephone out to us. Of course, I'm not saying anything about the *probability* of a husband telephoning his wife under such circumstances as you have mentioned, but I am interested in the *possibility* which is what you are discussing."

"Exactly," Benton replied. "There's a trick about that telephone."

"What?"

"The system of telephones on this yacht is something of a makeshift. I didn't want to have a switchboard which would require the services of a telephone operator. Therefore, I put

61

in a call system. But the number of connections which I could get on it were limited. So I solved the problem by putting in *two* systems."

"Go ahead," Mason said. "You interest me."

"The system which is in the guests' staterooms has only certain outlets. The staterooms can all communicate with each other and with the steward, but they can't communicate with any other part of the ship. In only one stateroom are there phones from both systems."

"Yours?" Mason asked.

"Mine," Benton said. "I can communicate with the pilothouse, phone the engine room, the galley, and the lookout station on the crow's-nest as well as the bow of the ship. I can, of course, also communicate on the other system with the various staterooms and with the steward. Scott Shelby could *not* have called his wife from the bow of the ship."

Mason asked, "That box up there in the bow containing a telephone holds an instrument that can call only one stateroom?"

"That's right," Parker Benton said. "It is on the circuit which communicates with my stateroom, with the pilothouse, the engine room, the galley, etc. It can't reach any stateroom other than mine."

"Therefore?' Mason asked.

"Therefore," Benton said positively, "*if* Marion Shelby received any such call as she says she did, it must have come from one of the other staterooms or from the steward's desk."

"Well?" Mason asked.

"The other staterooms," Benton said dryly, "were all occupied."

"And the steward's office?"

"The steward on duty is a man who has been with me for some time, one whom I can trust absolutely. With that number of guests aboard the yacht I felt that it would be wise to have a steward stay on duty until two o'clock in the morning. This man volunteered to sit up. I saved his life once. His loyalty to me is almost a religion with him."

"Was he asleep?"

"He was sitting at his desk reading when the thing happened. He didn't hear the scream, but he did hear the sound of a shot and the sound of something bumping against the side of the yacht as the current swept it on past.''

"And so?" Mason asked.

"And so," Parker Benton said, "I find myself in a very embarrassing position. Apparently one of my guests has disappeared. His wife tells a story which on its face is impossible.''

"I don't see anything impossible about it," Mason said.

"She says that her husband telephoned her from the telephone station at the bow of the yacht. You can see what happened. When I was showing my guests around, I pointed out that little boxed-in telephone at the bow. The guests naturally assumed that the telephones would have been connected on one circuit. It makes a nice story but it simply doesn't stand up.''

Mason said, "Pardon me, Benton, I know something about evidence. You haven't proved a falsity of the wife's story.''

"No?"

"No," Mason said crisply.

"What's *your* theory?"

"Her husband may have *told* her that he was telephoning from the bow of the ship. It may have been the *husband* who had made the mistake about the telephone circuit. He was there when you showed the guests the phone.''

"In that event," Parker Benton said dryly, "he was telephoning from one of the other staterooms or from the steward's office. And I know he wasn't telephoning from the steward's office.''

Mason said, "That makes it a most interesting problem. What became of the gun Mrs. Shelby was carrying?''

"I thought I'd better take charge of it. The officers will want it. One of the chambers holds an empty cartridge case. The others are loaded.''

Mason said, "Some persons always keep a gun loaded that way—an empty shell under the hammer of the gun.''

"We'll leave that for the officers," Benton said. "You seem to be sticking up for Mrs. Shelby. Has she retained you?''

"Heavens no! I'm sticking up for her because I like her, and because I know absolutely what attitude the officers will take. They'll crucify her. That's why I'm trying to see if there isn't some other factor we haven't considered."

"I'm afraid there isn't."

"You're doing everything you can to locate the body?"

"Everything. I have both boats out and we're combing the water. There isn't the slightest chance the man is alive and swimming. He must have gone to the bottom, and it's more than twenty feet deep right here."

"Was the husband dressed or undressed. In other words, did you find his clothes in the stateroom?"

Benton said, "Shelby and his wife went to bed. There are twin beds in that cabin. She is rather a sound sleeper. Sometime after she got to sleep, Scott Shelby evidently got up and dressed. The peculiar thing is he didn't put on his socks, or his underwear, just slipped on trousers, shirt, shoes and a coat and went up on deck."

"Hat?" Mason asked.

"That's the strange thing. He put on his hat, but he left his underwear, his socks, his tie and scarf. Apparently he had dressed in a great hurry, but no one knows. The last anyone admits seeing him was when he turned out the light after he had got into bed. His wife says that he was morose and angry. He had fully expected that he would make a satisfactory settlement."

"On his own terms?"

"Apparently. He considered that four thousand dollars was ridiculously small and moreover he felt that I had caused him to lose face by the manner in which I approached the subject. I haven't all the details as yet, but that's the general sketch as his wife gave it to me."

"And then what happened?"

"She was sound asleep. The telephone rang. She answered it, but says she was only half awake. Her husband's voice poured an urgent message into her ear, to come at once to the bow of the ship, to take his gun from the top of the dresser and bring it to him. He shouted at her to hurry, to get up there as quickly as possible, not to try to dress. And then she heard someone who she thinks was her husband, grunt, as though he had been making some great effort or had been struck by a blow. She thinks there was a sound such as the impact of a blow, but she can't be certain. She was only half awake at the time.''

''And what did she do?''

''She says that without even stopping to think, she hung up the receiver, grabbed the gun, and dashed up to the deck, attired only in her nightdress.''

Mason said, ''You'll notify the police?''

''Just as soon as I feel I can spare one of the boats from the search.''

''When will that be?''

''As soon as I reach the conclusion it's really useless to continue a search for the body—perhaps five minutes, perhaps ten. Then I'll send the launch over to that town and telephone the sheriff's office. In the meantime I'm going to make certain no one leaves this yacht.''

Mason nodded.

''You haven't any suggestions?'' Benton asked.

''No.''

''And no criticisms?''

''None.''

''Thank you. This is my first experience with anything of this sort, and I wanted you to see if my plan of procedure was proper.''

''I would say it was eminently proper.''

''Thank you,'' Benton said, and moved away.

Chapter 10

An ominous sense of restraint settled upon the yacht. The guests huddled about, then went back to their cabins, only to return to the cold deck, restless, uncomfortable, and a little frightened.

The crew in the rowboat kept up their fruitless search for the body and from the fog-filled night there could be heard the *thunk . . . thunk . . . thunk* of the oars in the oarlocks. Occasionally the sound of a voice called out a hoarse command.

Mason, accompanied by Della Street, kept himself isolated in the bow of the yacht. The chill dampness of the fog had begun to penetrate and Della Street, giving a little shiver, asked, "What's the idea, Chief? Why can't we go where it's warm?"

Mason said, "I want to stay here until the officers come, Della."

"What's the reason?"

"In the first place, I don't want any tampering with whatever evidence there may be in the bow of the boat. In the second place, I have an idea that by keeping somewhat isolated this way we may invite the confidence of some of the others."

"You want me to stay here with you."

"Not if you're cold."

Della Street began flexing her knees, lowering and raising her body.

"It's the fact that my circulation is sluggish. I'll start the blood circulating," she said. "After all, being roused in the middle of the night this way and then standing out in the fog . . . But my stateroom seems ghastly . . . Chief, what about the status of the property now?"

"How do you mean?"

"Will Parker Benton go ahead and buy it?"

"Probably not."

"Then you mean if Scott Shelby is dead . . . Well, let's suppose he's murdered. His death didn't do the murderer any good?"

"Not so far as this particular deal is concerned. In fact it had just the opposite effect. Parker Benton now has notice of the lease. If he took the property, he would take it subject to the lease, regardless of the fact that it hasn't been recorded. And with the death of Scott Shelby, there's no opportunity of reaching a compromise, at least until some administrator has been appointed and a lot of red tape unwound. . . . That probably wouldn't suit Parker Benton at all."

Della Street ceased her flexing exercises as the full import of this statement soaked into her mind.

"Go ahead," Mason said, laughing. "Say it."

"Then the murderer couldn't have been one of the people who . . . Chief, that upsets my entire theory of the case . . . I had supposed, of course . . ."

Her voice trailed away into thoughtful silence.

Mason said, "I'm telling you the law, Della. But that doesn't necessarily affect the motive for murder."

"What do you mean?"

Mason said, "The murderer may not have known the law, may not have reasoned the thing out, may have felt that Scott Shelby was standing between the murderer and a nice profit on the sale of the property—or perhaps the property itself."

"Why that last?" Della Street asked.

"Because," Mason said, "if . . . Wait a minute, Della. We have a customer."

A figure silhouetted itself against the lights surrounded by their little fog auras.

Lawton Keller tried to make his manner casual.

"Oh, hello. I didn't know there was anyone up here."

"Looking for something?" Mason asked.

"Just taking a stroll to get warmed up . . . I suggested to Benton that it might be a good thing to serve a hot toddy but he doesn't want the officers to come and smell liquor on our

67

breaths. Personally, I'd give a lot for a good hot buttered rum.''

"Sounds very tempting," Mason said.

"Provided we had the butter," Della Street observed.

"And the rum," Lawton said, laughing.

"And the hot water," Mason supplemented.

They all joined in laughter which seemed a little forced. Then Lawton Keller said, "Has anyone found out what Shelby was doing up here in the bow of the ship?''

"Apparently not," Mason said. "I don't know. I haven't been around where the others were talking. I preferred not to hear the various theories.''

Lawton Keller said, "Well, I suppose I should be sorry. Personally I think the man was a crook and a blackmailer. Of course, even so, I wouldn't want to have the deal go through as the result of such a price as that.''

"Has it ever occurred to you," Mason asked, "that Shelby's death hasn't changed the situation in the least?''

Lawton Keller was evidently surprised. "Why, no," he said, "I thought . . . Well, to tell you the truth I hadn't given it a great deal of consideration.''

"Better ask Parker Benton what he intends to do," Mason said. "I think you'll find that Benton has given it plenty of consideration. . . . No, on second thought, you hadn't better ask him. It might show an undue eagerness.''

Keller was quite evidently completely nonplused. "You mean that his death doesn't clear the thing up?''

"Makes it more complicated than ever," Mason said.

Keller was silent for several seconds, then he absentmindedly took a cigarette from his pocket, struck a match, and lit the cigarette. The hand which held the match was unsteady.

Della Street noticed a slight tremor and flashed a quick glance at Mason.

The lawyer cautioned her with a slight frown against making any comment, and then the match went out and they were once more in half darkness.

Obviously jarred by the import of Mason's statement, Keller started to turn away, then after a moment swung back to

68

face Mason. "One thing," he said, "that may or may not be important."

"What?"

"Marjorie Stanhope was wandering around the deck shortly before the thing happened."

"How do you know?" Mason asked.

"I saw her."

"Where?"

"From the porthole of my stateroom. I couldn't sleep. I got up to smoke a cigarette . . . wondered if the fog had lifted and whether we'd get back early in the morning or perhaps be held here for a while. I went over to the porthole of the stateroom . . . my stateroom looks out on the port side of the deck."

"Lights were on?" Mason asked, making his voice sound as casual as possible.

"No, but there was some illumination. It wasn't pitch dark."

"And what did you see?"

"I saw Marjorie Stanhope walking along the deck."

"Toward the bow or toward the stern?"

"Toward the stern."

"Walking as though she were strolling around or as though she had been some place."

"As though she'd been some place."

"Said anything about this to anyone?"

"Just you, that's all. Do you think I should?"

Mason said, "Let your conscience be your guide."

"Well, I'm wondering. I suppose the officers will ask a lot of questions."

"Undoubtedly."

"And should I tell them?"

"Well," Mason said, "if they ask you if you saw anyone, you certainly couldn't lie to them."

"No, I'd hardly want to do that."

"Of course," Mason went on, "you're not called upon to volunteer any information. But if they should take a statement from you now and you neglected to mention a fact as important as that and then had to recall it later in response to some specific question, you might find yourself in something of a fix."

"Yes, I can see that," Lawton Keller said. "I'd prefer to have Marjorie Stanhope questioned first. Then if she mentions being on deck, everything will be all right."

"And if she doesn't?" Mason asked.

"Well, of course . . . My gosh, Mason, I never thought of *that*. If she doesn't. If she tries to conceal it and then I come along . . . Gosh, that's virtually the same as accusing her of something, isn't it?"

Mason said, unsympathetically, "Well, that's your problem. I definitely don't want to advise you."

Keller said, "I . . . Gosh, I don't know whether to go to Miss Stanhope and tell her that I saw her or . . . or . . . just wait and see what she says. Perhaps I'd better go to her."

Mason stretched, yawned, said, "Well, I guess you won't have much longer to deliberate on it. Unless I'm mistaken, these are the officers coming."

The sound of an air whistle came from the distant fog and the yacht answered with a short blast of its own whistle and swung the searchlight out over the water so that it was boring a milky tunnel into the night, a tunnel in which fog moisture swirled and gyrated in a kaleidoscope of misty motion.

Keller said, "Yes, I guess these are the officers all right," and rapidly moved away.

Della said, "Shall I see if he goes to talk with Miss Stanhope, Chief?"

"I don't think he'll have much time," Mason said. Even as he spoke the speedboat came roaring out of the fog into the illumination of the searchlight.

A man in the bow of the speedboat tossed a line to the deck of the yacht. It was caught and drawn up. A rope was attached to the end of the line, and a moment later the speedboat was secured.

The two officers who came aboard the yacht were rural deputies who were quite evidently impressed by the importance of the occasion.

The passengers assembled in the dining salon. The two officers sat at the head of the table. One of them asked the

70

questions in a nasal voice. He was in the late sixties, thin, sparse, and with blue eyes that seemed covered with a film as they peered out through spectacles, the lenses of which were badly soiled with finger marks. But his mind covered all the various angles of the situation.

"Now then," he said, "I want to know whether anyone *knows* anything about this."

There was a moment's silence which greeted his blanket question; then Mrs. Shelby said with grim determination, "I think I'm the one who knows all there is to know about it. I've told my story before, but I'll tell it again."

She went on and told her story in detail.

The deputy sheriff listened to her attentively, said, "Well, I guess that covers it," glanced at his companion, cleared his throat, turned to Perry Mason and said, "You were out on deck, Mr. Mason?"

"That's right."

"What do you know about what happened?"

"My recollection conforms substantially to the statement made by Mrs. Shelby."

"Anyone else on deck?" the deputy asked.

There was a period of uncomfortable silence.

"If it hadn't been for that shot," the second deputy interposed, "we'd think there wasn't anything to it, just somebody falling overboard. That shot makes things kinda different. Are you certain you heard a shot, Mrs. Shelby?"

"Yes."

"You had a gun?"

"That's right."

"But you didn't shoot it?"

"No."

"You're sure of that?"

"Yes."

"There's one empty shell in the cylinder."

"I know that."

"How do you know that?"

"Mr. Benton broke the gun open after I told him what had happened and he told me there was an empty shell in it. I didn't know it."

"All the others were loaded?"

"I believe that's right, yes."

The deputy sheriff once more glanced at his companion, then turned to Mason. "Just why were *you* out on the deck, Mr. Mason?"

"I couldn't sleep."

"You didn't have any idea that . . . Well, you know, something was going to happen?"

Mason smiled. "My telepathy isn't that good."

The deputy sheriff didn't smile. "The first thing we've got to do," he said, "is to find the body."

"We're searching for it now," Parker Benton said. "We've kept up a continual search . . . I can assure you of one thing, there was no struggling man in the water . . . I believe you said your husband could swim, Mrs. Shelby?"

"Yes, he's a *very* good swimmer. he wouldn't have gone down . . . I mean even if he'd fallen overboard, he could have stayed on the surface of the water indefinitely if it hadn't been for . . . you know, something else."

"You mean a gunshot wound?" the deputy asked.

"Yes."

"Know any reason why anyone should have wanted him dead?"

The woman hesitated while her eyes sought those of Parker Benton, then looked at Lawton Keller, then swung back from those of Jane Keller to the deputy. "No," she said.

Abruptly, Margie Stanhope spoke up. "I was on deck."

The deputy looked at her. "You were?"

"That's right."

"Doing what?"

"Walking. I couldn't sleep. This business meant a lot to me—meant even more than anyone will ever realize."

"What business?"

"The business Mr. Benton had with Scott Shelby."

"I'll explain that to you later," Benton interposed, speaking to the deputy.

The deputy looked at Marjorie Stanhope.

"See anyone?" he asked.

"Yes, I saw Mr. Shelby."

"Where?"

"In the bow."

"What was he doing?"

"Standing there. He acted as though he was waiting for someone, as though he had an appointment."

"You talk with him?"

"I tried to. He asked me to leave. Said he had a date to discuss something."

"Did he say who he was waiting for?"

"No."

"Why didn't you tell us before?"

"This is the first chance I've had."

The deputies exchanged whispered comments, then the one in charge turned to Mrs. Shelby and said, apologetically, "Guess we got to ask you a personal question. . . . Leave any insurance, did he?"

"Yes."

"Much?"

"Quite a lot."

"When was it taken out?"

Marion Shelby took a deep breath. "Sixty days ago," she said.

The deputy looked at the other passengers, said, "I guess you folks better go to your rooms now. There's a few more questions we got to ask Mrs. Shelby here, and it might go better if we're sort of by ourselves."

Chapter 11

Marion Shelby tapped timidly at the door of Mason's state-room. "Come in," Mason called.

She entered the room, said, "I hope you'll forgive me for disturbing you like this but . . . I simply had to see you."

She had been crying and her eyes were swollen and red.

"What's the matter?" Mason asked. "Have they been getting rough with you?"

"Yes."

"Make any specific accusations?"

"Nothing that's specific. They might just as well have, as to say the things that they did. And then back of all that, there was . . . you know, the manner . . . the way they did things."

Mason nodded.

"Mr. Mason, I want you to . . . Well, in case anything should come of it . . . You know what I mean."

"Go on," Mason said as she stopped.

"I want you to take care of me. I want you to represent me and see that I'm protected. I just don't know what's happening. I don't know what I'm getting into."

Mason said, "Your husband told me that he had been poisoned."

"Yes, we had had food poisoning, we both got it, but . . . now it seems there was something in the food."

"Your husband had enemies?"

"Yes."

"A good many?"

"I think so, yes."

"How did you and he get along?"

She heaved a long sigh, said, "All right, I guess . . . I guess it's about the way things go nowadays. But, I tried to be broad-minded."

"You mean there were other women?"

"I don't know. I didn't ask questions."

"But you *think* there were?"

"He had been staying out quite a bit lately. He was hardly ever home nights until very, very late. And when he did come home, he didn't want me even to talk to him. He had things on his mind. I could see that and I tried to do the way he wanted me to do. When he wanted to be left alone, I left him alone."

"Didn't ask any questions?"

"Not a question. I think that's where a lot of marriages split up. People begin to get too nosy about each other. After all, you can't stop a person from doing what he wants to do. I think that people like to have the power of decision, the freedom of action. The minute a man, in particular, begins to think that his freedom is being curtailed, he resents it."

"So you were becoming just a bit disillusioned about marriage?"

"Just a little disillusioned about Scott Shelby if you want to be specific."

"Was there any other man as far as you were concerned?"

She met his eyes steadily. "No," she said.

Mason said, "I want to know one thing, Mrs. Shelby. Are you telling me the truth about what happened tonight?"

"Absolutely, Mr. Mason. I swear to you on my word of honor."

Mason gave the matter thoughtful consideration for a few seconds, then asked abruptly, "Did you telephone Parker Benton and suggest to him that a conference on this yacht with you along might bring about a settlement of the case?"

Her eyes showed surprise. "Who said I did?"

"Did you?"

"Yes. How did you know?"

"I didn't. I'm asking."

She said, "My husband asked me to. He seemed very much upset. He said he had a chance to settle a case with a lawyer who he felt was really representing Parker Benton and that he'd kicked that chance to make a settlement out of the window. So he went on to say that it *might* not be too late,—if I'd telephone Mr. Benton and pretend I was just giving him an anonymous tip and not let on who I was, and tell him that while Scott was erratic and headstrong, his wife was the balance wheel, and that if he'd invite . . .''

Mason interrupted. ''Now this may be terribly important—to you. Had there been any *previous* discussion between you and your husband about a yachting trip on this yacht?''

''Why no.''

''You're sure?''

''Of course. He hardly knew who Parker Benton was.''

Mason frowned.

''He had wanted me to go on a yachting trip this weekend,'' she went on. ''There was a yacht he was going to try out and buy if he liked it. He and a friend of his were arranging a party and I was to go—a week-end cruise, but that was a yacht he was buying, or planning to buy, and . . .''

She broke off as knuckles pounded on the door.

Mason crossed over and opened the door. The deputy sheriff, looking somewhat startled, stood on the threshold and beside him was Sergeant Dorset.

''Well,'' Mason exclaimed, ''what are *you* doing here? Isn't this somewhat out of your jurisdiction?''

Dorset said crisply, ''I tried to get here before it was too late. I see that I didn't.''

''Before it was too late for what, Sergeant?''

''To keep Scott Shelby from being murdered.''

''You knew that he was in danger of losing his life?''

Sergeant Dorset said, ''I had collected enough evidence so that I felt free to act.''

Mason's eyes were probing. ''Come, come, Sergeant, there's no need to be so secretive about it.''

Sergeant Dorset said, ''All right, if you want the lowdown I'll give it to you. I came here because I had a warrant to serve.''

''On whom?''

''A warrant,'' Sergeant Dorset said, ''arresting Marion Shelby for an attempt to commit murder by means of poison. She is the one who administered the arsenic which would

76

have finished her husband off if it hadn't been for the prompt medical attention he received."

Marion Shelby recoiled as though the officer's words had been bullets, pounding at her with a physical pressure. She came over to stand beside Mason. "You . . . you can't say things like that. It's not true . . . it's not . . ."

"Take it easy," Mason said, "let's hear the rest of it, Sergeant."

"Isn't that enough?"

"If there's any more, we may as well hear it."

"You'll hear it at the proper time," Sergeant Dorset said.

Mason said slowly, "Under the circumstances, Mrs. Shelby, in view of the fact that you have been arrested, I think it would be a good plan for you not to do *any* talking."

"But I'm going to deny those charges," Marion Shelby said indignantly. "They're absolutely absurd. They're false. They're malicious."

"That's all right," Mason said, "deny the charges. Remember now, Mrs. Shelby, if I'm going to represent you, I want you to have just one formula. For the press there will be only two words 'no comment.' For the officers you will simply say, 'I am not guilty. I have done nothing and the charge is unfounded, but I do not care to discuss it in the absence of my attorney. And, when my attorney is here, he will do the talking for me.' "

"I see," Sergeant Dorset sneered, "the old formula."

"The old formula," Mason told him. "And, whenever I have a client who is being framed, I revert to that formula."

"Framed?" Dorset said and laughed.

"That's what I said," Mason told him.

"Well, get a load of this," Dorset said. "She got her husband to insure his life in her favor, got him to sign over quite a bit of property to her, then, she went into a drugstore and bought some arsenic. Said she wanted it for rats. Next rattle out of the box, it shows up in her husband's food . . ."

"And I was poisoned at the same time, with the same sort of poison," Marion Shelby said.

"Sure," Sergeant Dorset acknowledged patiently, "that's an old stunt. Quite frequently they do that to divert suspicion.

77

You were careful to give yourself just a small dose, and your husband a deadly dose.''

"That's not true."

"Remember the purse you were carrying that day? The brown calfskin that went with your brown suit?" Scrgeant Dorset asked.

"Yes."

"Well, in that purse there's a little paper bag containing arsenic."

"Why there certainly isn't! There . . ." She stopped indignantly.

"And," Sergeant Dorset went on, "you'll have to admit that you bought the arsenic. You didn't even go very far to do it. Just three or four blocks from where you live."

"Why should I have gone anywhere? There was nothing to conceal."

"Why did you buy it?"

"Careful," Mason told her.

"I'm not going to be careful, Mr. Mason. I have absolutely nothing to conceal. I got that arsenic for rats because my husband asked me to."

"And what did you do with it when you got it?" Sergeant Dorset asked.

"I gave it to him."

Dorset laughed. "And I suppose he promptly proceeded to take you out to dinner, poison himself with it, put a little in your food and then put the rest of it in your purse."

"I . . ."

"You *may* have something there, Sergeant," Mason said. "You probably intended that to be sarcasm but I think perhaps you're getting rather close to the truth. And, I think we won't do any more talking, Mrs. Shelby."

"So tonight," Sergeant Dorset went on, "she decides that poison is a little too uncertain. She isn't going to try that any more. She brings along a six-gun she took from the dresser drawer in her husband's room, pushes him overboard, shoots him and then starts yelling for help."

"That's not so. I did not do any such thing. I have told the officer here exactly what happened."

"Yeah, I know," Sergeant Dorset said wearily, "it isn't even a good story."

"It's the truth."

"Look here," Mason said. "If you think this woman fired a gun, give her the paraffin test and . . ."

"Bosh on that stuff," Dorset said. "I don't believe in it where murder is deliberate. She wore a glove, pulled the trigger, then threw the glove away. That gun was fired within the last few hours, the barrel still smells of powder fumes. She admits she had it when her husband was shot . . ."

"And we insist on a paraffin test," Mason interrupted.

"Got any paraffin?" Dorset asked.

"No, of course not. But there may be some on the boat."

"There isn't any, and I don't like the way you're yelling about that paraffin test. There's lots of ways of beating that."

Marion Shelby said, "I did *not* fire that gun."

"You heard a shot?"

"Yes."

"Your husband telephoned you from the bow of the boat?"

"He *said* he was talking from the bow of the boat."

"Well, how did he get on the telephone?" Sergeant Dorset asked. "Where was he telephoning from?"

Mason said, "Now, Sergeant, you're really beginning to get somewhere. Since you're here, and since you're a trained investigator of homicides, I suggest that you dust the receivers of every telephone on the yacht and see if you can find Scott Shelby's fingerprints."

Sergeant Dorset's smile was patronizing. "That," he said, "would be just a waste of good dusting powder, Mason. Scott Shelby didn't leave his fingerprints on any telephone receiver because he didn't telephone. He *couldn't* have telephoned. Her story is absurd on the face of it.—And she thought the insurance company wouldn't make any investigation but would cheerfully pay off the fifty thousand dollar policy where the holder was bumped off within sixty days after the policy was issued. She went down to her own neighborhood drugstore to buy the arsenic with which she tried to poison her husband. My God, but she's naive!"

Mason said, "Sergeant, I ask you once more, please dust the receivers of these telephones. Please give a paraffin test."

"Nuts!" Sergeant Dorset said and held the door open for his prisoner.

With her head high, Marion Shelby walked out of the room.

Mason hesitated a moment, walked over to the dressing table, opened his bag, dumped the contents unceremoniously in the drawer of the dressing table, went over to the telephone, took a sharp knife from his pocket, neatly severed the telephone wires and using great care not to get his fingerprints on the receiver, gently lifted the severed instrument, put it in his bag and snapped the catch.

A few moments later he had put on his hat and overcoat and, bag in hand, walked down the corridor and knocked on the door of Della Street's stateroom.

"Who is it?" she asked.

"Put your things on, Della," Mason said through the door, "we're leaving."

"But don't we have to wait until . . ."

"*We* don't have to wait for anything," Mason said. "The speedboat is going and I'm going with it. Sergeant Dorset has shown up with a warrant for the arrest of Marion Shelby. He got the deputy here to help him serve it."

"But will they let us go back?" Della Street asked.

Mason said, "If they think they're going to stop us, they'll have to give a damn good reason. Personally, I don't think they'll even try. My own idea is there'll be a stampede ashore. Sergeant Dorset thinks he's got it all solved. . . . Come on, Della, we've got work to do."

Chapter 12

Paul Drake, head of the Drake Detective Agency, had, like a doctor, learned to adjust his sleeping habits to the exigencies of his profession. He had learned to sleep with three telephones by the side of his bed. When he was working on an important case, he would waken with the ringing of one of these telephones, mechanically switch on the bedside lamp with one hand while he lifted the telephone receiver with the other. He would listen to some new development, correlate the matter in his mind, give instructions, hang up the telephone, slide back down into bed, turn out the light and be asleep almost as soon as he had reached the pillow.

A good detective, Drake frequently said, must have two essential qualifications. The first qualification is that not only must he not look like a detective, but he must look so much like a man in one of the other professions that he seems typical. The second qualification is that he must learn to take his sleep and his meals, when and if he gets them.

And then, Drake was wont to add with a whimsical smile, "If he has brains, it helps. But they're not *really* necessary."

Drake himself looked professionally sad, and whenever Della Street would tell him to cheer up, his stock rejoinder was, "Leave me alone, Della, I'm practicing looking like an undertaker. In my business it's my biggest asset."

Mason's knuckles beat a tattoo on the door of Paul Drake's apartment.

Almost instantly Mason heard bare feet hitting the floor, then steps coming to the door.

"Who is it?" Drake asked.

"Perry Mason, Paul."

A lock clicked on the inside of the door.

"Della Street's with me," Mason hastened to add.

"In that case," Drake said, "give me five seconds."

A few moments later the door opened. Drake, attired in a bathrobe and slippers, his tousled hair in complete disarray, regarded them with a jaundiced eye and said, "I presume you two have committed matrimony or something and have got me up to tell me about it."

"What an *interesting* way to spend a honeymoon," Della Street exclaimed.

Mason said, "Don't be silly, Paul. The husband who would let his bride look at you would be guilty of contributory negligence. If she thought men looked like that, she'd rush home to mother."

Drake ran his fingers through his hair, said, "If you'd telephoned first, I'd have had my hair all slicked down, and been shaved."

"And washed your eyes with cold water, I suppose."

"Sure," Drake said, "the sky's the limit. I'd even have cleaned my teeth. It's cold here. I'm getting back into bed. Find yourselves chairs and talk. Lift the pants out of that chair, Perry. Careful with them, my watch is in the pocket. What time *is* it, by the way?"

Mason looked at his wrist watch and said, "Five thirty-two."

"Almost daylight," Drake said. "What's the trouble?"

"We want you to find a corpse."

Drake slid into bed, pulled up the covers, punched the pillows up in back of his head, looked from Mason to Della Street and said, "Shucks, yes. When you come right down to it, a man should have known that it wasn't romance that has been keeping you two on a nocturnal expedition. It's crime that invariably furnishes the motivation for *your* gallivanting around."

Mason moved Paul Drake's trousers from the chair, said, "Sit down here, Della. I'll sit on the foot of the bed."

Drake moved his feet.

"You must admit that this is a novel variation," Mason said, sitting on the foot of the bed.

"I don't get it."

"Usually," Mason said, "we find the corpse and we want

you to find the murderer. This time, we have the murderer and we want you to find the corpse."

"Dragging a lake, or something I suppose," Drake said.

"It's not a lake, it's a river."

"And I have to drag it?"

"No, the police will be doing that."

"Where do I look for the corpse then?"

"In a blonde's apartment."

"Sure, nothing to it," Drake said. "I'm getting to be a genius at finding these things, Perry. You simply knock on the door . . . Let me see. It will be around six-fifteen. I'll knock on the door and say, 'Pardon me Madam. I'm the field representative of the Bureau of Vital Statistics. We're wondering if you have any old corpses around you'd like to turn in. We can give you a liberal allowance for a trade-in or, if you're tired of corpses, we can make an outright purchase.' Or, I might pose as a medical student looking for bodies to dissect. That would be a good line, 'Pardon me Madam, but I'm a young medical student working my way through college. There's a shortage of stiffs for dissection and I thought perhaps you could help me get my education.' For an approach like that, you mustn't wear a hat, cultivate an earnest, sincere smile . . . People are always willing to help someone through college. Hell yes, Perry, she'd dig up a corpse any time."

Mason said, "When you get done wisecracking, you might listen to facts. We may not have too much time."

"Okay, okay, go on. What's the story?"

Mason said, "The story is too long to give you *all* the details. But I want to sell you on my theory of what happened. I'll sketch the highlights."

"Start sketching."

"A man by the name of Scott Shelby. Something of a human enigma, plays them close to his chest and chisels around with oil leases. Married for the third time. Has a peach of a wife several years younger than he is. She's a good scout, easy on the eyes and has a beautiful chassis."

Drake said to Della Street, "It's all right, Della. He isn't entirely hopeless. You notice that he doesn't have much time to describe the murder, but when it comes to describing the guy's wife he really goes to town."

Della Street smiled. "You'd be surprised at what he notices, Paul."

"Wouldn't I?" Drake said. "Okay, Mr. Perry Mason, what about Mr. Shelby and his beautiful wife?"

Mason said, "We were on a yachting trip with them. The wife is wakened from a sound sleep by a telephone call. Her husband tells her to grab the gun that is on the dresser by the bed and rush up to the deck, to come quickly—it's a matter of life and death."

"So she calls you on the telephone, rolls over and goes to sleep," Drake said, "and you want me to find the corpse."

"No. She jumps up out of bed, doesn't even stop to put a wrap around her or put on slippers, grabs the gun, runs in her bare feet toward where her husband told her to meet him. She's just in time to see him floundering around in a peculiar way and then there's a splash and he's overboard. Just about that time she hears a shot, she lets out a scream and runs up to the bow of the boat. She sees her husband down in the water, making a few feeble struggles. He calls her name in a faint voice, then he is swept by the current under the overhang of the boat. She thinks he's going down the starboard side. As a matter of fact, he evidently drifted down the port side, gave a few spasmodic kicks and struggles, hitting against the side of the boat as he went downstream."

"And the wife?" Drake said.

"Ran slap into my arms," Mason said.

"What time?"

"Around midnight."

"Nice going," Drake said to Della Street. "In my early childhood I used to practice penmanship by copying over and over 'It's the early bird that catches the worm.' But look what happens to the guy who's standing out on the starboard side of the boat, just waiting for wives to come along. He probably has been standing there three or four hours, and then his patience is suddenly rewarded. A beautiful wife clad only in a diaphanous silk nightgown, rushing along the deck, pops right into his arms. Nice going, Perry. No wonder you took

84

so much time describing the anatomical charms of the wife. Any sign of the murderer?''

"Only the wife."

"Tut, tut. . . . Oh, by the way, Perry, what about the gun? Was she still carrying the gun?''

"She was still carrying the gun."

"Any shells fired?''

"One."

Drake raised his index finger and slid one across the other. "Naughty, naughty, Perry. You've let the gal's sex appeal ruin your judgment. If she had approached you in your office, you'd have taken one look at the case and said that it stunk. But, because she comes charging into your arms, you look down into her eyes and decide you're going to protect her from the bold, bad police.''

"You think so?'' Mason asked.

"Think so!'' Drake exclaimed. "My gosh, Perry, if you're telling me the story the way it happened, look at how absurd it is. In the first place, if someone had fired a shot, who fired the shot? The husband was down in the water mortally wounded, drifting past the boat, kicking at the sides as he went past. Where was the murderer? He'd hardly have been in the water, swimming around with the husband. Apparently he wasn't on deck. Put yourself in the position of the jury. A woman smiles sweetly at them and says, 'There I was, on deck, clad only in my nightdress, with a gun in my hand, and my husband was down in the water below me mortally wounded. There was no one else in sight, but it's a perfectly natural predicament for a devoted young wife to be in. My lawyer will stand up and give you a complete and perfect explanation.' And then she crosses her knees and smiles at you, Perry. That will be your cue to stand up to the jury and tell them how it happened.''

"You don't know anything yet,'' Mason said grimly.

"Well, go ahead. I'm always anxious to learn.''

"About sixty days ago she insured her husband's life for fifty thousand dollars.''

"Oh-oh,'' Drake observed.

"And four days ago she went to a drugstore and bought some arsenic."

"Wanted to poison rats, I presume."

"Exactly."

"And what happened to the poison, Perry?"

"It turned up in papa's soup."

"I suppose he jumped up on the table and made squeaky noises like a rat and she thought that rats always ate soup and that would be a good place to put the poison."

Mason said, "You see what I'm getting at, Paul?"

"Good Lord, yes. You're tired of winning murder cases. You want to get one where you don't stand a chance on earth. Hang it, Perry, I'm only half kidding. Why the hell don't you sit in your office and let people come to you fully clothed. If you'd seen that girl with her clothes on, you'd have kicked her out on the street. I only have one suggestion to offer."

"What's that?"

"Let her put her nightgown back on and go to court in that. Perhaps she can do as much for the jury as she did for you.—But I doubt it."

"So do I," Mason said.

"Well, it's your only chance."

Mason said, "Look at the case a little more closely, Paul."

"I hate to do it, Perry. It hurts me every time I consider it. And if you think the Drake Detective Agency is going to be sucker enough to get all worked up over a client like that, you're nuts. I don't want to touch the case with a ten foot pole, Perry. Much as I like your business and all that, I'm damned if I want to try and convince myself that a woman like that is innocent. Get someone who is more gullible and don't tackle him so early in the morning."

"Quit it," Mason said. "We haven't time."

"Okay, but I'm just telling you how I feel. I don't want any part of it."

Mason said, "The woman is beautiful."

"You told me that before."

"Her eyes have that little half-humorous twinkle that you find in the eyes of beautiful women who have looked over life, have seen all there is to it, and are just a little amused by it all.''

"I know the type," Drake said. "They are so beautiful that every man pursues them and they become faintly amused by the unvarying, universal response of all masculine mankind; so after a while they decide they can get away with anything, including a murder, if they just put on thin night clothes and manage to run into the arms of a famous lawyer.''

"The point I am getting at is that she's intelligent," Mason said. "At least, she thinks.''

"With all due respect to Della Street here, who is probably the only one I know who combines beauty and brains, the two are not necessarily inseparable," Drake said.

"So," Mason said, "we begin to consider the case against a woman.''

"It's about time," Drake muttered.

"She has a husband take out a tidy little insurance policy. She goes down to a drugstore, a drugstore in the immediate neighborhood where the police will be certain to look in case they start any sort of an investigation. She buys arsenic. She says she wants it for rat poisoning. Then her husband has a near fatal case of arsenic poisoning. It happens at a time when he is dining at a restaurant with his wife and no one else in the restaurant gets any poison, only the husband. And oh yes, Paul, something I almost forgot to tell you.''

"Don't tell me that it's more circumstantial evidence against the wife?''

"But it is.''

"What?''

"When the police examined the purse the wife was carrying the day the husband became ill from food poisoning, they found a little paper bag still containing some arsenic.''

"Well, *isn't* that nice," Drake said. "Really, Perry, I must go to court and hear you when you're arguing that case to the jury. That's going to be something!''

Mason said, "Now let's forget the obvious for a minute and look at the thing from a common sense standpoint. If a woman were going to put a slug of arsenic in her husband's soup while he went to answer the telephone or something, she would have taken along the necessary dosage and dumped the whole thing into the soup and stirred it up. She wouldn't have sprinkled a little in and then very carefully left some in the bag so that the police could find it.''

"Oh, I see," Drake said. "That's going to be your defense. She couldn't possibly have been that dumb. Is that it?''

"That's it.''

"I don't like it.''

"Why not?''

"About the arsenic, for instance. She might have dumped half of it in the soup and intended to save the rest of it for dessert. Then hubby decided that he didn't want any dessert or perhaps he didn't go answer the telephone after the dessert was served or he might have held the telephone in a position where he could keep looking at the table; so she didn't dare to raise the upper crust of his pie and dump the rest of the nice little white powder that would make it so the insurance company would pay mama the money so she could run away with the other man.''

"Okay," Mason said. "That's fine. Now then, having done all of those dumb things and having gone home, she doesn't dispose of the rest of the arsenic but leaves it in the purse for the police to find.''

"Well, of course," Drake said, "you're acting on the assumption that she looks ahead and sees that the police are going to realize that it's arsenic poisoning, and most smart little women like that think that the doctor will make a death certificate of acute indigestion and that's all they need to worry about.''

"So then," Mason goes on, "she takes him out on a yachting trip and tries to kill him. In order to do that she waits until midnight, goes up to the bow of the ship, carrying a gun. She has evidently lured her husband up there. She gets him near the rail, gives him a push, and as he hits the water, leans over and gives him a nice little lead pill. Then she runs down the deck, still carrying the gun with one chamber fired, and runs into me.''

"Of course," Drake said, "she didn't know that she was going to run into you. Or did she?"

"Figure it either way," Mason said. "She still couldn't have been that dumb."

"You can't tell. Suppose she didn't know you were on deck. She might have had a chance to run back to her stateroom, climb into bed, and be sleeping the sleep of the innocent when the captain knocked on the door and said, 'I beg your pardon, Ma'am, but have you lost a husband?' "

"Sure," Mason said, "that would have been perfectly swell. And there she would have been, lying so sweetly innocent, with the murder weapon on the dresser. Of course, no one would have suspected. It would have been the perfect crime."

Drake scratched his head. "You're beginning to get me sold," he said. "Even a dumb cluck who depended on her curves to get her out of trouble would have thrown the gun into the drink."

"As far as she could have chucked it," Mason said.

"Go ahead," Drake told him. "I'm getting interested now. What happened after that?"

"After that," Mason said, "they threw out a life preserver with a flare attached to it. Nothing happened. They launched boats, rigged up a searchlight and cruised all around. No body."

"Of course with a lead pill in him," Drake said, "he'd have gone to the bottom."

"Remember that he floated past the boat and managed to keep kicking at the side of the boat, pounding it so that people who hadn't been awakened by the shot and the woman's scream would be roused from their slumber by the jars on the side of the boat.—You know how it sounded. That sound was magnified along the water line of a trim yacht."

"Even so," Drake said, "the absence of the body doesn't bother me so much. It could have sunk down to the bottom. A wounded man drifting past the ship naturally would try to cling to the side of the boat. He'd keep groping with his hands trying to find something to hang onto."

Mason said, "Now we come to something else. He was

buying a yacht, going to try it out over the week end. His wife and a few friends were going along.''

"I don't get it, Perry."

"And then this deal with Benton came up," Mason went on, "and he had his wife phone Parker Benton suggesting this yacht trip. Get it?''

Drake frowned. "Deal me one more card, Perry. I'm beginning to get the idea."

"All right," Mason said, "now we come to something else. A short time before the murder I had been walking around the deck of the yacht and up in the bow I'd stumbled over a piece of rope, a rope about twenty feet long, about one inch rope."

"What about it?"

"I kicked it out of the way."

"I don't get it," Drake said.

"When I went back there a while after the shooting and the splashing, the rope was gone."

"Go on," Drake said. "You went up to take a look?"

"I went up to take a look."

"No one there?"

"No one."

"If the wife didn't fire the shot, who did?"

"Don't you get it, Paul? There's only one person who could have fired it."

"Who?"

"The husband."

"You mean he shot himself?"

"Not himself. He just fired one shot in order to pass the buck to his wife. He had already fired one shot out of the gun that he left on the dresser for the wife to bring when he telephoned her. Now then, he had to work his timing just right. He had to wait until he saw her coming along the deck and then he had to struggle and sway in a peculiar manner and then topple overboard. Then he had to fire a shot and be in such a position that just as she leaned over the bow of the boat she'd look down and see him. He'd even call her name so that there could be a positive identification. Then he'd slip out of sight and drift along the side of the yacht, pounding and bang-

90

ing against the sides, so he'd be certain to waken witnesses, then he'd completely disappear."

"Let's hear more about the rope," Drake said. "What does the rope have to do with it?"

"You see, Paul, the man had to go overboard, falling in a rather peculiar way. Then he had to be where his wife would see him when she reached the bow of the boat. There's quite an overhang on the bow of a yacht that's built along those trim lines. He had to be certain that the current didn't sweep him away until after his wife had seen him. And in addition to that, he had to be where he could have one hand out of the water and fire a gun, and be sure it went off. He didn't want that gun to get wet or have the barrel filled with water. He had to drop off the yacht in such a way that he could keep his right hand out of the water until after he'd fired the shot."

"And you mean that accounts for the rope?"

"That accounts for the rope," Mason said. "The best way to have done all that was to have looped a twenty-foot rope over the bow of the yacht. Then when he leaned over the side, he could manage to fall in just that peculiar manner. He could hit the water with a splash, but it would be a controlled splash. He'd have hold of the rope with his left hand and the gun would be held in his right hand. He'd fire the gun then let go one end of the rope and pull the rope down with him. Then he only needed to kick himself up against the current and the confused motions of a wounded swimmer would keep him in just the position he wanted until he looked up and saw his wife looking down at him. Then he could drift along the side of the boat."

"Gosh," Drake said, "he really must have loved his wife."

"That's the point," Mason said, "I think he loved a nice little blond real estate agent by the name of Ellen Cushing. He'd been divorced twice and had had the bite put into him for alimony. He didn't want any more of that; so he decided he'd die this time. But when a person dies, there are certain formalities that have to be taken care of before he's marked dead officially. Someone has to see the body and identify it. So why not pass the buck to his wife? Why not let her be the one to identify the body? And just to make sure that she was kept thoroughly occupied, he'd leave her framed with a nice little murder rap.

"You see the thing had all been planned for this week-end yachting party, but it wouldn't have looked so good if he'd gone bye-bye overboard at a time when he was surrounded only by his own friends. Then along came this deal with Parker Benton, and, of course, Benton's been known as a yachtsman for years—pictures of his yacht in all the yachting magazines. . . . If Shelby could get aboard that yacht and leave Parker Benton to do the explaining to the police . . . Get it?"

"I'm beginning to, okay. But why didn't he compromise his case, get the dough and . . . ?"

"Because he could never in the world have got a dime out of Benton until the escrow was closed. Benton would have demanded a quitclaim deed from Shelby, then given Shelby an order on the escrow. So, by playing it this way, and leaving the case wide open, Shelby felt certain the true facts would never have been even suspected, let alone uncovered."

Drake ran his fingers through his hair, looked at Della Street, scratched the hair on top of his head, rubbed the palm of his hand along his temple, said, "Gosh, Perry, you *almost* convince me. I have to hand it to you. It's the best story I ever heard to account for a woman running barefoot along a deck carrying a gun and saying, 'Oh, dear, something terrible has happened. My husband has just been murdered, but I don't know what happened to the murderer. And the similarity of my having a gun in my hand is purely coincidental. No resemblance to any murderer living or dead is intended.' It's a hell of a swell story, Perry, but remember I'm only listening to your side of it. Something seems to tell me that if I were on a jury, when the district attorney got up and began to make his argument, I would fall for it like a ton of bricks. I'd bring in a verdict of guilty of murder in the first degree. I can imagine that a good district attorney could pour on a lot of nice sarcasm and before he got done, the jurors would all be laughing at you."

92

"That's just the point," Mason said. "The district attorney has the closing argument. *I* think that's what happened, but we've got to get some proof."

"And the proof?" Drake asked.

"The proof," Mason said, "lies in the fact that the man must have had an accomplice, someone to help him out, someone who was camped downstream with a rowboat anchored out of the deep channel but where the current was strong. Scott Shelby must have kicked past the side of the boat, then gone on downstream, swimming under water, come up to the surface, quit swimming, turned over on his back and floated until he saw the signal of his accomplice in the rowboat, probably a shielded flashlight. Then he climbed aboard over the stern of the rowboat and his accomplice promptly cut loose from his anchor and silently sculled the boat to shore where they had an auto waiting. They'll be working according to a tight little schedule. Scott Shelby will be on an airplane headed for the East or perhaps some place in Mexico. He'll show up under the name of Scott Cushing and after a while his blond wife will come to join him. Now that's where you come in, Paul. I want you to get the best operatives money can buy. I want to get a whole flock of people scrutinizing the passengers who go out on airplanes. I want detectives to cover the morning outgoing trains at the depot. I want detectives to comb the river bank and see if they can find some trace of a blond girl who rented a rowboat, And above all, Paul, if the scheme worked out according to schedule, Scott Shelby must have changed from his wet clothes to dry clothes in the girl's automobile. I want to get hold of her automobile and see if we can find Shelby's wet clothes. That's why I'm in a hurry and that's why we've got to work fast."

Paul Drake came out of bed with a bound. "Give me those pants, Perry . . . It's all right, Della, sit still. I'll dress in the bathroom . . . Tell you what you do, Della. You can save some time. Ring up the agency and tell the night telephone operator to call the list of numbers on the emergency card that she'll find in my upper right-hand desk drawer. Those are some men I can depend on. Let's see, Perry. I'd better start some of them out before we . . . Della, look up Ellen Cushing's address first and leave word for three of the operatives to meet us there. The first thing we do is to take a look at that blonde's automobile.''

"That's the way I figure it," Mason said.

"Well, it will take those people probably an hour to get out of bed and assembled at the office. Okay, Della, you put through the call. I'll dress."

Chapter 13

The dawn was cold and chilly and Della Street drew her coat around her as the automobile slid to a stop.

"What's first on the program?" Drake asked Mason.

Mason surveyed the apartment house standing on the silent residential street, as though waiting for the warm morning sunlight to bring it to life.

"Like a sleeping horse standing on three legs with his head down," Mason said. "You can't believe this neighborhood is jammed with people."

"Another hour you'll see curtains going up, smell the aroma of coffee, see the people dashing down the steps running for the streetcars," Drake said.

"I wish I were certain we had an hour," Mason told him. "Well, there's only one thing to do. Find out first where her apartment is and next where her garage is."

"That garage business may be tricky," Drake protested. "Some early riser could be looking out of the window and . . ."

"I know," Mason said.

"I hate to take chances that way, Perry."

"How *would* you go about it?"

Drake thought for a while and said, "I'm darned if I know. But if you went to Sergeant Dorset . . ."

"He'd laugh at me."

"How about Lieutenant Tragg then?"

"Tragg would refer it to Dorset. He wouldn't let me go over Dorset's head, not the way things are now. Later on perhaps, but not now."

"Well, why not wait?"

"Water," Mason said dryly, "has a habit of evaporating.

I want to take a look at that automobile before the cushions have had a chance to dry out."

"All right," Drake said. "If you feel that way about it, let's go. Every minute makes things that much more dangerous."

They left the automobile, walked up to the apartment house and by consulting the directory found that Ellen Cushing had apartment 16B.

As they turned back to the car Mason said, "Now, Paul, you take the car, drive up the driveway, and we'll pretend that we're looking for a stall to put the car in. If there's any trouble, we can claim that some friend told us we could use his garage for a couple of days because he was going to be away."

"And then if they ask us about the friend and where he lives," Drake said, "it will be just another one of those things."

"We'll just have to talk fast and try to talk our way out of it. Be a sport."

Paul Drake went back to the automobile, started it, backed into a half turn, then drove slowly up the driveway. Mason and Della Street walked ahead of him.

The driveway went around to the back of the apartment house, where there was a large cemented yard flanked with garages.

"Begins to look better," Mason said. "Look, the garage doors even have the numbers of the apartments on them."

"And padlocks," Della said dryly.

Mason said, "We'll leave that to Paul Drake. What's a detective good for if he can't pick a lock once in a while."

"Isn't that breaking and entering?" Della Street asked.

"It is," Mason said, and then added, "I believe it's a felony. I wouldn't do it for a million dollars if there were any other way."

Drake brought the car to a stop, climbed out, and looked at the padlock. "I don't like this, Perry."

"I don't like it myself. Got those skeleton keys handy?"

"Not for this job, Perry. There are times when you have to draw the line."

"Got those skeleton keys?"

"I have . . . Yes, there are some in the car."

"All right. Get them for me."

Della Street said, "Let me do it, Chief."

"I'll do it," Mason said.

"Look, Perry," Drake pointed out, "the windows of those back apartments look out here on the court and . . ."

"The longer you talk, the more chance there is someone will hear the discussion and look out to see what it's all about. This is no time to get weak-kneed. We have to go ahead as though we owned the joint and we're just putting the car in for the night. Get me those keys."

Drake walked back to the glove compartment of his automobile, reluctantly took out the bunch of skeleton keys, handed them to Mason, said, "These are the padlock keys."

Della, walking over to the door, stood so that her body shielded the large bunch of keys from any casual observer who might be looking out of the window. Drake took two lagging steps toward the door, then abruptly changed his mind and turned back to the automobile, apparently trying to disassociate himself from what was going on.

It took five keys before Mason found one that would open the padlock.

The lock clicked back and Della Street calmly opened the door and stood as though waiting for Drake to drive in.

Mason moved inside of the garage, after a moment called out, "Oh, Paul, come here."

Drake hesitated a few moments, then reluctantly entered the garage.

Mason had the sedan doors open, was feeling the seat cushions and the carpet on the floor.

"Look at this rear cushion, Paul. Doesn't that feel damp to you?"

Drake put a reluctant hand on the cushion.

"The left side," Mason said.

"It feels sort of damp," Drake admitted.

Mason frowned thoughtfully.

"But it would have been soaking wet if your theory was right, Perry."

Mason hurriedly searched through the automobile. Disappointment showed on his face.

"Clean as a hound's tooth," Drake said with relief in his voice.

Mason said, "I guess we're off on a wrong trail, Paul. The only thing to do is to get out of here fast. Hang it, I can't get over that damp place in the seat cushion. What do you suppose caused it?"

"Darned if I know, Perry, but if it had been what you think it was, it would have been wetter than that."

"I suppose so. Let's take a look at the motor temperature."

Mason clicked on the switch and then looked at the electric gauge.

"Cold as a cucumber," Drake said.

Mason flicked off the switch, said, "Okay, I guess we're licked."

Della Street entered the garage. "No soap?"

"No soap, Della."

"Do you suppose she could have used another car?"

"Darned if I know. I just know there isn't the evidence here to back up my theory, and if it isn't here I don't know where we're going to look for it."

Drake said, "All right. Let's get out and do our talking afterward. I never did like this idea in the first place."

Mason started for the door and Della Street, who had been making a quick survey of the garage, suddenly said, "Chief, look here!" Her voice was filled with excitement.

"What is it, Della?"

"Over here. Quick."

The tone of her voice brought Mason and Paul Drake to her side.

Della Street was bent down over a dark corner which was under a workbench.

"What is it?"

Della Street straightened. She was holding an army blanket in her hands. "Feel this."

Mason felt of it, then whistled.

"Soaking wet," Drake exclaimed.

98

"And look under here."

Della bent over and picked up a pair of men's oxford shoes. "These," she said, "were directly under the blanket."

The shoes themselves were soaking wet.

Drake said to Mason, "You win, Perry. By gosh, I'll hand it to you."

"Thanks to Della," Mason said.

"Well, what do we do?" Drake asked. "Take the evidence?"

"No," Mason said, "we put everything back the way it was, get out of here, and let the police make the discovery."

"Do you think they will?"

"They will after we get done with them, Paul."

"Just put them back the way I found them, Chief?"

"Yes, but first look on the inside of those shoes. See if there's a manufacturer's name. See if you can get his size."

Della Street said, "Do you want to read me the letters that are on the inside here, Chief? I'll write them down."

Mason picked up the shoes, held them so the light shone down on the figures which were stamped on the lining. He read off the numbers and the name of the manufacturer.

"Nothing to show the retail store which sold them?" Della asked.

"Nothing," Mason said. "Just the shoe. Eight and a half B as I interpret the meaning of these numbers. However, we'd better check up with a shoe man on that."

"And get out of here," Drake said.

"Okay," Mason said. "Put the shoes back, Della."

Della Street put the shoes back, put the wet blanket over the shoes. Drake was the first out of the garage, Mason the last.

Mason locked the door of the garage and once more Della Street shielded what he was doing with her body so that no one in the apartment house could see Mason wiping fingerprints off the padlock with his handkerchief.

Mason helped Della Street into the car, then climbed in beside Drake.

"Now what?" Drake asked, turning the car and going out

of the driveway much faster than he had entered. "Do we call on Ellen Cushing?"

"I don't think *we* do," Mason said. "I think that's a job for the police."

"And how do we go about getting the police on the job?"

"We first try to get more evidence. If we can get it we're okay. If we can't, we've got to take a chance."

"How do we get this evidence?"

Mason said, "That's where your operatives come in, Paul."

"I don't get it. What do you think happened?"

"Drive around the corner," Mason said, "and we'll park the car. Your operatives are on the way?"

"They should be here almost any minute now."

"Okay," Mason said. "Drive around where we can see the front of the apartment house and park the car."

Drake drove around the corner, backed up in a driveway, turned the car, came back to place it against the curb, and switched off the motor.

Mason said, "I'll give it to you in a nutshell, Paul. You can figure what must have happened. In the first place, Scott Shelby had everything all planned, down to the smallest detail. But he didn't dare to sneak any of his clothes out of the house so he'd have a dry change."

"Why?"

"Because the insurance company is going to make an investigation."

"Even if they pin it on Marion Shelby?"

"No matter what they do, the insurance company is going to look into the thing. The murder story is improbable as hell, unless you look at it on the theory the wife bumped him off in order to get the insurance. It will be duck soup for the insurance company. They'll start an investigation to try to get out of paying the policy."

"Naturally."

"All right. If in their investigation they should find anything that looks like collusion, then the fat will really be in the fire."

"I don't get it."

"It's this way," Mason said. "As far as the police are concerned, they're perfectly willing to make a murder out of it, pin the thing on the wife and get a conviction. But an insurance company is always afraid of a collusion between husband and wife, by which at the last minute the wife would pull something that would get her acquitted."

"Okay. So what?"

"So the first thing the insurance company does is to start looking around for collusion. That's their routine. Naturally they're good at it."

"Yes, I suppose so."

"So they'll start checking on every suit of clothes, every pair of shoes the guy had."

Drake nodded.

"And if they find any of his clothing missing, they'll want to know where that clothing is. They'll then be off on the theory that maybe Shelby isn't dead after all."

"And Shelby didn't want that?" Drake said.

"That was one thing he couldn't afford to have happen. That was where he was most vulnerable. So he decided he'd get along with his wet clothes. So you see what happened. He went overboard. He fixed everything up so that he had framed a murder case on his wife. Then he climbed into a boat that was rowed by Ellen Cushing. She put him in her automobile. And she had taken along one or perhaps two blankets. She bundled him up in those blankets and drove just as fast as she could to get him to her apartment. They dumped one blanket in the corner of the garage, perhaps had another blanket around the outside where it didn't get as wet. That's why the seat cushion was only a little damp."

"And how about the shoes?"

"I haven't figured out the shoes. Probably she had been able to pick up a pair of slippers for him and he had his feet in the slippers. It wouldn't be so bad sitting in wet clothes if he had himself all bundled up with blankets. But there was no reason to stay in wet shoes. My guess is she'll be out to get the shoes within an hour or two, take them in and dry them out."

101

"Why didn't she take them in with her when she went in with him?"

"Darned if I know. Probably because she forgot 'em."

"So what do we do?"

Mason said, "We do two things. We put operatives on the job where they can watch the front entrance to the apartment house. We find out which apartment 16B is, and we stake out men with binoculars to watch those windows."

"For what?"

"For a man. We watch the front entrance of the apartment house to make certain no one goes in who presses the bell of apartment 16B. And we watch the windows of that apartment. Pretty soon someone will be stirring around. Then if we see a man in there . . . Well, then we start moving in. Get it?"

Drake nodded. "It's taking a chance, Perry. It's sort of making two and two add up to six."

"Hell's bells!" Mason exclaimed. "This is no time to be conservative. The guy disappears under circumstances that fairly shout a frame-up. The little blond cutie has a half interest in the oil lease and has been carrying something wet in her car, all wrapped up in a blanket—and there are a man's wet shoes . . . What more do you want, Paul?"

A car swung around the corner, hesitated a moment, then veered sharply and swung into the curb behind Drake's automobile.

Drake said, "Here's a car with three of my operatives now. What do we do first?"

"Put them out the way I said, so they can watch the apartment, the garage, and the windows."

"Okay. Then what?"

"Then," Della Street interposed with firm determination, "we get a cup of hot coffee and if there's any brandy in the car, we spike it with brandy. My chattering teeth are chipping all the enamel off."

"That," Mason agreed, "is an idea."

Chapter 14

Mason and Della Street sat in Mason's private office. Mason had passed out word that he would see no one during the morning. They both showed somewhat the effects of the cold, sleepless night, a night packed with excitement, perplexing problems, and risks. Mason had not as yet been shaved and now that the excitement was over Della Street's eyes showed she was dog tired.

"I don't know how you and Paul Drake take it the way you do," she said. "When I lose a night's sleep and have a lot of excitement—and then the letdown—gosh, Chief, I feel all in."

"Why don't you go home and go to bed, Della? There's nothing you can do now."

"Not me. I'm going to see it through."

Mason ran his fingertips over the angle of his jaw, felt the bristling tips of his stubble, and said, "There was a time when you could get a barber to do a shaving job in the office. The best antidote for a sleepless night is a Turkish bath and the second best thing is a shave and a massage with plenty of hot towels."

"I could use a massage myself," Della said. "Gosh, Chief, it's after eight o'clock. You'd certainly think that if she were in the apartment she'd have been moving or . . ."

The phone rang with sharp insistence.

Della Street pounced on the receiver, said, "Yes? Hello . . . Oh, yes. Just a minute, Paul."

She handed the receiver to Mason, said, "Paul Drake. He's excited."

Mason picked up the telephone, heard Drake's voice saying, "You win all along the line, Perry."

"What?"

Drake said, "They started moving around in the apartment about ten minutes ago. The blonde was in a robe. She came to a window, closed it, raised up the curtains. That makes that window a bedroom window, doesn't it?"

"I'd say so," Mason agreed, his voice showing excitement. "How about anyone else?"

"One of my men picked up a man standing in the window."

"Description?"

"About thirty-five as nearly as my man could tell by using his binoculars and of course taking into consideration that he's looking into a room where the illumination isn't too good."

"Go ahead," Mason said, eagerly. "Give us the rest of it, Paul."

"My operative figures this guy at around five feet eight, about a hundred and sixty-five to a hundred and seventy pounds, dark hair, and as nearly as he can tell dark eyes."

Mason said, "That's just about Shelby's description, Paul. How about the front door? This bird didn't come in . . . ?"

"No. He's been there all the time—at least she hasn't had any visitors. My men have been watching the front of the apartment house. No one has rung her bell. A lot of people have gone out, but no one that answers this bird's description has gone in, and there's been absolutely no one for apartment 16B."

Mason said, "That's all we want, Paul. We're off."

"Can I help?"

"Better come along and be a witness," Mason said.

"Okay. Where do I pick you up?"

"You don't. Are you at the office now?"

"Yes."

"I'll come by the office."

"Going to Sergeant Dorset?"

"Lieutenant Tragg," Mason said, "I think we can go to him now. Dorset will be antagonistic."

"Okay. I'll be ready."

Mason hung up, said to Della Street, "It clicks."

"What?"

"Scott Shelby is in her apartment."

"You're sure?"

"A man's in her bedroom and he answers Shelby's description as nearly as Drake's operative can pick him up through binoculars, looking through the window. He didn't come in through the front door. He's been there all night."

"Gosh, Chief, that's swell. This really *will* be something."

Mason said, "That shows the danger of relying on circumstantial evidence. There was an airtight murder case built up against Marion Shelby. The only trouble with it was that it was just *too* airtight. You can't imagine a woman being that obvious, being that naive, and being that stupid. Anyone who reads the newspapers, goes to the movies, or reads a detective story would know that those methods were just too crude to pay off. Marion Shelby isn't that dumb."

"You said you wanted Lieutenant Tragg?"

"If you can get him," Mason said.

Della Street called Police Headquarters, asked for Homicide, and then for Lieutenant Tragg.

"Just a moment, Lieutenant. Mr. Mason wants to speak with you."

She held the receiver out to Mason.

Mason picked it up, said, "Hello, Lieutenant. What's new?"

"I understand you have another client in a murder case," Tragg said.

"That's right."

"I think you're going to get stuck this time, Mason. Take my advice and bail out."

"In too deep now," Mason said. "I want to talk with you, Lieutenant."

"When?"

"Right now. Just as soon as I can possibly see you."

"Is it that urgent? I'm working on this . . ."

"It's that urgent," Mason said.

"It would have to be terribly urgent," Tragg went on.

"It is."

"What's it about?"

"About that murder."

"Well, what about it?"

"I have some new evidence I want to put in your hands."

"Now, look, Mason, if you've got something that indicates your client is innocent, and you're just wanting to outline some theory so that I won't 'make a fool of myself,' forget it. It will keep. The thing I'm working on now is important."

"This won't keep," Mason said. "This is evidence."

"What sort of evidence?"

"Evidence that will make it bad for the whole department if you go any farther on that Marion Shelby business."

"Bunk! Marion Shelby is so guilty she doesn't even dare to talk. She can't even try to explain the facts against her. They're too black."

"I don't care how black the facts are," Mason said, "but if you go ahead without listening to me, you're going to be the sorriest man in town."

"Well, tell me what the evidence is."

"I can't very well over the telephone."

"It'll keep," Tragg said. "Nothing is going to happen to the girl. She is sitting tight in jail and it won't make any difference if I see you this afternoon or tomorrow or . . ."

"The hell it won't!" Mason interrupted angrily. "I've got something to dump on the table for you."

"Well, what is it?"

"Very well, if you want to know, it's the corpse," Mason said.

"What corpse?"

"The corpse of Scott Shelby."

"Now then," Tragg said, suddenly suave and interested, "you have something, Mr. Mason. While we probably can establish a *corpus delicti* independent of the statement of the defendant, we nevertheless would like to find the corpse very very much."

"Well, that's what I'm going to do. I'm going to hand you the corpse."

"Where is it?"

"If you want to know," Mason said, "it's walking around

very much alive and well, and it's in a girl's apartment. If you go ahead and hand out any stuff to the newspapers about Marion Shelby, you're going to be the sorriest man in town when you have to put handcuffs on the corpse."

Lieutenant Tragg whistled. "Insurance?" he asked.

"Partially."

"Wife in on it?"

"I don't think so."

"You're not kidding me?"

"No."

"How soon can you get here?"

"Ten minutes."

"Ten minutes hell," Tragg said impatiently. "Make it five. Step on it. My God, I can go from one end of town to the other in ten minutes."

"*You* have a siren," Mason said.

"Well, you've got something just as good," Tragg told him. "If you've got a lead on that corpse, you get here and tell any cop who tries to stop you that I said . . . Hell's bells, I'll come to you. Where are you?"

"My office."

"Sit tight until I get there," Tragg said. "Better yet go down and wait at the curb, and it won't be over five minutes."

Mason heard the phone slam at the other end of the line, grinned at Della Street, said, "I'm going down to Paul Drake's office, pick him up, go down and be waiting at the curb for Tragg. You wait here to make sure that we make connections. In case anything should happen, you can contact us down at the lobby."

"How long do I wait?"

"Tragg said he'd be here in five minutes. Give him ten. Give us that much margin of safety. If you don't hear from us in ten minutes, go on down to the lobby. If we're gone, that will mean we're with Tragg. So go home and go to sleep."

"And I can't go with you?"

"Not a chance. This is official. This is police stuff."

"I'd like to see it through."

"I know you would, but there's nothing we can do about it. I'll take Tragg around there and you go on home and get some sleep. Go to a beauty parlor and get all the facial massages, and whatever it is they do to make a woman feel good, and put the bill on the expense account. Get the whole works."

"When will I see you?" Della asked.

"Probably tomorrow," Mason said. "I'm going to get this thing cleaned up, go to a Turkish bath, get a shave, face massage, sleep for about fifteen hours, and then get up and have something to eat."

"Okay, I'll be seeing you."

Mason grabbed his hat, opened the door, and went down the corridor to Drake's office.

Drake was waiting in the reception office as Mason opened the door. His hat was on the back of his head and he was giving some last-minute instructions to the girl at the switchboard.

Mason said, "Okay, Paul, we're ready to go. Tragg is coming here. He thought he could get here quicker than we could get up there."

"Gosh," Drake said, "you must have made a sale."

"I did."

"How did you do it?"

"I had to lead with my chin."

"What?"

"Told him I was going to show him the body of Scott Shelby."

Drake grinned and said, "I'll bet that got him. They must have been worried about their *corpus delicti*."

"I think they were, but I went farther than that."

"What?"

"I told him I'd show him the body walking around alive and well."

"I'll bet *that* got him."

"That got him," Mason said. "Let's go down and wait in the lobby. He'll be in a hurry when he gets here."

"Gosh, I'd like to go in my car. I hate to go screaming

around corners with Tragg when he's in a hurry. He certainly does bear down on the siren."

"It's all right," Mason said. "Let's not let him stop long enough to think."

"Why?"

"Because if he does, he'll think I'm going over Sergeant Dorset's head or something and will insist on referring me back to Dorset or else having Dorset in on the play."

"Well, what's wrong with that? We've got the play sewed up."

"I don't like it," Mason said. "I want to get Tragg on the job. Tragg can handle a thing of that sort. He has brains. Dorset is an opinionated cuss. Come on, Paul, let's go."

Drake said to the girl at the switchboard, "I'll call in just as soon as I can get to a telephone. Keep those reports all piled up and keep everybody on the job. They all have their instructions but I want to make certain they stay put. Okay, Perry, let's go."

They went down in the elevator and had been standing at the curb for less than thirty seconds when they heard the scream of a siren and a moment later Lieutenant Tragg shot through the frozen traffic, slammed the Police Department car to a stop at the curb, said to Mason, "Hop in. Hello, Drake. You in on this too?"

"He's in on it," Mason said.

"Get in," Tragg said, and then after a moment added, "Hang on."

Mason and Drake settled themselves. Mason barked out the address of the apartment house.

"Okay," Tragg said. "I hope you boys aren't nervous."

"We aren't," Mason said.

"Speak for yourself," Paul Drake announced, bracing himself and hanging on to the robe rail. "Some people haven't got sense enough to be scared. I'm smart. I'm frightened."

"Then hang on tight," Lieutenant Tragg said, "because you're going to be more frightened by the time you get to where we're going. I'm in a hell of a hurry."

The siren throbbed and rose into a crescendo of strident demand for the right of way. The car gathered speed.

From time to time Tragg threw comments back over his shoulder. "Getting so they try to chisel on a siren. I'll have to send some of the boys out to pick up a few of these guys . . . That's the worst of civilians. They think there isn't any emergency that can compare with their own requirements . . . Look at this bird trying to sneak around the corner . . ."

"Look out!" Drake screamed.

A car coming fast down a side street slammed on brakes and went into a skid as it saw the police car flashing into the intersection, siren screaming, red light blazing.

Drake threw one look at the skidding car, saw that it was going to hit them, and dove to the floorboards.

Tragg swung the wheel with a deft twist of his wrist, sent the police car into a skid which swung it out of the way of the civilian sedan. Then he fought his way out of the skid and straightened out half way down the block.

"Damn fool," he announced over his shoulder.

From the floorboards Drake's voice came up pleadingly. "Please, please, would you mind going where you're going and doing the talking after you get there?"

Tragg laughed, said, "Tell your friend, the detective, to brace himself, Mason. We're taking a corner."

"Hold on," Mason warned. "We're taking a corner, Paul."

"Hold on?" Drake demanded indignantly. "Who the hell do you think is pulling this footrail out by the roots?"

The car swung wide, then lurched into a screaming turn.

"About four blocks up on this street, right-hand side," Mason said.

"Okay. I'd better cut out the siren."

Tragg cut the siren, slowed the car down. "What's the play?" he asked.

Mason said, "The woman is Ellen Cushing. He's in her apartment. She doesn't know Paul Drake and she doesn't know you. She knows me. I think I can get you in on the theory that I want to talk about an oil lease."

"Then what?" Tragg asked. "I haven't all day to fool around, beating about the bush."

"You want to get the evidence, don't you?"

"You said the evidence was in her apartment."

"Sure it is, but give her a chance to lead with her chin first," Mason pleaded. "Let her get herself tied up. I want to pin a conspiracy charge on her and I don't want it to be hashed up."

"Okay. You do the talking," Tragg said. "I'll be a clam but don't stall around too long because I'm in a hurry. I've got things to do this morning."

Lieutenant Tragg slammed the car to a stop. "Come on up for air, Drake," he called over his shoulder.

Drake, his face actually pale, jerked down the handle on the door, got out, and said, "If you think I'm going to ride back with you, you're crazy as a pet coon."

Mason, walking up the steps, said, "The apartment is 16B, Lieutenant. If you'll pretend you're interested in buying an oil lease, I think we can get her out on the end of a limb."

"Lead the way," Tragg said.

Mason punched the button.

The electric buzzer released the catch on the door. Mason pushed it open, held it open for Lieutenant Tragg and Drake.

"What's the floor?" Tragg asked.

"The second," Drake said.

"You've been up here before?"

"No, I've had men on the job spotting the apartment."

"Shelby sweet on her?"

"Apparently."

"How did he get here?"

"Your guess is as good as mine. My hunch is he swam downstream, she picked him up in a rowboat, put him in her car and brought him here."

"Then there should be some evidence in the car. Wet clothes or something."

"Could be," Mason said noncommittally. "Takes a police officer to get all the angles on a deal like this, Paul."

"We should make certain no one tampers with her car," Tragg said.

"My men are on the job all over the place," Drake assured him.

"Okay. You do the talking, Perry."

They left the elevator. Mason found the apartment and jabbed the button. The door was almost instantly opened by Ellen Cushing. She looked fresh and fit, ready for the street.

"Oh, good morning, Mr. Mason," she said. "You're *just* the man I wanted to see."

"And I wanted to see you. This is Mr. Tragg and Mr. Drake. They're associated with me in a matter on which I'm working.—I presume you heard about Mr. Shelby?"

"Yes, I heard about it this morning," she said. "I rang his office and a detective answered the phone. He wanted to know all about me and who I was, took my number. Tell me, what are the details, Mr. Mason?"

Mason said, "He went out on a yachting trip with Parker Benton."

"Yes, I know. Weren't you along?"

"That's right."

"He was going to try to make some settlement on that oil lease, I understand."

"That's right."

"And what happened?"

"He apparently fell overboard."

"Was his wife along?"

"Yes."

"Oh."

"Why did you ask?"

She smiled and said nothing. "Please come in. Let's sit down."

They entered the apartment. Tragg looked around in a swift survey. There was nothing to indicate that anyone else was in the place.

"You have a two-room apartment?" Mason asked.

"They call it a three-room, but the kitchen isn't much more than a good sized closet. There's a living room and bedroom and this kitchen."

Mason said, "It was most unfortunate that Mr. Shelby

112

died just as he did. But he told us before he died that he was representing you, that you had an interest in the oil lease."

"Yes."

"He said a half interest."

She laughed and said, "That was a little window dressing we'd agreed on."

"Then that wasn't true?"

"It didn't represent the *entire* facts. No."

"Then what did?"

She said, "I own it all."

Mason flashed Lieutenant Tragg a quick glance, said, "Mr. Shelby said it was only a half interest."

"Yes. I wanted him to pose as the owner of at least a half interest because I thought he could carry on negotiations better than I could. You know how it is. A man can do things that way that a woman can't. Mr. Shelby was very clever at that sort of thing."

"Known him long?" Mason asked.

"About six months."

"This the only business deal you'd had with him?"

She laughed and said, "Really, Mr. Mason, don't you think your questions had better be confined more to the exact matter under discussion? I take it you're interested in working out some sort of a settlement on that lease?"

"I might be."

"Well, I'm open to propositions."

"Of course," Mason said, "I had acted on the assumption that you only had a half interest. The fact that you have a whole interest might change the situation."

"Wouldn't that make it less complicated?"

"Yes."

"Therefore, you could make a better offer."

Mason smiled. "My client might or might not look at it that way. But, of course, there's the question of proof."

"Proof of what?"

"That you have the whole interest in the lease."

She said, "I can answer that very simply."

"It would have to be rather simple," Mason said, "because in view of Mr. Shelby's declaration that you owned

113

only a half interest the administrator of his estate would naturally claim that that was the only interest you had, and under the law you can't testify."

"*I* can't?" she asked in some surprise.

"No. It's a general rule of law that when the lips of the one party are sealed by death the law seals the lips of the other party and he can't testify to anything."

"Oh, I see."

Mason said, "It would therefore take Mr. Shelby's signature on some document to enable you to establish your claim."

"Oh, that's very easy."

"It is?"

"Yes. I have his signature."

"Oh."

"So," she said, "we can go right ahead discussing the compromise proposition."

Mason took a cigarette case from his pocket, selected a cigarette thoughtfully, tapped it on the edge of the cigarette case, said, "It might not be that simple. My client would naturally want to know something about that instrument by which all rights in the oil lease were assigned to you. Did his wife sign that transfer?"

"What does she have to do with it?"

"It was probably community property."

"No," Ellen Cushing said with some feeling, "she didn't sign it, and I don't think we need her signature. Marion Shelby certainly didn't enjoy her husband's confidence in business matters—or in anything else."

"You know what?"

She said, "Of course I know it."

"How?"

"By keeping my eyes open and by little things that Scott let drop here and there. If you ask my opinion, I think *she* was the one who gave him the poison."

"That's rather a broad statement to make," Mason said.

"Yes, I guess it is," she amended hastily. "I didn't mean it in *exactly* that way. But . . . Well, I just don't like her. That's all."

114

"Why?"

"Because I think she's a double-crosser. I think she was double-crossing Scott . . . But come, Mr. Mason, that doesn't have anything to do with this oil lease."

"The point is," Mason said, "that I'd want to see that assignment and pass on it. If it was an assignment made covering that one particular oil lease, the question would naturally arise why Scott Shelby said last night that he only owned a half interest in it and you owned the other half. If it was a blanket assignment providing that you should, after his death or in the event anything happened to him, be considered as owning everything . . . Well, that would be a gray horse of another color."

"What would be wrong with that?"

"In the first place," Mason said, "it would probably be invalid. In the second place, it would quite probably result in my client taking a radically different position."

"Well, there's no need for us to beat around the bush," she said. "Now that the cat's out of the bag, I can tell you the whole story."

"What is it?"

She said, "Scott Shelby actually never did own anything in that lease—that is, not for the last few months. He had decided to let the lease go by the board. I happened to be in his office and talking over oil propositions and he told me that he had a lease that I could have cheap if I wanted it. All I would have to do would be to pay up the back rentals and reinstate it, then I would have to pay a hundred dollars a month. He said it as sort of a joke."

"Go on," Mason said. "What happened after that?"

She looked at him defiantly and said, "What's the use of lying to you, Mr. Mason?"

"There isn't any."

"All right. I'll come clean. I'm in the real estate business. I happened to know that the island had been sold to Parker Benton and that the deal was in escrow. I didn't tell Scott Shelby anything about it."

"Why not?"

"Because I didn't think I had to. I didn't think that was

anyone's business. After all, Mr. Shelby was in business and I was in business."

"Go on, what happened?"

"I told him that I would be willing to take the lease up and pay him one hundred dollars for his rights in the lease. That he'd give me a blanket assignment of the lease and I'd pay him the one hundred dollars and then pay the owner of the property five hundred dollars in order to reinstate the lease."

"What did he say?"

"He told me I could if I wanted to. He said that there had been some oil excitement, but that it had mostly died down."

Mason nodded.

She said, "I'm putting all the cards on the table, Mr. Mason, because I want you and your friends to understand the situation." She smiled at Lieutenant Tragg and Paul Drake, trying to turn on the magnetism. Drake smiled back. Tragg gave no faintest change of his facial expression.

Mason said, "It begins to shape up. The way you tell it, it sounds a lot more convincing than as if you had simply relied on your naked assertion that 'now that Scott Shelby was dead you controlled the entire property.' "

She said, "I put up the money. Shelby agreed that he was to go ahead and handle it in his name but that he would simply act as my trustee, that anything that came from any settlement of the lease would be held by him in trust for me."

"Then what?"

She said, "Then I hired a man to offer the five hundred dollars to Jane Keller. I coached him in what to do. Of course, I knew she couldn't accept it. I wanted witnesses and I wanted her to take the money, at least to have it in her hands. So I arranged to have my man wait for her at the bank and catch her there. He had to wait for two days before she showed up."

"Why the bank?"

"That's where reputable people stand in line. That assured me of good substantial witnesses. What's more, a person will accept money if you push it at her in a bank. Otherwise she might not have touched it."

116

"I see. You're rather clever in your knowledge of applied psychology. That was very cleverly thought out."

"I try to get by."

"That offer was made in Scott Shelby's name."

"Naturally, I wanted to keep in the background as much as I could. You see, I'm in the real estate business and . . . Well, a deal like this wouldn't do my reputation any good but I thought there was a chance to clean up several thousand dollars on it. But it was chiseling. You know it and I know it. I'd have preferred to have Shelby out in front instead of me."

Mason said, "You're being very frank with us."

"Because the way I size you up, I think it's the best way."

"Go ahead. What happened after that?"

She said, "You got in touch with Mr. Shelby on the telephone. He came rushing to me. By that time I had given him a general idea of what the situation was, and after you telephoned I had to really let my hair down and give him all the details."

"And then what?"

She said, "Shelby got greedy. He thought he should get more money out of it. You were due to call on him within a few minutes. We didn't have much time."

"So what finally happened?"

"I agreed to pay him twenty-five per cent of anything I received by way of settlement as additional compensation for selling me the lease. I didn't think he was justified in asking for it, but he thought that I had taken advantage of our friendship and . . . Well, that's the way it was."

"He thought you had taken advantage of his *friendship*?" Mason asked.

"Yes. We have offices in the same building. I'd been able to do him a good turn once or twice and he had thrown a couple of prospects my way. There had never been any great financial benefit one way or the other. Just a matter of—well, what you'd call neighborly accommodation—a lot of little things."

"Some of these little things made money?"

"Some."

117

"No other dealings between you?" Mason asked.

She started to answer, then looked sharply at him, and said, "After all, Mr. Mason, I'm trying to put my cards on the table, but that's no reason why I should bare my life's history."

Mason laughed. "You're doing quite all right. I'm beginning to get the picture now. I presume that inasmuch as you know a sale was pending, you demanded that Shelby execute an assignment?"

"An assignment and a declaration of trust providing that anything that he would do would be done on my behalf and for me."

"Who drew those documents up?"

"I did."

"In writing or on a typewriter?"

"On a typewriter."

"What happened to them?"

"Scott Shelby signed them and gave them to me."

"Let's take a look at them."

She got up, started for the bedroom door then suddenly caught herself, whirled, said, "Perhaps, before I put any more of my cards on the table, Mr. Mason, it might be well to look at some of *your* cards."

Mason said, "I might be in a position to offer you a cash compromise."

"How much?"

"I don't know yet."

She said, "Mr. Shelby thought I could get ten thousand dollars."

"Shelby was mistaken."

"I thought he might be."

She waited a moment and then asked abruptly, "How much *could* I get, Mr. Mason?"

"I don't know."

"Then don't you think you'd better have your people make me an offer?"

"They won't make any until they know that you have the power to accept or reject it."

"Why not? What does that have to do with it?"

Mason said, "It's just the way some people play the game. They aren't going to make an offer unless they feel certain it will be accepted, and even then they won't make it unless they know that when it is accepted, they'll be able to get what they pay for."

"Yes, I can see that. They might not want to tip their hands."

"So," Mason said, "you might make us an offer."

She said, "The figure I always had in mind was three thousand dollars net to me. I told Scott that was every cent I thought he'd be able to get."

"You mean that he was to settle for three thousand and . . ."

"*Four* thousand," she interpolated. "You forget that he was to get twenty-five per cent of whatever was actually paid by way of settlement. Personally, I thought that four thousand dollars was as high as anyone would go and was as high as we should ask them to go."

"And Shelby thought otherwise?"

"Shelby insisted that he could get more than that."

"Therefore," Mason said, "he acted a little bit peeved last night when it appeared that four thousand dollars was the absolute top that Benton would even consider."

"Oh, did Mr. Benton offer four thousand?"

"No, but there were some figures discussed and it appeared that Benton might be willing to put in two thousand if Jane Keller would put in two thousand."

"That's *exactly* the way I wanted Scott to play it," she said. "I had told him I thought we should ask for four thousand dollars and let each side pay two thousand. That wouldn't be very much and it wouldn't be missed. Parker Benton could add two thousand dollars to the price he was paying for the property and Jane Keller could consider it sort of in the nature of . . . well, you know, a second real estate fee."

Mason nodded.

"Go on," she asked breathlessly, "what happened? What became of it? Did they agree to the four thousand dollars?"

"Shelby wouldn't listen to it. He insisted on going after something big."

"I was afraid he might do that. Personally, I'd rather have had the bird in the hand than gone chasing round after the two in the bush."

"Well, it's all over now," Mason said, then added, significantly, "It's a most peculiar coincidence that your figure agrees so identically with the figure Benton named last night."

"What's so peculiar about it?"

"Because you couldn't know of what was said there on the yacht."

"Oh, I see. But I'm accustomed to sizing up people and deals. I instinctively know about how high anyone will go."

"I see."

"So Mr. Benton and I can really get together then?"

"I don't know. I'm not here for Mr. Benton. I don't want you to think I am."

"Then whom are you representing?"

Mason said, "I'm sorry that I'm not at liberty to answer that question but I *would* like to see that assignment and declaration of trust."

She glanced toward the bedroom, hesitated a moment, said, "Could you let it go for an hour or two? I'll bring it to your office."

Mason glanced at Lieutenant Tragg. "How about it, Mr. Tragg?"

Tragg shook his head firmly. "As I told you, Mason, I'm in a hurry. If we're going to do anything, we're going to do it right now."

Mason looked back at Ellen Cushing.

She got up, said, "All right, wait here just a moment."

She walked toward the bedroom, opened the door an inch or so, said in an unnecessarily loud voice, "You gentlemen wait right here and I'll get it and bring it back. Just wait right there, please."

She pushed the door open some eighteen inches, squeezed through it sideways and hurriedly pushed it shut.

Mason motioned toward the bedroom and said, "There you are, Lieutenant."

"You're sure he's in there?"

Mason said, "I'm sure a man's in there and the description fits that of Scott Shelby."

Tragg said, "That isn't what you told me over the telephone."

Mason said, "How much do you want for ten cents?"

"Ordinarily, about two bits' worth," Lieutenant Tragg said, "and when I'm dealing with you, I want a dollar's worth."

"So I've noticed."

Tragg glanced at the bedroom. "I hate to go busting in there if . . ."

Mason said, "There's only one way to handle a deal like this when it gets to this point," and got to his feet, strode across the living room to the bedroom door.

Mason put his hand on the doorknob, gently turned it, placed himself in the position to ease his weight against the door, then pushing open the door, said, as the door was opening, "On second thought, Miss Cushing, I don't think that . . ."

She had been standing just in front of the door. She suddenly whirled. "Just a moment, Mr. Mason!"

The lawyer pushed against the bedroom door.

Ellen Cushing shoved up against Mason, pushing papers at him. "Here are the papers," she said. "Here they are, let's go over to our chairs and look at them."

Mason tried to look past her into the bedroom but the door only opened just enough to let Ellen Cushing out. When Mason pushed a little harder against it, the door was pushed back from the other side.

Mason returned to the others. Ellen Cushing held out a signed document.

"Will one of you take this please?"

Mason made a gesture toward Lieutenant Tragg. "You take it, Tragg."

Tragg took the papers and inspected them thoughtfully. "This is Mr. Shelby's signature?" he asked.

"Yes."

"You saw him sign it?"

"Yes."

"How long ago?"

"Around . . . Oh, I guess a week ago. Whatever the date is on there."

"This date is right?"

"Yes."

"You're certain these weren't signed later? They were signed on this date?"

"Yes, of course, why?"

Tragg said, "Oh, it might make some difference—legally."

She said hurriedly, "Well, that's all there is to it. I have an appointment with my beauty shop. If you have any offer to make, I'll be glad to receive it, or if you want to take time to think it over, now that you've seen the papers, you can think things over. But I've got to get out of here right now."

Mason glanced significantly at Tragg.

Tragg said, "Well, all right, we won't detain you. I think these papers are in order, Mr. Mason. You want to look at them?"

Mason glanced through the papers, saw that they were an assignment of the lease and a declaration of trust, rather amateurishly drawn, but still covering the ground.

Mason nodded, said, "When will you be back home, Miss Cushing?"

"Oh, I should be home along the first part of the afternoon."

"I'll give you a ring."

"All right."

They got up, moved over to the door. She held the door open for them and gave them her most magnetic smile.

Mason followed Tragg and Drake down the corridor. In the elevator Mason said indignantly, "Why didn't you back my play, Lieutenant? What are you waiting for?"

"So far," Tragg said, "there hasn't been any evidence except your statements and deduction, Mason."

Mason said, "There was someone in that bedroom.

122

Someone who was on the other side of the door, keeping it from being opened."

"Ellen Cushing had her hand on the doorknob pulling it shut," Tragg said.

"Exactly, but she didn't have enough strength in her arm to account for the pressure on that door. There was someone on the other side of it, I tell you."

"Well, suppose there was . . . Hang it, Mason, I'm beginning to get cold feet on this thing . . . I have an idea that I'll take a look at her car but that's just about as far as I'm going unless some more evidence turns up."

"Have it your own way," Mason said angrily.

"I intend to," Tragg assured him dryly.

"Well," Drake said, "when she goes to the garage to get her car out, you can walk over and ask her some other question."

"Or stop her on the street when she drives out," Tragg said.

"It would be better to get her in the garage," Mason observed. "There might be something in the garage, some evidence."

"Yes, I suppose so but I'm not going to do any searching without a search warrant."

"You're a helluva lot more considerate of some people than you are of *my* clients."

Tragg grinned and said, "I usually have more against your clients than I do against this baby."

"All right, play it your own way," Mason told him. "As far as I'm concerned, go ahead with your murder story if you want to. You make the afternoon editions, and I'll make a monkey out of you on the front page of the morning papers."

The elevator came to a stop. Tragg slid back the door, said, "And that also is something I'm afraid of, Mason."

In silence they walked out to the front of the apartment house. Then Tragg abruptly turned, walked up the driveway and stationed himself out of sight just around the corner of the apartment house. Mason and Drake followed, stood by his side.

They had been there some two minutes when they heard

123

the rapid click, click of a woman's heels and Ellen Cushing walked past them to the garage, moving so fast she was almost running. And, so intent was she on what she was doing, she didn't even notice them. Mason waited until she had opened the garage doors. Then he nudged Tragg and said, "Come on, Lieutenant."

Mason moved up. "Miss Cushing, would you consider four thousand dollars? Not as an offer but just asking you the question. Would you consider it?"

She paused and looked at them. Now her manner seemed much less embarrassed. "Why yes," she said, "I think I would. I'd prefer to have it made as an offer."

Mason, smiling said, "Well, you're in a hurry. Suppose you let Mr. Tragg ride with you as far as your beauty shop and you can talk in the car."

"That'll be fine."

She walked around and opened the door on the driver's side. Tragg walked around the other side.

Mason opened the rear door, said, "In here, Tragg, I'll get in with you."

Tragg pushed in the back of the car. Mason picked up Tragg's hand, placed it on the damp spot in the seat.

Tragg pushed down on the damp cushions and as he felt that bit of moisture, suddenly changed in his manner. He pushed open the door on the other side of the car, got out and said, "Nice little garage you have here, Miss Cushing."

She started the motor. "I find it very comfortable."

"You don't have many tools around."

"No."

"What's that over in the corner?" Mason asked.

She followed the direction of his eyes, said, "I don't know . . . Oh, it's a blanket."

Mason said, "So it is," and got out of the car.

Abruptly Ellen Cushing opened her own door, demanded, "Say, what is this?"

Without a word, Tragg walked over to the corner and picked up the wet blanket. Then he peered down in a corner, then once more felt the blanket. He put the blanket down, stooped and retrieved the wet shoes.

"Okay," he said, reaching a sudden decision. "Come on back up to the apartment with me. I want to ask you some questions."

"You and who else?" Ellen Cushing demanded angrily.

Tragg pulled back his coat to show her the star. "Me and the whole metropolitan police force, if you want to put it that way," he said.

Chapter 15

Ellen Cushing opened the door of her apartment and stood holding the door as Lieutenant Tragg, Mason and Paul Drake entered the room. Then she closed the door and said, "Sit down."

"Mind if we look around first?" Lieutenant Tragg asked.

"Are you making a search of my apartment?"

"I'd just like to look around. That is, if you have no objection."

"I certainly have objections."

"Of course," Tragg said, "if you want to get tough about it, I can get a warrant."

"Go ahead and get a warrant then."

"That isn't going to buy you anything."

"Why not?"

"Because," Tragg said, patiently, "you have certain things to explain, Miss Cushing. It's going to be a lot better for you if you make an explanation."

"What things do I have to explain?"

Tragg said, "Let's look at it this way. You were friendly with Scott Shelby. Last night Scott Shelby is yachting and goes overboard. The presumption is that he's drowned. There is some probability that he was murdered but the body hasn't been recovered. The water in the river wasn't too deep and the searchers last night and also this morning haven't been able to find any trace of the body."

"Isn't there a current in the river?"

"We're making allowances for that."

"So what?" she asked.

"So," Tragg went on rather patiently, "we find that you are in a position to step into the negotiations which Shelby was carrying on for making a settlement of an oil lease. We

126

find that in your garage there's a blanket that's soaking wet. There are a pair of soaking wet men's shoes, and it's quite apparent that some wet object has been on the seat of your automobile.''

"What if it has?"

"It makes no difference at all," Tragg said, "if it weren't for the fact that that wet object just *might* have been Scott Shelby.''

"That's absurd!"

"And," Tragg went on, "apparently you have a man in your bedroom.''

"How *dare* you say such a thing!"

"Haven't you?"

"No."

"Are you willing to let me look in the bedroom?"

"I . . . I see no reason why you should.''

They had arrived at a conversational impasse. Tragg glanced to Mason for reinforcements.

"Perhaps," Mason said suavely, "Miss Cushing would like to explain how that blanket got wet and what it was she was carrying in her automobile that was wet.''

She looked at him angrily and spat words at him. "Miss Cushing has nothing to say. Apparently, Mr. Mason, I owe this predicament entirely to you!''

"All right," Mason said, "if you want to be that way about it. Let's be more specific.''

"I wish you would."

Mason said, "Well to begin with, you have a man in your bedroom. He's around five feet eight, about a hundred and fifty-five and has dark hair and dark eyes. That's Scott Shelby's description.''

She looked at Mason strangely. "In my bedroom?"

"Yes."

Suddenly she threw back her head and emitted peals of laughter, a nervous, almost hysterical laughter.

When she had ceased laughing, Mason said patiently, "There's a man in your bedroom, Miss Cushing?"

"Heavens, no."

"Mind if I look?"

"Certainly I mind."

"May Lieutenant Tragg take a look?"

She was thoughtful now, her knees crossed, her free foot kicking nervously. She hesitated for several seconds, then said, "No, I don't want him to look."

Lieutenant Tragg said smoothly, "Well now, as I understand it, Miss Cushing, you're absolutely certain that there isn't any man in your bedroom?"

"Yes."

"Well now, that complicates the situation," Lieutenant Tragg said, "because witnesses have seen a man standing at the window of your bedroom and if you're certain there's no one in there, then the man must be a prowler, and as an officer of the law it is my duty to arrest any burglar who has made an unlawful entry of the premises."

"Who saw him in my bedroom? Who has been spying on me?"

"You have been under surveillance for some time," Lieutenant Tragg said. "Now, I want to know whether there is some man in your bedroom. Whether you have some guest in there. Someone who is authorized to be there. If you have, then of course I won't search the bedroom without a warrant, but if you tell me that there is no one in there, no person who is authorized to be there and that therefore anyone who is in there would be unlawfully present, it becomes my duty to put that man under arrest."

She looked from Mason to Lieutenant Tragg, carefully following every move they made, every expression on their faces.

"Suppose I should tell you that . . . that I had a guest?"

"Under those circumstances, of course, we wouldn't enter the bedroom without a warrant."

"Well, I . . . What *would* you do?"

"Under those circumstances," Tragg said smoothly, "we'd put a guard right here in the corridor to see that the man didn't leave this apartment and then we'd get a search warrant and search the entire place. We would also take you into custody for questioning."

She lowered her eyes, studied the carpet for some five

128

seconds and suddenly raised her eyes and said, "All right, I'll tell the truth."

"I think it would be better."

"There's a man in my apartment."

"Scott Shelby?" Tragg asked.

She hesitated for a thoughtful second, then said, "No, and he isn't in the bedroom. He's in the kitchen."

Tragg exclaimed, "The deuce he is!"

Mason smiled. "He may be in the kitchen *now*. He was in the bedroom when we were here before."

She flared angrily, "Mr. Mason, I wish you'd mind your own business. That's a lie! He was in the kitchen all the time. He was cooking breakfast, and now he's washing the dishes . . . Come out, Art."

The swinging door of the kitchen opened. A sheepish looking man, five feet eight inches tall, dark hair and eyes, his weight around a hundred and fifty-five pounds, grinned at them in embarrassed greeting.

Ellen Cushing said, "This is Art Lacey. He's the man to whom I'm going to be married. We're getting married just as soon as we can get the necessary red tape unwound. This morning, after I'd got back from the beauty parlor we were going to go to the clerk's office and get whatever it is we have to have to be married. He came in and cooked breakfast and washed the dishes so I wouldn't have to bother with doing that. In that way we saved time, or would have if you hadn't shown up."

The man nodded a greeting, said, "How are yuh, folks?" and sat down.

Mason said, "Suppose you try again, Miss Cushing."

Tragg nodded. "I think you'd better, Miss Cushing. This man was seen at your bedroom window."

"He wasn't. He couldn't have been. He was at the kitchen window after I let him in."

Mason merely smiled.

Drake asked abruptly, "What window did you go to and close when you first got up, Miss Cushing?"

"The kitchen window. Arthur knocked at the door and I let him in. He was going to cook breakfast and I went right

129

to the kitchen with him, and closed the window and told him to make himself at home. Then I went back to dress. I had a robe on when I closed the window."

Drake gave Mason a lugubrious glance.

Mason said, "That won't go, Miss Cushing. This man was in your bedroom when we were here a few minutes ago."

"How do you know he was?"

"Because he was pushing the door closed when I went to the bedroom door, where you were reluctantly getting those papers."

Ellen Cushing once more raised her voice. "I guess you've got to come out, Mother."

The bedroom door promptly pushed open. A dour-faced woman with stringy white hair hanging haphazardly over her ears, a voluminous bathrobe wrapped about her, came out and said, "Land sakes, I'd say it was about time! What's the matter with you people, anyway? I never heard such goings on in my life."

"Gentlemen, my mother," Ellen Cushing said, simply.

Tragg's jaw dropped. "You been in there all the time?"

"All the time. I spent the night there. Ellen and I slept together. I don't know what's the idea of all this, but I think you people owe my daughter an apology. She's a *good* girl."

Ellen Cushing said, "My mother came to visit me last evening. I met her at the eight o'clock train. She's been with me ever since. She likes to sleep late, and she hasn't been a bit well. That's why Art agreed to come in and cook the breakfast. He got things ready, brought Mother her breakfast in bed, and Art and I ate in the kitchen."

Mason asked the older woman, "Could you hear what we said in the bedroom, Mrs. Cushing?"

"Almost every word," she said, then added, "I was at the door listening when this man pushed against the door, he almost pushed me over . . . Land sakes! I forgot my teeth!"

She jumped up from the chair, scurried into the bedroom and emerged a few moments later with her false teeth in place. Her face now looked more full, more square jawed in its belligerency.

"How about you?" Tragg asked Arthur Lacey. "Could you hear what we said while you were in the kitchen?"

Lacey, apparently somewhat inarticulate in his embarrassment, nodded, "Some things. I quit work . . . didn't want to be caught washing dishes."

Mason said, angrily, "Well, this runaround was handled fast and cleverly, but it won't work."

"Why won't it work?" Ellen Cushing spat at him.

"Because your apartment house has been watched since before daylight this morning. This gentleman didn't come to the door. No one rang your bell."

"Oh, is that so? Well it happens that Art Lacey lives right here in the same apartment house . . . Oh, you never thought of that, did you? Elementary, my dear Watson. If you'd try minding your own business for a while . . ."

"That will do," Tragg interrupted. "I'm investigating a crime, Miss Cushing. I want to know how those wet shoes and the wet blanket happened to be in your garage."

Ellen Cushing's mother said, "Well, I can tell you one thing, Ellen didn't go no place last night except with me. And you don't need to take my word for that, either, young man. We went visiting right after we'd had dinner, maybe about nine o'clock. Went over to see my old neighbor, Mrs. Turlock, who lives right next door, and we were there until midnight. Then we came home and went to bed . . . Only thing I can't understand, Ellen, is why you didn't tell me you and this young man were getting married. You never said a word to me."

"I wanted to tell you after you'd seen him, Mother."

"You a sound sleeper?" Mason asked Mrs. Cushing.

"Heavens, no. I jump out of my skin if a mouse runs across the floor. Last night I was so excited I hardly closed my eyes until almost daylight."

There was a period of uncomfortable silence.

Tragg said, "I still want to know about those wet shoes and the wet blanket."

Ellen Cushing turned to Lacey. "Tell him, Art. We may as well. Guess we aren't going to have *any* privacy."

Lacey opened his mouth, started to say something, then

apparently couldn't find just the right place to begin. Ellen Cushing laughed, said, "Art's easily embarrassed. We went on a picnic yesterday. They're Art's shoes. He got them wet."

Tragg said, 'We've gone this far. We may as well hear *all* the details."

"And we might take a look in the bedroom," Mason said, "just by way of making sure."

Tragg nodded, got to his feet. "Any objections?" he asked Ellen Cushing.

"Help yourself," she told him. "I don't mind you, but I'm not going to have that lawyer messing around the place. He's caused enough trouble already," and she glared at Mason.

Tragg moved into the bedroom, opened the closet door, looked under the bed, went to the window, even opened it and leaned out. Then he came back, settled himself in his chair, said wearily, "All right, let's hear about the picnic . . . Wait a minute. Do you know Scott Shelby, Lacey?"

Ellen Cushing said, "He met him for the first time yesterday morning. It's because of that he proposed. I'm trying to tell you, if you'll let me."

Tragg said, "All right. Go ahead. Get it all straightened out while you're at it. I'll probably have to make a report on this, and," he added bitterly, "so help me, this is the last time any damned amateur gets me stampeded. Go right ahead, Miss Cushing."

Ellen Cushing took a deep breath. "All right, if you insist on prying into my private affairs. I am going to marry Art Lacey. He proposed to me yesterday. I accepted him. We went on a picnic into the country. We both of us wanted to get away from business and have just one carefree picnic. We were in a hurry. We wanted to take along some sandwiches and beer and ripe olives and a few things like that and have a picnic."

"Why the sudden urge for a picnic?"

She said, "I was walking on air. I have loved Art for a long time. I didn't know that he . . . Well, that he felt that way about me. So, we went out in the country."

"And how did the seat of your automobile and this blanket get so wet?"

"I'm coming to that. We went out on one of those helter-skelter affairs where I hurriedly put up some sandwiches and we stopped by a delicatessen store and picked up a few more things. And then we bought some beer and got started, and suddenly realized we didn't have any way of keeping the beer cold. I guess we were both a little flustered and we'd completely forgotten about it. And then I remembered that I had a blanket in the back of the car and we just stopped and got some ice and wrapped it up in the blanket and went out and had our picnic."

There was a moment of silence while Lieutenant Tragg thought that over.

"You went on a picnic up by the river?" Mason asked.

"We did not," she said turning on Mason angrily, "and I wish you'd mind your own business, Mr. Perry Mason!"

"Are these wet shoes yours?" Mason asked Arthur Lacey. He nodded.

"If you want to know," Ellen Cushing said, "we went out by a lake. And Art found an old board on the bank and launched it and pretended he was going to be a pirate and got his feet wet."

"And then you separated last night and he came to call on you early this morning?"

"That's right. We were going to get all the red tape in connection with our marriage fixed up. You see, Mother was coming on the eight o'clock train last night. Art had an eight-thirty appointment, but he wanted to meet Mother. So Art and I drove to the depot and then the train was fifteen minutes late, so he had to rush back. And we agreed he'd come in and cook breakfast and get things straightened up while I went to the beauty shop, and then we'd go to the County Clerk's office to get the license."

"Then you met your mother at about eight-fifteen?"

"That's right."

"And she's been with you ever since?"

"Yes."

"You saw a Mrs. Turlock last night?"

"After dinner, yes. You see, Mother has loads of friends here. She is only going to stay a few days and she wanted to see as many of them as possible. A Mrs. Starr had driven down to the depot to meet Mother. She had to be back to pick up her husband when he got off shift at nine o'clock; so when Mother got in, we three grabbed a quick dinner together right there at the depot. Mother simply won't eat on the train. Then we went with Mrs. Starr to Mrs. Turlock's place and had a visit with Mrs. Turlock. She lives in a flat right next door. You can ask her about it. We were there until midnight. Mother and Mrs. Turlock were gabbing like a house afire and I was afraid Mother wouldn't sleep a wink . . . So now you know the whole story."

Mrs. Cushing said, "I swear I gulped my food as fast as ever I could. I didn't want Edith to be late when it came to meeting her husband, but it was five minutes to nine when we got to Fanny's—that's Mrs. Turlock—and blessed if Fanny and Edith didn't get to gabbing and . . ."

Tragg turned to Lacey, interrupted Mrs. Cushing's rapid-fire chatter, "And these are your shoes?"

"Absolutely."

"Any way of proving it?"

Lacey kicked his shoes off, put on the wet ones, extended his legs toward Tragg. Tragg felt the shoes, said, "They fit."

"Sure, they're mine."

"You knew Shelby?"

"I'd just met him."

"When?"

"Yesterday morning."

Mason said, "You must have had a busy morning. You proposed to Miss Cushing yesterday morning, I believe . . ."

Ellen Cushing said, "Don't pay any attention to him, dear. He's just a slick lawyer. He's representing Shelby's wife. She killed him, and this lawyer is trying to scare up some scandal that will take the heat off the wife."

"What'd she kill him for?" Lacey asked Ellen, apparently feeling more at ease.

"Don't be silly! What do you guess?"

134

"She should have, I suppose," Lacey said.

"What do you know about it?" Tragg asked Lacey.

He grinned. "I guess the guy was sort of a W. O. W."

"What's that?" Tragg asked.

Ellen answered the question, "A Worn Out Wolf."

Tragg grinned.

Lacey said, "I got nothing against the guy. He made me sore, though, the way he treated Ellen."

"What was wrong with the way he treated Ellen?" Tragg wanted to know.

"The general idea of the old buzzard."

Ellen laughed. "You'll have to get over that, Art. Actually he was only seven years older than you are."

"I wasn't sore," Lacey said. "It was just the idea of the thing. Shucks, soon as I saw him, I knew he was just a rundown alarm clock trying to keep on ticking. I don't care how few birthdays he'd had, he could never have held a girl like Ellen . . ."

"Better tell me about that," Tragg said.

Ellen Cushing said, "I've loved Art Lacey for a long time. I met Mr. Shelby about six months ago. Mr. Shelby was married. I knew that he was something of a . . . Well, he was something of a wolf."

"Make passes?" Tragg asked, showing that he was interested.

Ellen Cushing said hurriedly, "He didn't get anywhere."

"Of course he didn't get anywhere," Lacey interposed, "but it was the idea of the thing. You know the way a nice girl would feel about a thing like that. They had some business deals and he was always trying to make her. I've been in love with her for a long time. I always felt a smart, clever woman like her was too far above the likes of me for me to be getting foolish ideas—but I never even touched her. I never dared. I had too much respect for her. You can imagine how I felt about this guy trying to take advantage of her."

"Then why did she keep seeing him?" Tragg asked, trying to draw Lacey out.

It was Ellen Cushing who answered the question. "I was

in the real estate business. Mr. Shelby was able to throw things my way once in a while and I wanted to keep on good terms with him. I wanted to be friendly. I had a living to make.''

''That's no sign he had to keep trying to paw you over,'' Lacey said.

She said angrily, ''He didn't do a lot of pawing.''

''Well, he wanted to.''

''Lots of men want to,'' Ellen Cushing said, and giggled.

''I can believe that,'' Tragg said smiling, ''but go on. Tell me about Shelby.''

''Well, that's about all there was to it. Mr. Shelby kept trying to throw business my way because . . . Well, I think he wanted to establish the contact, and I'm quite certain that if he thought he could have got anywhere, he'd have really gone overboard in a big way.''

''You mean he'd have left his wife?''

''I think he'd have tried to, yes.''

''So, as far as Shelby is concerned, he might have gone to any lengths in order to get rid of his wife and be free to marry you?''

''He might have, yes . . . I guess he wanted to, all right.''

''And Mr. Lacey resented that?''

''I did,'' Lacey said simply.

''Did you ever tell Shelby so?''

''Yes.''

''When?''

''Yesterday. That's what I keep trying to tell you.''

''You started out on this picnic yesterday morning?''

''Late morning. That was afterwards.''

''It was like this,'' Ellen Cushing said, ''he went up and . . .''

''Let me tell it,'' Lacey said, his voice slow and dogged, in the manner of an inarticulate man who wants to be certain that he is not misunderstood.

''All right, you tell it,'' Ellen Cushing said, smiling.

Lacey said, ''There was some stuff over this oil lease and Shelby started to put pressure on Ellen. Told her that he was responsible for putting quite a bit of money in her hands and that he'd had a reason for doing it and that sort of stuff. Ellen left his office, and I was waiting to see her in her office. Well, she told me about it and . . . Well, I got mad. So I went into Shelby's office and told him that as far as he was concerned, he could leave Ellen alone.''

"What did he say?"

"Well, I guess he was sore anyway. He'd just had a run-in with some guy who was leaving the office as I walked in—a crippled chap who thought Shelby had been cheating him out of a grocery store or something. Shelby got rid of him and turned to me, and asked me what *I* wanted—still half mad. And I was mad, and so I spoke my piece.''

"And what did he say?" Tragg asked.

"Well, he said that it was none of my business and that Ellen was able to handle herself and take care of herself and pick her own friends and I didn't have any right to stick *my* nose into something that was none of my business. And so I told him I was going to put myself in a position where I did have the right. At least, I was going to *try* and put myself in that position and then if I did get in that position, I was coming back and punch his nose.''

"So then what did you do?" Tragg asked.

"Then," he said, "I went right down to Ellen's office. She's got an office in the same building. And asked her to marry me.''

Ellen Cushing laughed suddenly, a peal of spontaneous merriment. She said, "You can imagine how *I* felt. I'd been in love with Art for a long time but he had never said anything . . .''

"I thought she was so darn far above me that she'd laugh at me if I'd ask her to marry me," Lacey blurted.

Ellen Cushing said, "After all, a man doesn't understand how a woman feels about those things. I didn't object to the fact that Scott Shelby found me attractive, just so he kept his hands off me and kept his . . . Well, you know, didn't proposition me too badly . . . And I'd mentioned to Arthur the fact that Shelby was getting a little insistent because . . . Well, because . . .''

"Because you thought it might bring things to a head with Lacey?" Tragg asked, his eyes twinkling.

"Because I thought that it would be a good way to find out whether Art really cared for me or not."

"And you found out?" Tragg asked.

She smiled and said, "I'll say I did! The door of my office burst open and Art entered the room, slammed the door shut behind him, walked over to my desk and I could see that he was still angry. He looked down at me and almost yelled, 'Ellen, will you marry me?' "

"And then what?"

"And I looked up at him and shouted, 'Yes.' Just like that. It certainly was the devil of a way for a man to propose and for a woman to accept. I'd always had romantic dreams about how it would be to have Art propose to me. I'd lie awake at night sort of half asleep and half waking and drift off into dreams that were part wishful thinking and part really dreams . . . And it would always be that we were out on a picnic somewhere and Art would be sitting over close to me and I'd lean over against him and put my head on his shoulder. And then he'd smooth my hair and ask me to marry him . . . And then the man came bursting into my office, walked up to my desk and bellowed at me, 'Ellen, will you marry me?' and I shouted right back at him, 'Yes.' And then the absurdity of the whole thing dawned on us and we both began to laugh."

"And then you went back to punch Shelby's nose?" Tragg asked Arthur Lacey.

"I didn't," he grinned. "I had other things to do. The minute she said, 'Yes,' I got over being mad . . . I wasn't mad at anyone. I felt at peace with the whole cockeyed world. If I'd had time, I'd have gone back and bought the guy a drink. I guess after all he wasn't such a bad egg. You can't blame him for wanting Ellen."

Ellen laughed and said, "I'd tried to use Shelby to find out how Art felt, and I guess I'd given Art a rather distorted picture of the man."

Lacey nodded. "I'd sort of pictured him as a sleek, irresistible millionaire—and then I saw this droop with the brooding sunken eyes. I guess he's okay. Only," he added, angry again, "I didn't like his way of getting in solid—or trying to."

Ellen picked up the conversation. "So then, after a half hour or so, I told Arthur how I'd always dreamed about the way he would propose to me and that was when we decided to . . ."

"I was going to propose all over again the way *she* wanted it," Lacey said. "And so we went about it like a couple of kids. We left her office and dashed up to the apartment here and she put up some sandwiches and I went down to the delicatessen store and picked up some cold roast chicken . . ."

"And *was* it tough!" Ellen exclaimed.

"And so we piled in the car and went out on this picnic," Arthur Lacey went on.

"And you proposed to her all over again?"

"I'll say I did!"

"*Most* satisfactorily," Ellen told him. Her eyes were starry and sparkling now. She had thrown aside all of her reserve and had forgotten her anger. And Lacey, having recovered from his embarrassment and the strangeness of the situation was acting more naturally, giving to Lieutenant Tragg the confidence of a man who is slow and inarticulate but once he has lost his self-consciousness, manages to express himself clearly.

"Well," Mrs. Cushing started rattling, "it's a great howdy-do when a girl's own mother has to learn all this because a lawyer and a policeman . . ."

"One more question," Mason interposed. "Why didn't you put the ice in the trunk instead of wrapping it in the blanket and putting it on the rear seat of the car?"

She turned to him and instantly her eyes became angry. "That," she flared, "is none of your business."

"Just to close the thing up," Tragg said, "*I'd* like to know the answer to that too."

She said, "I don't like to have him prying into my affairs. I think he's responsible for this whole business."

"But I'd like to know the answer to that one," Tragg said.

139

She said, "It's just like I told you. We were halfway there when we realized that we had forgotten the ice. This place was a little private country estate that had been listed with me for sale and there's a lake on it with some woods running down to the lake. We were spinning along when I suddenly realized I'd forgotten to bring any ice, and the other stuff, the boxes of sandwiches and the delicatessen stuff and everything were in the trunk and . . . Well, I told Art we'd forgotten the ice and we didn't know what to do. We thought we'd get some ice and put it in the trunk but we'd have had to move all the other stuff out and . . . Well, we were in a hurry."

"I was in a hurry," Lacey said and grinned, that slow good-natured grin that changed the entire expression of his face.

She laughed and said, "I guess we were a little bit rattled. Anyhow, I didn't realize that I was going to have to explain everything I did. Art simply took the blanket and went into the icehouse and got the ice wrapped up, came out and opened the car door and threw it on the seat."

"Why not on the floor?" Mason asked.

Lacey said, "It's too narrow down on the floor. There wasn't enough room down between the back of the front seat and the front of the back seat, but on the back seat there's lots of room, and it's got just the right slant to it so the ice wouldn't spill around out of the blanket, and so I just dumped it in and we were on our way."

"Don't talk to *him*, Art dear," Ellen said. "He doesn't have any right to ask questions."

Lieutenant Tragg got to his feet. "Well," he said, "thanks a lot. I'm sorry I bothered you."

"Not at all. Are you going to take us to the courthouse and to the district attorney?"

Tragg grinned. "I'll take you to the courthouse if you want to go with me but I'm in a hurry. I've got lots of things to do this morning and I'll give you a fast ride."

"You're not in any bigger hurry than we are," Lacey said.

"And as far as the district attorney's office is concerned," Tragg announced, "that's out. I guess when you come right down to it, someone handed me a button and told me that the vest belonged on the button and I was trying to sew the vest on the button.''

Ellen Cushing glared at Mason. ''I can make one guess as to who that was.''

Tragg said, ''Well, come on, if you're coming with me.''

Mrs. Cushing said, ''You young folks run along. I'll straighten up the kitchen.''

''It's all straightened,'' Art Lacey said, grinning. ''Just one cup and saucer that . . .''

''Come on,'' Tragg said.

''See you later, Mumsey,'' Ellen announced, getting her hat. ''If you get lonesome, give Mrs. Turlock a ring and . . .''

''I ain't giving no one a ring until I get my hair done. I s'pose I'm a holy show. The way . . .''

Tragg opened the door.

Lacey grinned at the older woman. ''Bye, Mother.''

''You be careful of Ellen—Son!'' she snapped back.

''Come on,'' Tragg said.

They rode in cold silence down in the elevator. Tragg held the door of the squad car open for Ellen Cushing and Art Lacey. He said to Paul Drake, ''Sorry to leave you boys stranded, but I'm in a hurry. I'm headed back for Headquarters.''

''No need to apologize to *me*,'' Drake told him cheerfully. ''Getting out of riding back with you is one of the few good breaks I've had all day.''

Tragg slammed the car door, glanced at Mason, bowed ironically and said, ''So long—*Sherlock*.''

Chapter 16

When Della Street returned to the office, four hours' sleep and a short session at the beauty parlor had done wonders for her. She fitted her key in the exit door of Mason's private office, clicked back the lock and was two steps in the room before she suddenly recoiled in surprise at the sight of the figure slumped over in the swivel chair at the desk.

"Chief! What's the matter?"

He shook his head.

"You haven't . . . My gosh! You haven't shaved, you haven't slept . . . What happened?"

"I stuck my neck out and got it stepped on. I'm trying to think, and I can't make the grade. I can't get a starting point."

"You mean that Scott Shelby wasn't there. Gosh, I've been so worried about it I'd've called up but I felt certain you'd be at a Turkish bath and asleep."

Mason shook his head, said, "It's the damnedest thing you ever ran into, Della."

"What is?"

Mason said, "All my life I've been claiming that circumstantial evidence didn't lie, that people simply put it together wrong, and then I went off half cocked and swallowed a whole mess of circumstantial evidence, and it's given me legal indigestion."

"But what about the man in the bedroom, and . . ."

"It wasn't the bedroom. It was the kitchen. Her mother was in the bedroom. She met her boy friend at the door, took him into the kitchen. He was going to cook breakfast for them. They were getting married and he wanted to get in solid with the old lady, I guess."

"You mean she went to the *kitchen* window in her robe?"

"That's right. It was the kitchen window all right. Tragg

stuck his head out of the bedroom window later, and Drake's operative figured that was the kitchen window. He'd got 'em mixed because Ellen Cushing went to the kitchen window in her robe. I guess she was wrapping it around her as she put down the window. The only thing I found out from the whole business is that probably Marjorie Stanhope's boy friend, the crippled soldier, went to Shelby's office and bawled him out.''

"When?''

"Apparently yesterday morning, shortly before the invitations to the yachting trip were issued. But I can't make anything out of that. They were having a row.''

"How do you know that?''

"Arthur Lacey, Ellen Cushing's boy friend, saw the crippled soldier—but I'm even afraid to trust the circumstantial evidence on *that*. It was just some cripple who was bawling Shelby out because he'd lost a chance to buy into a grocery business.''

Della said, "That must have been Frank Bomar, all right.''

"I suppose so. Can't see that it makes such a lot of difference. I'll have Paul Drake check on it.''

Della perched herself on the corner of the desk. "Tell me everything that happened.''

Mason said, "I made myself ridiculous. I ran into a whole flock of coincidences. I certainly led with my chin. If Dorset hears about it, and he will, he'll probably talk the girl into doing something that'll make headlines.''

"Why?''

"So it'll hurt my case. You know, make it look as though I had been trying to draw a red herring across the trail.''

"What about Tragg?''

"He's sore.''

"Do you mean to tell me there's an explanation for those wet shoes of Scott Shelby's being found.''

"They aren't his shoes. They're Lacey's.''

Della Street sighed. "Begin at the beginning and tell me the whole business. Will you, please?''

Mason told her. When he had finished her face was bleak with disappointment. "Gosh, Chief, and I thought you had it solved.''

Mason nodded gloomily. "I thought so myself—and here she turns up with alibis and witnesses. The whole thing is just one of those traps circumstantial evidence will set for you once in a while. So far it's been the district attorney's office that has walked into 'em. Now I know how they must have felt when I've showed 'em up. I feel like hell myself, now that the shoe is on the other foot."

"Look, Chief, you can't do any good for anyone sitting here and thinking around in circles. Go get shaved, and then get that Turkish bath. Tomorrow you'll be able to see a way out."

"I'm not certain that I will, Della. This is one of those nightmare cases . . . Gosh what a day! Everything I touch goes sour . . . Friday, the thirteenth! I'll say it's unlucky."

Della said, "Okay, if it's unlucky, let's just sit it out. The big rush is over now. Anything that's left will wait until tomorrow."

"I'm not so certain."

"Perhaps," Della said, "you had the right idea, but the wrong woman. Remember, the man is a gay Lothario. If he's trying to get out from matrimony and skip away with a siren he doesn't necessarily have to go with the Cushing woman."

"But she has the oil lease."

"What about it?"

"Don't you see? He'll need someone who can act as his stooge to salvage what cash can be squeezed out of the things he couldn't peddle before he made his plunge. That means his accomplice will have to be able to cash in. Hang it, it all points to the Cushing woman, but I sure ran into an avalanche when I tried to nail it down."

"Any chance any of that could have been framed?" Della asked.

"Not a chance. The mother looks like her. There are witnesses. I'm having Drake check on them, but it's just one of those things—that kitchen window! And Drake's man jumped at the wrong conclusion, thought it was the bedroom. I tell you, Della, the thing is hoodooed. It's jinxed, the whole case."

She laughed. "That's the way it looks now, but . . ."

The telephone rang.

Mason said, "See who it is, will you Della? I don't want to see anyone unless it's terribly important."

"I'll tell the world you don't want to see anyone," she said, looking at him critically. "You'd frighten all your business away from the office. They'd think you'd been on a drunk for a week."

She picked up the telephone, said, "What is it, Gertie? I just came in. The Chief doesn't want to be disturbed . . . What? . . . Oh, just a minute, I'll ask him."

She turned from the telephone and said to Mason, "There's a deputy sheriff out there. Says that he has to see you on a matter that's very important, that it will only take a minute but that it may make quite a difference to you."

Mason said, "Show him in. It may be a break."

"Shoot him on in," Della said and hung up the telephone. She walked over to open the door to the outer office.

The deputy sheriff, a short stubby man with keen gray eyes and a yellowish gray mustache, came marching into the office. He held papers in his hand. And, something in the manner in which he walked towards Mason's desk, tipped the lawyer off to the nature of his errand.

"Oh, oh," Mason said. "Here it comes, Della."

The deputy sheriff said, "I'm sorry, Mr. Mason but I have to serve papers on you. It's all in a day's work. You're a lawyer, you know how it is."

"What's the case?" Mason asked.

"Ellen Cushing versus Perry Mason and Paul Drake. Suit for two hundred and fifty thousand dollars defamation of character."

Mason looked bored. "Tell me some more about it," he invited.

"Well, she claims that you attempted to make a frameup and use her as a red herring in order to get Marion Shelby out of a murder charge and she doesn't intend to stand for it. One hundred and twenty-five thousand dollars in actual damages and a hundred and twenty-five thousand dollars for exemplary or punitive damages. Claims that she's about to be married and almost lost her husband on account of it. That

145

you pried into her private affairs, insisted on searching her apartment without a warrant, conspired to get officers to falsely accuse her of crime, claimed she'd spent the night with a man in her bedroom. It's quite a smear. Guess you know the lawyers on the other side. Attica, Hoxie and Meade. A firm of smooth shysters."

"Served Paul Drake yet?" Mason asked the deputy.

"Not yet, he wasn't in his office. I'll get him."

Mason said, "Drake's going to hit the ceiling. I suppose the newspapers know about it."

"I'll say they do! They're giving the gal a great play. Taking pictures with a lot of cheesecake and romantic stuff. Her and her future husband getting a marriage license and all that sort of stuff."

"Where is she now?"

"Last I heard she was in Sergeant Dorset's office. He's sort of master of ceremonies. That was one o'clock, I guess."

"I gathered he might be," Mason said.

The deputy sheriff, having disposed of his official duty said, "If you ask me, I think it's a crummy trick. From all I could gather, you tried to give the officers a little help and they turned it into a boomerang and then did everything they could to get publicity so it would put you in the doghouse. Attica sure rushed this case."

"Oh, well," Mason said shrugging, "when you start fighting a man, you have to expect to be hit. I've dished it out a lot in my time and I guess I should be able to take it."

The officer shook hands, said, "Well, you know where I stand, Mr. Mason."

"Thanks," Mason said.

"No hard feelings over the papers?"

Mason laughed. "Heavens no!"

"Okay, just wanted to be sure you felt that way about it. Good afternoon."

"Good afternoon," Mason said,

The man went out. Della Street looked at Perry Mason with dismayed eyes. "My gosh, Chief, two hundred and fifty thousand dollars!"

"Sure," Mason said bitterly, "it doesn't cost anything to

put lots of ciphers after figures and that makes it look better for the newspaper notoriety."

"What will this do?"

"It depends on whom you're thinking about."

"Marion Shelby."

"It won't do *her* any good," Mason admitted. "And if you want to think in terms of Paul Drake . . . *There's* something for you. Imagine Drake when this bird serves the summons on him."

Mason picked up the papers, glanced through the complaint. Once or twice muttered under his breath, "The damned shysters. . . . Oh-oh."

"What is it now?" Della asked.

"Just found something."

"What?"

"Listen to this," Mason said, and read from the complaint, "Plaintiff is informed and believes and upon such information alleges the fact to be that the said defendants and each of them wilfully, unlawfully and feloniously, and without proper authorization, by means of skeleton keys or otherwise, surreptitiously entered the plaintiff's garage, and while in said garage, and by means of such unlawful entry, uncovered certain articles, and that the basis of the said accusation made as aforesaid to the said Lieutenant Tragg was entirely founded upon this so-called evidence, produced and inspected at the time of such unlawful and illegal entry. All of which, plaintiff alleges, constitutes circumstances of oppression sufficient to warrant the imposition of punitive or exemplary damages."

Della said, "Well you're going to get out of here and go get some sleep before Paul Drake comes in to cry on your shoulder."

Mason shoved the papers in his pocket. "On the contrary, Della, we're going on a picnic. Sleep can wait."

"A picnic?"

Mason nodded. "We're going to the same place where Ellen Cushing went yesterday. It's a country estate that she has listed for sale."

"Well?"

Mason said, "The property has a lake on it."

"And you want to go there?"

Mason said, "I want to go there very very much. I'm going down and get a shave. I'll be back in about twenty minutes. You try to get the information. She is probably advertising the place in the papers. If you can get a description that looks good, find out how to get there."

"What's the idea?" she asked.

Mason said, "People who go on picnics leave paper plates and empty cans and papers and all sorts of things. I'm going out and look over that picnic place. I want to see if they were telling the truth."

"Suppose you don't find anything? Then what?"

"Then," Mason said, "I'm going to slap a subpoena on her for a deposition, and when I take her deposition, I'm really going to ask questions."

"And suppose you find they actually were out there on a picnic?"

"Things can't be any worse than they are now."

Della Street smiled, "Okay. You go get your shave. I'll start digging out information."

Twenty minutes later Mason returned to find Della Street studying a map.

"Get it?" he asked.

"I think I have it. It's a place out about fifteen miles back of Pleasantville, four hundred acres in it and they want twenty thousand dollars."

"A lake?"

"A lake, some woods, and a spring. I don't think it's too much of a lake. The spring feeds it but it's described as something that can be fitted up into a nice swimming pool."

Mason said, "Let's go."

"It will be dark before we get back."

"What do we care? I've got some flashlights in the car."

"Chief, you *should* have some sleep."

"I'll sleep when this is over," Mason said. "Let's get going."

She recognized both his restlessness and the seriousness of the situation so made no further objection.

Mason crowded the speed limit all the way to Pleasant-ville, then followed Della Street's directions and after a mile and a half of dirt road, they came to a rustic gateway and a sign FOR SALE—*Inquire of* E. B. CUSHING, LICENSED REAL ESTATE BROKER and below that was her office address.

As they turned in through the rustic gate, Della Street said, "There's been a car in here recently."

Mason nodded. "I noticed the tracks. Doesn't look so good, Della."

"No?"

"No," Mason said. "Ellen Cushing's car had one brand new tire on the right front and the left front was worn almost smooth. Apparently her car made those tracks."

The sun had reached that point in the western heavens where it seemed to pause before taking its final dip below the horizon. The valleys were filled with purple shadows, while the tops of the rolling hills were tinged with reddish gold illumination. The light also was at just the right angle to bring out most effectively the characteristics of tire tracks. Mason studied them briefly.

Mason stopped the car and helped Della Street out. "Where," he asked, "do we go for our picnic, Della?"

She said, "I think the lake is off here to the right. It is supposed to be up a trail through a patch of woodland."

They followed a trail which wound up a slope beneath huge live oaks. The trail curved to the right and then doubled back sharply to the left.

Della Street exclaimed at the sheer beauty of the scene before them.

The lake, some hundred and fifty feet long by a hundred wide, reflected the reddish glow of massed clouds in the western heavens. Back of the lake on the east was a hill and from this hill a spring fed a small stream which trickled down over granite rocks under oak trees. There was no wind and the lake was a vivid mirror of growing color.

Della Street stood drinking in the beauty of the scene. Mason, at her side, slipped his arm around her shoulders, held her close to his side as they stood watching the sunset.

"What a perfect place for a proposal!" Della Street exclaimed, then laughed nervously. "*I'm* beginning to think she was telling the truth, Chief."

Mason said, "The cold feeling in the pit of my stomach still persists. Let's take a look around, Della, before it gets dark."

They walked around the shore of the lake, found no difficulty whatever in locating the spot where the picnic had taken place.

The picnickers had been careless, not unusually so, but paper plates were still in evidence, an empty tin which had contained olives caught the reflection of the clouds and glowed with reddish brilliance. An attempt had been made to dispose of surplus garbage by digging a hole, but the hole had been left uncovered and Mason, using a little chip of wood as a scoop, carefully brought out the remnants of a meal, bread crusts, olive pits, and a quantity of what had evidently been creamed tuna, below which was macaroni and cheese of the type dispensed by delicatessen stores; there were also some bags which had contained potato chips and the peeled shells from hard boiled eggs.

After a few minutes of studying the results of his scavenging, Mason tossed the chip away, got to his feet, said, "Well, Della, this Friday the thirteenth certainly has been *my* unlucky day."

Della Street slipped her hand into his. "I hate to add to it Chief . . . But the board's over here, the one he used for a raft."

Mason saw a rough slab of board floating in the lake, a board which had originally been cut to generous proportions, eighteen inches wide, two inches thick, and perhaps some five feet long. Some round limbs from a dead oak had been crudely lashed to the bottom in order to form a raft which looked capable of supporting one's weight.

Mason turned abruptly away.

Silently they walked around to the far edge of the lake, then paused to look at the after colors of sunset. Della Street glanced questioningly at Mason.

The lawyer wearily settled down on the grassy slope, looked up at the clouds which had now turned crimson.

150

They sat there in silence, close together, each preoccupied with his own thoughts. Mason turning over and over in his mind the murder case, Della Street from time to time glancing up at Mason's granite-hard profile, his level-lidded concentration.

At length Mason lay back, put his hands under his head, looked up at the heavens and said wearily, "Let's wait for the first star, Della. Then we'll go."

She moved around, raised his head, put it on her lap, smoothed back the thick wavy hair from his tired forehead.

Mason closed his eyes. "That feels swell," he muttered.

She placed the tips of her fingers over his eyelids, softly drew them around the edges, then gave a gentle pressure against the sides of his head just back of the eyes.

Mason drew in a deep breath, exhaled it in a sigh, relaxed until the furrows left his forehead, said almost dreamily, "Call me when you see the first star, Della."

Ten seconds later he was asleep.

Della let him sleep until the stars were blazing brilliantly, until the evening air began to have a suggestion of chill, then she wakened him.

"The first star, Chief," she said.

"Della . . . Good Lord, what time is it?"

"I don't know. It's not *too* late."

"You should have wakened me."

"I was asleep myself," she lied.

"Honest?"

"Uh huh."

"Gosh, Della . . . Where are the flashlights?"

"Over here."

"It's going to be dark."

"That's all right. We can find our way down the trail."

"Well," Mason said, "let's go back and call it a day, Della."

Della said, "You know, Chief, I've been thinking."

"What?"

"The fact that this Cushing woman was telling the truth, the fact that they *did* come out here and *did* have their picnic doesn't necessarily affect anything that Scott Shelby did or

151

didn't do. After all, he'd made a perfect setup to duck out and leave his wife framed with a murder."

"But why?" Mason asked.

"That's something we'll have to find out. I can't help but think your reasoning is correct. We just tied it up with the wrong party, that's all. He must have had some other woman."

"Perhaps, yet, somehow I doubt if he did. I'm beginning to feel now that there's something I've overlooked . . . And yet the case against Marion Shelby is just *too* bulletproof. I can't help but think Shelby is alive."

Della Street said, "You *could* be wrong?"

"Of course. Why do you ask in just that tone of voice?"

"Because, somehow, I feel he was murdered. I have a hunch he . . . well, you know . . . The murder was committed on the yacht. It must have been."

Mason said, "If he's really dead, I'm licked, Della—and licked good and plenty. Oh well, let's go. We'll see what turns up tomorrow."

Mason played his flashlight along the ground in front, said, "You walk ahead, Della, and I'll hold the flashlight slightly to one side and . . . What's that in your hand?"

She said, "A hollow tube of lead. It's a sinker. Someone evidently was fishing. I picked it up for luck." She handed it to him. "Keep it and see if it doesn't give us a break."

"Luck on Friday the thirteenth?"

"Why not? After all, Chief, Scott Shelby was a man of parts. He didn't confine his attentions to one woman. His whole record shows that. Ellen Cushing *thought* that she was the whole show, but the probabilities are that he was making passes at her just to keep his hand in. Let's see if some other woman wasn't the one who waited out there in a rowboat and picked him up."

Mason said, "You *might* have something there. The thing that makes the Cushing woman so plausible is that oil lease."

They walked silently down the pathway. Mason held the door open for Della, fumbled for his ignition keys.

"Okay?" she asked.

"I think I forgot something," he said.

"What?"

He grasped her shoulders, pulled her towards him, kissed her, then held her close to him.

She sighed when he released her. "It should have gone with the sunset," she laughed, but her voice was wistful.

"Better late than never," he told her. "I'm going to quit taking my cases so seriously if they make me unable to concentrate on the things that are worthwhile in life."

"Don't go to extremes," she laughed. "Just dismiss it from your mind until tomorrow."

Chapter 17

Perry Mason entered the elevator with a smile twitching at the corners of his lips. His shoulders were back, his head up. The worry of the day before had completely vanished and his step was light, his eyes twinkling.

He stopped on his way to his own office to look in at Paul Drake's office.

"The boss wants to see you just as soon as he possibly can," the girl at the switchboard told him. "He's in there, waiting."

Mason grinned. "In other words, I suppose the papers have been served on him. Okay, I'll go on in."

Paul Drake looked up as Mason entered, "Hello, Perry. Seen the papers?"

"What about 'em?"

"We're being sued for two hundred and fifty thousand smackers."

Mason stretched, yawned, "Lawsuits are cheap."

Drake said bitterly, "I'm going to throw away those skeleton keys and never carry them again as long as I live."

"You've said *that* before, Paul," Mason replied, "but you know you can't throw them away. It's too complete a collection."

"Don't kid yourself. I'm going to go down to the longest wharf on the waterfront and throw 'em as far as I can hurl. Tell me, Perry. What is this case? How serious is it?"

Mason said, "Probably publicity on the part of the police."

"See the pictures of the picnic, Perry?"

154

"No. Where?"

"The Times has an exclusive on 'em. The gal had a camera along."

"The deuce she did!"

"Uh huh. The gal must be a good photographer. She got some swell pictures. One of 'em even shows the ice on the blanket. A nice jolt for us, eh? The pictures were taken with a delayed action release, shows them both. A jury will like 'em—nice pictures."

Mason said, "Cheer up, Paul. It's all a part of yesterday's tough luck. Yesterday was Friday the thirteenth. It's gone now. We've got a new day, Saturday the fourteenth. Get your fingerprint outfit, will you? I want you to come into the office and do a job."

"On what?"

"On the telephone I took from my stateroom on Parker Benton's yacht."

"Did you use the telephone?"

"Yes. But I think somebody else used it after I did."

"Who?"

"Shelby. Apparently mine was the only vacant stateroom."

Drake said, "For the love of Mike, Perry, wake up. Forget that telephone business. That woman never did get any telephone call. She knew that her husband was on deck. My guess is that he was on deck with that Marjorie Stanhope. The wife was doing a little eavesdropping and probably heard plenty. I guess Shelby was quite a rounder. He may have been using the oil lease as a little leverage to help him make a noise like a wolf. Marion Shelby simply parked around there until after the party broke up and then bumped her husband off."

"Come on," Mason said, "we'll conduct our postmortems after we know more. Let's see if we can develop some latents on the telephone."

"How the heck are we going to get Shelby's fingerprints for comparison when they haven't got the body?"

"The police will have developed a set of fingerprints from his apartment."

155

"Maybe. But they won't turn them over to anybody. After the body is discovered, we can get the fingerprints from the coroner's office."

"Well," Mason said, "come on, let's go down and take a look at that telephone instrument anyway."

Drake picked up a small satchel, said, "I suppose you'll want a fingerprint camera too. Anyhow I'll take one." He picked up a long, oblong black covered box.

Mason held the door open for him and they went down the corridor. Mason unlocked the door of his private office, smiled at Della and said, "How are you feeling this morning, Della?"

"Like a million dollars. Seen the picnic pictures, Chief?"

"Not yet. Where's that bag with the telephone, Della?"

Della Street opened the safe, took out the bag. Mason opened the bag and took out the telephone, being careful not to leave his fingerprints on the instrument.

Drake dusted the instrument with a white powder while Mason looked at the picnic pictures in the newspaper.

At length Drake said, "Well, we've got some nice latents here—whoever made 'em. They're sharp as a tack, and . . ."

He broke off as the telephone rang and Della answered it.

"For you, Paul," Della Street said, pushing the telephone at Paul Drake.

Drake picked up the receiver, said, "Hello . . . Huh? . . . The hell they did . . . When?"

He cupped his hand over the mouthpiece of the transmitter, looked up at Perry Mason. His face held stupefied surprise. "They've recovered Scott Shelby's body, Perry! Dragged it out of the river."

"The devil they did!" Mason said incredulously.

"A thirty-eight bullet in the base of his skull," Drake went on.

"What time?" Mason asked.

"What time?" Drake asked into the telephone.

He turned to Perry Mason. "Eleven-fifty-nine last night, Perry."

Mason said whimsically, "Friday the thirteenth had to take one last wallop. This looks like the pay-off, Paul."

Chapter 18

The district attorney, thinking back on the unexpected pitfalls which Perry Mason had injected into previous cases, embarked on the trial of The People vs. Marion Shelby with the leisurely thoroughness of a connoisseur who is not going to be hurried through a most pleasant experience.

Paul Drake had delivered a final report as the court recessed after a jury had been selected. "They've got a mathematical case, Perry, one of those dreams of the district attorney, a case where there isn't any single possible solution other than that of guilt."

"Did you get a report on those fingerprints?"

"Yes."

"Were any of those prints of Scott Shelby?"

"Yes, they were," Drake said.

Mason grinned. "I think, Paul, that's all the break I want. If I can find something that will substantiate Marion Shelby's story . . ."

"But you can't, Perry."

"What do you mean?"

"There are other fingerprints on there, those of Parker Benton, the fingerprints of a woman that haven't as yet been identified. Benton says he has no idea who she could have been. There's some possibility it was a woman who had occupied the stateroom some time previously and Benton doesn't want to have her name brought into the case."

"I don't care about the other fingerprints, Paul. If Scott Shelby's fingerprints are on that telephone . . ."

"Wait a minute," Drake said. "I'm coming to something else. Parker Benton says that originally Scott Shelby was put into that stateroom. Then, Benton decided to put Shelby and his wife in the other end of the yacht. He thought they would

158

be more comfortable in a larger stateroom. So he moved them and put you in there. Shelby could have used the phone in the five minutes or so he was in there. At any rate, the D.A. will claim he did and that will knock your theory galley west."

Mason made a wry face. "How about the bullet, Paul?"

"They're keeping mum on that, Perry. The D.A. feels there's been a leak on some of his other cases, so he's sewed this up so tight I can't find out a darn thing."

"Well there's one thing," Mason said with an air of conviction, "the bullet couldn't have been fired from that gun. That's *one* break I can count on."

"Don't be too sure, Perry."

"Phooey! If she saw him alive and on the deck, and she had the gun all the while. No, Paul, they'll claim the bullet was too battered to identify or that she had two guns. That's *one* break they'll have to give me."

The bailiff called for the jury. Paul Drake thrust out his hand, gripped Mason's. "Well, here's luck. You're going to need it regardless of the marks on the bullet."

Mason sat down beside his client for a brief whispered conversation, and then arose as Judge Maxwell entered the courtroom and the bailiff called court to order.

District Attorney Hamilton Burger leisurely started laying the ground work for proving the *corpus delicti*, and skillfully paving the way to blast the defendant's story in the event she took the witness stand.

A draftsman introduced plans of the yacht, showing the location of each stateroom, the side elevation, overhang of bow and stern, the amount of freeboard, and, finally a complete deck plan of the yacht.

These plans were one after another introduced in evidence.

Then Hamilton Burger said, casually, all too casually in fact, "Now, Mr. Adams, I notice on this plan which is introduced in evidence as People's Exhibit C a red line and also a green line."

"Yes, sir."

"Those lines seem to run pretty much through the diagram

and to branch out into several ends. Can you tell me what they mean—that is, what they stand for? Just explain to the jury, please."

The draftsman said, "These represent two lines of wires, two telephone systems."

"Will you please turn to the jury and trace them so the jurors can see them?"

"Yes, sir. Now this red line indicates a telephone system which has several stations on the yacht, one in the bow, one in a crow's-nest on the masthead, one in the engine room, one in the pilothouse, one in the owner's stateroom, one in the crew's quarters, one in the captain's stateroom, one in the galley."

"Making a total of eight in all?" Burger asked.

"Yes, sir."

"And the green line? I noticed that that also has eight endings or outlets."

"Yes, sir. That green line represents another independent telephone system installed in the staterooms."

"That has eight outlets?"

"Yes, sir. There is an outlet in each of the staterooms and one in the steward's office."

"Those systems are not connected in any way?"

"No, sir, they are not."

"I'm anxious to get that clearly established in the minds of the jurors," Hamilton Burger said, "because it will explain the use of two different colors in tracing these telephone lines on the map. Do I understand that it would be impossible to call any of the stations on the green network from any station on the red network?"

"That is right. Yes, sir."

"But any station on the red network can be called from any other station on the red network?"

"Yes, sir."

"And similarly, any station on the green network can be called only from any station on the green network?"

"That is right. Yes, sir."

"And there is no common point on the boat at which those calls could be transferred?"

160

"No, sir. Each system is separate and independent."

"I think that is all. Do you wish to cross-examine, Mr. Mason?"

"Yes," Mason said. "I'm interested in this telephone system."

"I thought you would be," the district attorney said ironically.

Mason said to the witness, "As I understand it, you have testified that it is an absolute impossibility for any station on the green network to be called from any station on the red network."

"That is right. Yes, sir."

"I notice, however, that the two stations meet in this stateroom which you have marked Number One."

"That is the only stateroom which has outlets from both lines, the one occupied by Mr. Parker Benton as a rule, and I understand he has to call . . . Well, I guess I hadn't better go into that."

"No," the district attorney said with a smile. "Just confine yourself to what is shown on these diagrams, if you please, Mr. Adams. The jurors will understand without your help that the owner of a yacht naturally has to call its various departments."

"Yes, sir."

Mason said, "These two telephone systems *do* meet, however, in this stateroom Number One?"

"They don't meet. No, sir. But stateroom Number One is served with both telephones, that is, a telephone from each system."

"And I notice that the end of the green line and the end of the red line in this diagram showing stateroom Number One are very close together."

"That's right. Yes, sir. There were two telephones within a few inches of each other on the telephone table. Experiments proved that one was connected with the red network—the one which you see on the right here—and the other with the green network."

"Exactly. Now let's consider one other possibility. It would have been readily possible for the occupant of stateroom

Number One to have called any station on either the green or the red network?''

''Yes, sir. Provided he used the proper telephone in each instance.''

''Exactly,'' Mason said. ''Now then, wouldn't it have been possible for an electrician to have removed the insulation from these lines and hooked up a wire which would, at least temporarily, have consolidated the two systems?''

The witness frowned. ''I see what you mean,'' he said, ''but I don't think it could have been done.''

''Why not?''

''Well, if it could have been done, it stands to reason the owner would have installed the system that way in the first place. As I get it, he wanted to have sixteen telephone outlets but he couldn't do that on the systems which he could secure and install. He had a maximum of eight outlets on each. So he . . .''

''Never mind what *he* had in mind,'' Mason said, ''or what you *think* he had in mind. What I am asking you now is whether it wouldn't have been possible to have removed the insulation from one of these lines on the green, bridged across to the lines on the red, and temporarily at least, joined the two systems.''

''Well, you have complicating factors there. The telephone in itself is simple but there's the question of call arrangement. You see there's a selective bell service by which you can call any one of the eight stations, and that's the thing that really complicates the installation of this system. I'm not enough of an electrician to know what would happen if you bridged the two. I would say offhand that you'd get your calls all mixed up. Your calling system would be thrown completely out of kilter.''

''You don't know whether it could be done or could not be done?''

''No, sir. I do not. I won't say positively. I don't *think* that it . . .''

''But you don't *know*?'' Mason interrupted.

''No, sir. I don't.''

''And you don't actually know the reason for the two systems having been installed. It is only your assumption that the facilities were installed in this way as a matter of convenience."

"I know what Parker Benton told me."

"Exactly," Mason said, "but you also know you're not supposed to testify to hearsay."

"That's right. Yes, sir."

"So you yourself don't know."

Adams shook his head and said, "I myself don't know."

"That's all," Mason said.

The district attorney called Parker Benton as his next witness.

Following the usual preliminary questions, Hamilton Burger asked the witness, "Mr. Benton, did you know Scott Shelby in his lifetime?"

"I did."

"Where is Mr. Shelby now?"

"He is dead."

"You are certain?"

"Yes, sir."

"You saw his body?"

"I did. Yes, sir."

"Where?"

"At the morgue."

"And did you identify that body?"

"I did. Yes, sir."

"You had seen Mr. Shelby in his lifetime?"

"I had. Yes, sir."

"There can be no question about your identification?"

"No, sir. None."

"And you identified that body in the presence of officers and of an autopsy surgeon?"

"I did. Yes, sir."

"A Mr. Robert P. Noxie was also present?"

"The ballistics expert. Yes, sir."

"And did you give a firearm to the officers sometime prior to the time you viewed this body?"

"I did. Yes, sir."

"What was the description of that firearm?"

"A .38 caliber Colt Police Positive."

"Was there a number stamped on that gun?"

"There was. Yes, sir."

"What is it?"

"One-four-five-eight-one."

"Where did you obtain that gun, Mr. Benton?"

"It was given to me by Marion Shelby, the defendant in this action."

"And under what circumstances did she give it to you?"

"It was on my yacht."

"Did she make any statement to you at the time the gun was given to you?"

"She did."

"What was it?"

"Just a moment, Your Honor," Mason said, "I object on the ground that this is incompetent, irrelevant, and immaterial, that no proper foundation has been laid."

"You refer to the *corpus delicti*?" the judge asked.

"Exactly," Mason said. "The evidence so far shows that Scott Shelby is dead. There is no evidence indicating that he was murdered. There is no evidence indicating that he met his death by other than purely natural means. It is a well-known principle of law that the *corpus delicti* must be established before any declaration of the defendant can be admitted in evidence, and that the declarations themselves cannot prove the *corpus delicti*."

"Of course, as to that last point," Judge Maxwell ruled, "there are certain qualifications, if not exceptions. However, it would appear that the district attorney has it within his power to produce the proof in a conventional and orderly manner; so I will sustain the objection as to what the defendant may or may not have said until after the *corpus delicti* has been more conclusively established."

"Very well," Hamilton Burger said, yielding to the ruling of the court with somewhat bad grace. "This will necessitate my putting the witness on the stand twice."

"That is not a fatal objection," Judge Maxwell said calmly. "There is no reason why it can't be done."

164

"Very well," Hamilton Burger said. "You did receive this weapon from the defendant?"

"I did. Yes, sir."

"And what did you do with it?"

"I turned it over to the officers and obtained a receipt from them for it."

"Would you recognize that weapon if you saw it again?"

"I would. Yes, sir."

"I hand you a .38 caliber Colt Police Positive and ask you if that is the weapon."

"It is. Yes, sir."

"That's all for the time being. I will ask you to step down and will recall you later on. Are there any questions, Mr. Mason?"

"None," Mason said. "Not at this time. I will reserve my cross-examination."

Hamilton Burger hesitated, then said suddenly, "I'm going to ask one or two more questions in order to pave the way for the evidence that will be introduced."

"No objection," Mason said. "That is, to your asking additional questions. I may object to the questions themselves."

Burger said, "Mr. Benton, there was a yachting party aboard your yacht the night of the . . . the night the defendant gave you this gun? The evening of the twelfth?"

"Yes, sir."

"Will you describe the occasion of that yachting party, please?"

Parker Benton said, "I was buying some property from a Jane Keller, an island. The deal was in escrow and I understood the escrow was on the point of being completed when I was advised there was an unrecorded oil lease outstanding on the property and that Mr. Shelby claimed some rights under this oil lease."

"Go ahead."

"Frankly, I was rather anxious to secure the property. While I had paid what I thought was a very generous price, I would have gone a little higher if I had had to do so."

"So you approached Mr. Shelby?"

"I did. Yes, sir. I suggested that Mr. Shelby and the owner of the property, Jane Keller, her brother-in-law who is acting as her adviser, a Mrs. Martha Stanhope and a Marjorie Stanhope, the sister and niece of Mrs. Keller respectively, and who seemed to be interested in the deal, and Mr. Mason who was acting as attorney for Jane Keller, and Mr. Mason's secretary, Miss Della Street, have a conference aboard my yacht. My wife was also present and Mr. Shelby brought his wife, the defendant in this action."

"You cruised up the river to the approximate location of this island?"

"About five hundred yards below the island. Fog had settled down and I was a little afraid to go right on in to the island."

"You anchored downstream from the island?"

"I did. Yes, sir."

"In what depth of water?"

"Twenty-two feet."

"And there was a current?"

"Yes. There's a channel of the river at this place, a channel which goes past the island. It is not the main channel of the river, but it is a well-defined navigable channel. That was one of the reasons I was interested in the island. There was a fairly deep water anchorage on the south shore of the island."

"Now, without going into details, was there generally some discussion on the yacht that night in regard to this oil lease?"

"There was. That was the evening of the twelfth. I had thought that I might get everyone together, give them a good dinner, get them over their antagonism to each other, and see if the case couldn't be compromised."

"And that was the general background of this gathering on the yacht?"

"It was. Yes, sir."

"I think that's all."

"Just a moment, on that last phase," Mason said. "I have a question to ask."

"Yes, sir?"

"There was some discussion with Mr. Shelby about the conditions under which he would be willing to relinquish his oil lease?"

"There was. Yes, sir."

"A question of money being involved?"

"Yes, sir."

"And a discussion of amounts?"

"That's right. Yes, sir."

"And did Mr. Shelby at that time make some statement in regard to an interest in the property being owned by a Miss Ellen Cushing?"

"That's incompetent, irrelevant, and immaterial," the district attorney objected. "It's not proper cross-examination."

"I think it's very proper," Mason said. "You have asked him about the circumstances and about the conversation which took place."

"Not about the specific conversation, only general questions as to the field covered by the conversation generally."

"I could have objected to questions concerning the general conversation," Mason said, "on the ground that answers to such questions embodied the conclusion of the witness and not the best evidence. However, to save time I didn't do so; but the fact remains that so far as the scope of this cross-examination is concerned, it is exactly the same as though you had asked for specific conversations in the words of the participants. And it is an elementary rule of cross-examination that when a part of a conversation is introduced in evidence on direct examination, the cross-examiner has the right to bring it all in."

"The objection will be overruled," Judge Maxwell said.

"Answer the question," Mason said.

"Yes," Parker Benton said readily enough, "Mr. Shelby stated that Ellen Cushing, a real estate agent, had acquired a one-half interest in and to this lease. Subsequently I discovered that . . ."

"Never mind what you discovered subsequently," Burger interrupted irritably. "Confine yourself to the conversation. Answer counsel's questions and stop when you are finished."

167

"Yes, sir."

"That," Mason said, "is all."

"That's all, Mr. Benton Call your next witness, Mr. Burger," the judge said.

"My next witness will be Dr. Horace Stirling."

Dr. Stirling took the stand, qualified as an expert physician and surgeon, stated that he had been present when Parker Benton identified a body as that of Scott Shelby and that he had performed an autopsy on that body.

"Did you determine the cause of death?"

"I did, yes sir."

"What was the cause of death?"

"A bullet."

"Where did you find that bullet?"

"The bullet had struck the vertebrae."

"Where?"

"Between the first and second cervical, or as they're more specifically known, between the axis and the atlas. The bullet had penetrated the spinal cord and the odontoid process of the axis."

"Death had not been caused by drowning?"

"Death had not been caused by drowning, no sir."

"You would say that the bullet wound was the cause of the death?"

"Yes, sir."

"You recovered that bullet from the body?"

"I did. Yes, sir."

"And what did you do with it?"

"I identified it by scratching my initials on the base of the bullet and then turned it over to Robert P. Noxie, the ballistics expert."

"You may cross-examine," Hamilton Burger said.

Mason said, "As I understand it, Doctor, fracture dislocations of the axis and atlas frequently occur as the result of a trauma, associated with a fall from a height, a dive into shallow water or something of that sort."

"It can so occur, yes."

"Now, the mere fact that a bullet may have lodged in the spinal cord does not necessarily mean that there could not have been a fracture dislocation of the cervical vertebrae caused by a fall.''

''In this case, there was no such fracture dislocation of the spinal cord. A backward luxation of the odontoid process of the axis in the cervical canal would be due to the tearing of the ligaments which held this bone in place, and I found no such tearing. On the other hand, I did find the bullet embedded in the spinal cord and lodged against the odontoid process of the axis. I therefore am of the opinion that death was due entirely to this bullet wound.''

''Where had the bullet entered the body, Doctor?''

''The man had been shot in the back of the neck.''

''Were there any powder burns?''

''There were no powder burns.''

''Does this indicate anything in connection with the position of the weapon when the shot was fired?''

''Ordinarily, powder marks are not found beyond two or three feet from the muzzle of the gun. When the weapon is held closer than that, we encounter powder marks, depending somewhat upon the condition of the weapon and the nature of the ammunition.''

''The neck is rather a small target, is it not, Doctor?''

''Comparatively small.''

''So that if the weapon were held at some distance away, a person intending to commit deliberate murder would hardly have aimed at the neck.''

''I am not qualified to state what a person would or would not do under those circumstances,'' the doctor said with slow deliberation. ''The person might have aimed at the head, shot low, and hit the neck, or, might have aimed at the back between the shoulders, shot high, and hit the neck. Or, the person might have aimed at the neck and hit the neck. I only know that I examined the body, that death was due to a bullet which had embedded itself in the spinal cord in a position which I indicated.''

There was a faint rustling of surreptitious levity in the back of the courtroom as the doctor so neatly and determinedly avoided the trap Mason had tried to set.

''The bullet had actually penetrated only a very short distance into the body then if it had lodged against the odontoid process of the axis and had been fired from a position directly behind the victim?''

"It had penetrated far enough to cause death," the doctor said dryly.

This time, there was an audible titter.

"There were no symptoms of death from drowning?"

"None. There were evidences that the body had been in the water for some hours, but no evidence that death occurred from drowning. Permit me to repeat: Death occurred, as I have said several times before, from a bullet which had penetrated the spinal cord."

"Were there any other marks of violence on the body?" Mason asked.

The doctor hesitated, glanced somewhat dubiously at the district attorney.

Mason said, "Go on, answer the question."

"I think that is hardly proper *cross*-examination," the district attorney ventured somewhat tentatively.

"Overruled," the judge snapped. "Answer the question."

The witness took a deep breath. "There was some evidence of a blow on the head," he said. "I cannot give you a definite statement as to the severity of that blow or its possible consequences, because of the fact that it had evidently occurred at approximately the time of death. But, there had been a rather severe blow on the head, a blow struck by some object which didn't tear the skin, but did leave evidence of a distinct traumatic ecchymosis."

Mason leaned forward, "A blow such as might have been struck by a body falling into water from a height of several feet, Doctor?"

"No. I would say not. A blow which was more sharply localized than that. A blow such as might have been made by a heavy blunt object with no sharp corners."

"A slung shot?" Mason asked.

"Very similar to a blow of that nature. Yes."

Mason was plainly excited now, but, nevertheless, feeling his way carefully, well aware that he was confronted with a hostile witness of no inconsiderable ability and forensic experience. A witness who was now being called upon to testify to something which quite evidently failed to fit into the theory of the case as advanced by the district attorney.

Mason said, "This blow, then, must have been struck by someone standing close to the decedent?"

The doctor cleared his throat. "Conceding of course, that the blow was struck by someone."

"It was a blow?"

"Definitely a blow."

"And a blow must be struck by someone. Must it not, Doctor?"

"Not necessarily. The man could have fallen and struck his head on something."

"Such as what?" Mason asked.

The doctor said, "If the man had fallen from a considerable height and had struck against a rope, the force of impact might have left a wound such as that which I discovered."

"That blow did not cause death, Doctor?"

"I would say that death occurred from the bullet wound, although the blow *may* have caused unconsciousness."

"But in the event the decedent had fallen and struck his head on a rope, you would then have found certain indentations caused by the strands of the rope?"

"Well . . . not necessarily."

"But you would have expected to?"

"The rope might have been covered, wrapped, or serviced as it is called in yachting circles."

"In other words," Mason said, "you are doing everything in your power to minimize the importance of this blow on the head."

"I am not," the doctor snapped testily.

"That's objected to as argumentative and is not proper cross-examination. It's incompetent, irrelevant and immaterial," the district attorney said.

Mason smiled, "It goes to the bias of the witness and it has already been answered."

"The question has been answered, gentlemen," the judge said. "Proceed with your examination, Mr. Mason."

171

Mason said, "Because of the absence of powder stains, you would say that the person who fired the shot was more than three feet distant from the victim?"

"Well, two or three feet."

"Which?"

"Well, more than two."

"Now in firing a revolver, the revolver is held in the hand. Is it not?"

"Naturally," the witness said sarcastically. "It is difficult to fire a revolver with one's teeth."

The courtroom burst into laughter which the judge promptly silenced.

"Exactly," Mason said. "So, a revolver is held in the hand. Will you please hold your hand in the position of a person firing a revolver?"

The witness promptly extended his hand.

"Now hold it right there," Mason said, "until I can measure the distance."

Mason produced a tape measure from his pocket.

The witness, suddenly realizing what Mason was after, dropped his elbow slightly, moving the hand a little closer to his body.

"No, no," Mason said, "you're moving your hand. Now put it back where it was."

"Well, I ah . . . am just getting my hand in the position that a person would hold a revolver," the witness said, moving his hand around and managing to get it a few inches closer to his body.

Mason smiled. "In other words, as soon as you realize what I'm after, you start moving your hand in. Is that right?"

"Not at all," the witness said indignantly. "I'm merely trying to answer your question, that's all. You asked me to hold my hand in the position of a person shooting a revolver."

"And you extended it out to about here, did you not?" Mason said, straightening the arm almost out to its full length.

"Well, if you were taking a sight, you would hold your hand more extended than if you were shooting blind."

172

"And do you think you could hit a person in the neck without taking a sight?"

"The murderer probably was aiming at the man where he was thickest and the bullet went wild and hit him in the neck."

"Now, you're qualifying as a mind reader," Mason said, "and putting yourself in the position of the murderer."

"Murderess," the man snapped.

"I thought you said 'murderer' the first time."

"Well, it was a murderess."

"How do you know?"

The witness became sullenly silent.

Mason smiled. "Obviously you're quite prejudiced in the case, but then, that's only to be expected. Just put your hand back, if you will, in the position of a man shooting and taking aim."

Reluctantly the witness extended his hand.

"Could you aim from that position?" Mason asked.

"I think I could."

Mason said, "Let's take this gun that's been introduced as an exhibit and put it in your hand. Now aim."

The witness lowered his head.

"Isn't it easier to raise your hand than to lower your head?"

The witness raised his hand, reluctantly yielding each inch.

Mason laughed, said, "All right. That will do, hold it!"

He snapped up the tape measure and measured the distance. "Twenty-eight and three-quarter inches from the tip of the gun to the point of your nose," he said.

The witness said, "Well, that's not exactly fair, because you're measuring to the *tip* of the gun."

"But when you say that the powder stains would appear if the distance had been closer than two feet, you mean from the tip of the gun, don't you?"

"Well . . . well, yes, I guess so."

"Your nose doesn't leave powder burns, does it?" Laughter rocked the courtroom. The judge silenced the laughter. District Attorney Burger said, "Your Honor, I consider that sarcastic comment was uncalled for."

"That was no sarcastic comment," Mason said. "It's a

question. The witness has said it's difficult to fire a gun with your teeth. If that wasn't sarcasm then I'm entitled to know if a nose can leave powder burns. If it *was* sarcasm, I'm entitled to give tit for tat. Right now, I want to know where powder burns come from.''

The judge smiled. "Proceed, gentlemen," he said good naturedly.

"So that the person who pulled the trigger on that gun, must have been more than four feet from the neck of the victim?" Mason asked.

"Well, perhaps . . . Perhaps an inch or two, either way."

"At least four feet, four and three-quarter inches. Isn't that right?"

"Yes."

"And that's the least," Mason said.

The witness was silent.

"Now then," Mason went on, "is it your contention that the blow which you discovered on the head of the decedent could have been hit with a club four feet long?"

"It could have been hit with a club twenty feet long."

"Exactly. It would have been rather awkward to have handled such a club, wouldn't it?"

"I don't know. I'm not a murderer. I'm talking about the conditions which I discovered."

"And you don't know whether the blow was struck first or the shot was fired first?"

"No, I don't. The blow may have been at about the same time. It probably was."

"The blow could have been struck with a hard object, such as a baseball bat?"

"Provided it . . . Yes, it could. Any object that was round and didn't have any sharp corners. If a baseball bat, it might have been wrapped with something or padded with something."

"It was about that shape of object? Something about that size? About that diameter?"

"Perhaps . . . Perhaps just a little smaller."

"Thank you," Mason said, "that is all."

The court adjourned for its noon recess and Mason picked

up Della Street and Paul Drake from the crowd which debouched from the courtroom. "Come on over and have lunch," he invited. "I want to talk things over."

Drake said, "That's something new, Perry. About the blow."

"Uh huh," Mason said, "but let's not talk it over until we get where we can have some privacy. What have you found out, Paul? Anything?"

"Not a darn thing," Drake said, "except that I've been tipped off. They're going to put Ellen Cushing on the stand to prove motive."

"To prove motive?" Mason said, frowning.

"Uh huh, they are going to introduce the oil lease through her.—Get the sketch, Perry? You'll have to take a lot from her or else bring out the fact that she's the plaintiff in a suit for defamation of character against us."

"I get it," Mason said. "All right. We'll handle it just any old way they want to handle it, if that's the way they feel about it. Let's go eat."

Chapter 19

When court reconvened at two o'clock, Hamilton Burger, in the manner of a lawyer calling his star witness, said, "Mr. Robert P. Noxie, will you please take the stand."

Mr. Noxie took the stand and qualified himself as an expert on ballistics with a wealth of descriptive detail which showed only too well the manner in which the man enjoyed an opportunity to discuss his technical qualifications in front of an audience.

When some twenty minutes had been consumed in relating the experience and studies of the witness, Hamilton Burger got down to the meat of the situation.

"I hand you herewith a piece of lead, shaped as a bullet, bearing certain identifying marks and ask you if you have ever seen that piece of lead before?"

"I have. Yes, sir."

"Was that in your possession?"

"It was. Yes, sir."

"Who gave it to you?"

"Dr. Stirling."

"And where were you when that was given to you?"

"At the morgue in the autopsy room. Dr. Stirling handed it to me almost as soon as it was taken from the body of Scott Shelby."

"Just what is that piece of lead, Mr. Noxie?"

"That is a thirty-eight caliber bullet. It has a weight of one hundred and fifty grains. It will leave the muzzle at approximately six hundred and ninety-five feet per second and will penetrate four seven-eighth inch pine boards."

The witness glanced at the court reporter to make certain his testimony was being taken down and smiled triumphantly

176

at Perry Mason, as much as to say, "Go ahead, see if you can trap *me*!"

"Now then," Hamilton Burger said, "I will ask you whether it is possible to tell from what particular weapon this bullet was fired."

"It is. Yes, sir."

"Now by that I do not mean, what particular type of weapon but I mean what individual weapon."

"Yes, sir. This bullet was fired from a Colt Police Positive revolver Number 14581."

The district attorney said, "I hand you a Colt Police Positive revolver which has been heretofore introduced in evidence and ask you if that is the weapon referred to in your testimony."

"It is."

"I will now ask you how you know that this bullet was fired from that gun."

"You want me to explain that to the jury?"

"If you will, please, yes, sir."

"That answer will take some little time."

"Go ahead," Hamilton Burger said with a wave of his hand, "we have all afternoon."

"In the first place," the witness said, "it must be borne in mind that there are certain lands in the rifle barrel. These serve to guide the bullet, imparting to it a rotary motion when the bullet is discharged. Now these lands naturally have certain microscopic variations. And, in the course of time, a barrel will become pitted or rusted so that there will be certain scratches, certain little projections, various little things which will leave marks or scratches upon the bullet as the bullet tears on past. In fact, every weapon imparts a distinctive marking to each bullet which is fired through its barrel. These markings are invariably sufficiently identical to make possible a definite identification.

"Now, when I first received this revolver in question, I proceeded to fire a series of test bullets through the weapon. I fired those bullets into a cylinder of water, taking care to fire the bullets straight down into the water so that there would be no distortion of the tip."

The witness turned and looked to the jurors and, quite evidently flattered by the interest he was arousing, said, "I then set up a microscope and photographed those various bullets. I have here a series of twelve photographs showing certain distinctive markings upon these six bullets, each photo showing two sides of each bullet."

The witness opened a brief case, produced a dozen eight by ten photographs, then said, "These photographs are micro-photographs, that is, they were taken through a microscope. They show the appearance of the bullet just as it was seen through the microscope with a relatively low power of magnification and a large field.

"I have arranged these photographs so that certain distinctive markings upon the bullets are in evidence. Each one of these first six photographs which I now hand you, Mr. Burger, is a photograph of a different bullet fired from the same weapon but taken at such an angle that it is possible to see identical surface scratches upon each bullet.

"And I now hand you a composite photograph which is a photograph composed of strips, taken from each bullet, and placed one immediately above the other so that the scratches or blemishes on the sides of these bullets form a continuous line upon the photographs."

Hamilton Burger said, "I ask that each of these photographs be properly identified and admitted in evidence."

"No objection," Mason said.

There followed a short interval during which each photograph was identified, introduced in evidence, and marked by the clerk of the court as an appropriate exhibit.

"Now then," Hamilton Burger said, "returning to my question as to how you know this fatal bullet was fired from this particular gun, I will ask that you resume your testimony to the jury, Mr. Noxie."

"Yes, sir. Having identified the individual markings of the gun barrel as they appear on the surface of the test bullets, so that I was acquainted with what one might term the idiosyncrasies of the weapon in question, I then turned my attention to the fatal bullet. There are, of course, some slight distortions about the head of the bullet, but these are very slight indeed when one considers that it penetrated bone. The bullet is, in fact, in remarkably good condition. It is in unusually good condition. I took this bullet, placed it under the microscope in my laboratory and proceeded to rotate it while I carefully photographed it. I then used a comparison microscope which fuses two objects into a single image. By placing the fatal bullet on one table of the microscope, and a test bullet on the other, I was able to match up the grooves and scratches in the manner such as you see them in *this* photograph.''

Hamilton Burger said, ''Just a moment, was this photograph which you now produce taken through the comparison microscope?''

''No, sir. This is a photograph which shows two bullets, the fatal bullet on the left hand and the test bullet on the right. The lighting is absolutely identical in each case and the photograph is taken so as to show the similarity in the grooves and scratches. You can very plainly see them but in order to make that more evident, I have prepared herewith a composite photograph of the two bullets. The lower half is the photograph of a test bullet, and above this line of demarcation shown on the photograph, the bullet is the fatal bullet. It will be noted that the scratches and grooves combine in such a way that it precludes any possibility of coincidence and proves, in fact it demonstrates absolutely, that this bullet was fired from this particular weapon.''

Hamilton Burger, showing that he was very much impressed by the testimony of the witness, said, ''Your Honor, I want this photograph to be introduced in evidence, and then I would like to have the jury inspect it.''

The witness said glibly, ''I have already arranged for that, Mr. Burger. I have had twelve duplicate prints of this photograph made. Each print is made from the same cut film negative and the prints are all absolutely identical.''

''Under the circumstances, Your Honor,'' Hamilton Burger said, ''I ask that each one of the jurors be given one of these prints and an opportunity to examine it carefully.''

The witness dove down into his voluminous brief case,

came up with twelve magnifying glasses. "I have some visual aids for the jurors," he said.

The district attorney gratefully accepted the magnifying glasses, passed a photograph and a magnifying glass to each of the jurors.

Mason watched the jurors keenly.

Some of them made a rather detailed examination. Some of them looked at the photograph for only a few moments, then raised their eyes to study the defendant, an infallible sign that they had made up their minds.

"Do you wish to cross-examine this witness, Mr. Mason?" Burger asked.

"Yes, certainly," Mason said, giving no external evidence of the shock he had received from Noxie's testimony.

"Then I suggest the jurors retain their photographs and magnifying glasses during the period of cross-examination so that in case there is any necessity to refer to these photographs they will have them handy."

"Is there any objection?" the judge asked Mason.

"None whatever, Your Honor."

"Very well, it will be so ordered."

Noxie turned to Perry Mason with a confident, somewhat patronizing smile. "Go right ahead with your questions," he said.

"Thank you," Mason retorted with exaggerated politeness. "Now as I understand it, Mr. Noxie, when a fatal bullet penetrates tissues and scrapes against bone, it has not only the scratches and markings of the rifle barrel which were etched into the lead as the bullet left the barrel, but it also has the flattening effect of impact and such other scratches as may have been received by penetrating bony tissue."

"That is, in the main, correct."

"Now, take for instance in the present bullet. There were certain scratches upon the fatal bullet which were not left by the barrel of the weapon."

"Well, there could have been, but this bullet is in very good condition."

"I believe you said unusually good condition."

"Yes, sir."

180

"Then this bullet is not what you would consider a usual fatal bullet."

"I didn't say that. I said the bullet was in unusually good condition."

"What is unusual about it?"

"Well, it shows very little flattening."

"What does that indicate?"

"Merely that we are particularly fortunate in having a bullet where it is possible to identify the distinguishing marks on small portions of it. Quite frequently, when a bullet is flattened or distorted, there will be one side that is almost valueless. But, in this case, there is only a very little flattening."

"The bullet penetrated bony substance?"

"So I understand."

"You were present at the post-mortem?"

"Yes."

"Did you see the bullet extracted?"

"I did. Yes, sir."

"And marked by Dr. Stirling?"

"Yes, sir."

"And then what was done with it?"

"I immediately took it into my possession."

"Then according to your testimony, there should be minor scratches upon this bullet which would have been the result of penetrating the body of the deceased."

"Well, there could have been."

"Have you found any such scratches?"

"I haven't looked for them."

"You have merely assumed that they were there?"

"Yes."

"You were very careful to look for scratches which proved that the bullet had been fired from the revolver which has been introduced in evidence."

"Naturally, that was the point I was called upon to establish."

"But you apparently took no interest whatever in finding any scratches which would indicate that this bullet had penetrated the body of the deceased and caused death."

"I took the doctor's word for what caused death. That is, for the effect of the bullet on the body of the deceased. I took the evidence of my own eyes that the bullet had penetrated the body of the deceased."

"You saw the hole of entrance?"

"I did."

"And were present while the doctor performed the autopsy?"

"Yes, sir."

"And saw the position of the bullet?"

"I did. Yes, sir."

"By the way, were any photographs taken of the bullet hole in the neck?"

The witness cleared his throat. "Well, I took some photographs, yes. But they didn't establish anything other than that there was a bullet hole in the back of the neck."

"Where are those photographs?"

"I have them in my office."

"You didn't bring them to court with you?"

"No."

"Why not?"

"Because I saw nothing to be gained by bringing them with me. I take many photographs which I don't use."

Mason said, "As I understood your testimony, this bullet is capable of penetrating four, seven-eighth inch pine boards?"

"That is right. Those are the statistical qualifications of this bullet fired from this type of firearm with this type of powder load."

"The bullet didn't penetrate very deep into the body of the deceased."

"The bullet struck against bone. When it strikes against bony substance, you can't tell what a bullet will do, particularly when the body is, perhaps, falling when the bullet strikes."

"Then you would say that Scott Shelby had been falling when the bullet struck?"

"No, sir. I wouldn't say that."

"What would you say?"

182

"I'm not an expert on that."

"You're an expert on ballistics. How do you account for the shallow penetration of this bullet?"

"Well," the witness said and fidgeted, "I have my own theory."

"All right, what is that theory? We want it."

"My theory," the witness said, "is that . . . Well, I guess I'm not supposed to go into that. I'm only supposed to identify the bullet."

"No," Mason said, "you're an expert on ballistics. You have a theory as to the facts which accounts for the shallow penetration of the bullet. I want that theory."

"Well, if you want to know it," the witness said, "it's *my theory* that the man was shot while he was in the water. Just about the time he'd hit the water."

"Well, now," Mason said, "that is very, very interesting. And what makes you think that, Mr. Noxie?"

"Oh, if the Court please," Mr. Burger said in a tone of martyred, weary protest, "if we're going to embark upon all of these irrelevant side matters, the case will take forever. We have already consumed a great deal of time and it seems to me that any mere theory as to where or how the shot might have been fired which this witness may have, a theory which has no particular proof to back it up, is merely taking up time."

"As you yourself remarked but a short time ago," Mason said, "we have all afternoon."

"And I don't propose to consume it with a lot of trivialities," the district attorney snapped.

"Are you making an objection?"

"I am. I object that it's not proper cross-examination, that it's incompetent, irrelevant, and immaterial."

The judge said, "The Court doesn't care for any argument, Mr. Mason. The objection is overruled. The witness will answer the question."

"Well," the witness said, "you have several things to account for in this case. One of them is the peculiar nature of the hole of entrance."

"Oh, there was something peculiar about that?" Mason asked.

"Well, it wasn't round. It was sort of oval in shape."

"And what does that mean?"

"Well, that usually means that the bullet had ceased to travel in a straight line. That is, it had started to wobble."

"Can you illustrate what you mean by that?"

The witness took a pencil from his pocket, said, "Now a bullet that is properly rotating travels in a straight line, like this. But, if a bullet is defective, or if there is something defective about the weapon that fires it, the bullet begins to wobble in this manner.—You will see that the point of the pencil is moving forward in a straight line, but the rear of the pencil, the part that is represented by the rubber eraser, has begun to move in a circle some two inches in diameter."

Mason nodded.

"Now then," the witness went on, "when that bullet strikes, it will not leave a round hole, but will leave what is known as a keyhole point of entrance, so called because of the fact that the bullet strikes partially broadside, and the description of it as a keyhole is very illustrative."

"Quite interesting," Mason said conversationally. "Now in this case, you have what is known as a keyhole bullet wound of entrance?"

"Yes, sir."

"And you also have some other unusual factors?"

"I've mentioned that the distortion or the flattening of the bullet was very, very small. You can see that this bullet has only a few chewed-up surfaces on the nose of the bullet. It hasn't flattened or mushroomed in any way."

Mason nodded. "What does that indicate?"

"That, plus the penetration of the bullet, indicates to my mind that the bullet had struck some smooth surface and glanced before it entered the body of the decedent."

"Oh," Mason said, "the bullet had glanced, had it?"

"That's only his theory, if the Court please," Hamilton Burger said.

"He's testifying as an expert," Mason pointed out. "His

theories are supposed to be the result of an expert interpretation of facts.''

"Well, I can't see that it makes any difference, myself,'' the district attorney said somewhat testily.

"You can't?'' Mason asked.

"No, I can't!'' the district attorney said angrily. "And if you weren't merely trying to grasp at straws, you . . .''

"That will do,'' the Court interrupted. "Counsel will refrain from personalities.''

Mason turned to the witness. There was something of a purring satisfaction in his voice. "You left the photographs showing this peculiar wound of entrance in your office?''

"That's right.''

"You didn't bring them to court?''

"No, sir.''

"You had this theory in regard to the bullet having glanced?''

"I did.''

"And did you communicate that theory to the district attorney?''

"Objected to as improper, irrelevant and immaterial, not proper cross-examination,'' Burger protested.

"On the contrary,'' Mason said. "I think it is proper cross-examination. It goes to show the qualifications of the witness as an expert. It goes to show the bias of the witness, and in the event it should appear the witness had communicated this theory to the district attorney, and the district attorney had advised the witness to say nothing about it unless he was asked to do so, and the district attorney had been the one who advised the witness not to bring those photographs to court, then it would go a long ways toward showing the bias of the witness.''

"Your Honor, I object to that. It assumes a fact not in evidence,'' Hamilton Burger said, "it touches the integrity of my professional reputation and I object to it as a matter of personal privilege. I ask that counsel be ordered to apologize to me for those remarks.''

"On the contrary,'' Mason said, "there's nothing to apologize for. If those are the facts, they speak for themselves.

185

If those aren't the facts, the district attorney can very readily let me get to the truth of the matter by simply asking this witness questions."

"It's absurd to take up time with such trivia," the district attorney shouted.

Mason smiled. "Look at the face of the witness if you think it's trivial, Your Honor."

The witness had shifted his position uneasily on the witness stand. His face was dull red.

"Your Honor, I object to that statement," Burger said. "The face of the witness is not in evidence."

The judge smiled. "The objections are overruled. I'm going to let the witness answer that question."

"Go ahead," Mason said, "answer the question."

"Well, yes, I did outline my theory to Mr. Burger and he didn't think . . ."

"Never mind what you think he thought," Mason said, "let's confine ourselves to what he *said*."

"Your Honor, this is all incompetent, irrelevant and immaterial," Burger protested. "It is not proper cross-examination and it relates to a conversation which this witness had with counsel for the prosecution. Certainly that is not evidence."

"I am inclined to think that it is not proper to introduce a conversation between this witness and counsel for the prosecution. That is, unless the conversation is specifically limited within certain designated points," the judge ruled. "But, this being cross-examination, you have the right to ask leading questions, Mr. Mason."

"Very well," Mason said. "I will ask you, Mr. Noxie, if it isn't a fact that you communicated your theory to the district attorney; that you pointed out to him that in your opinion the physical evidence proved conclusively that the bullet must have struck the surface of the water and glanced before embedding itself in the neck of the decedent, and the district attorney told you not to say anything about that and warned you that he didn't want that phase of the case brought into court."

"Well, not in those words," the witness said.

186

"Well, what were his exact words on that point?"

"Same objection," Burger said.

"This objection is overruled," Judge Maxwell said. "The question now calls for a specific part of a specific conversation."

"But what possible significance can anything that I told this witness in regard to his testimony have upon the facts of the present case?" Burger stormed.

Mason said, "It isn't what you told the witness, it's what the witness *did*. It's the fact that the witness came to court and, *following your suggestion*, left those photographs in his office. Following your suggestion, he didn't say anything at all about this matter on direct examination. In fact, he tried to avoid the issue until I pinned him down definitely to it and then he blurted out the truth.—Now then, Your Honor, I submit that any witness who permits himself to be guided in his testimony in a murder case by the direction of a district attorney, is a biased witness and that we have the right to show that bias to the jury."

"The bias, or lack of it, is already apparent to the jury," the judge said.

"But it isn't in the record," Mason pointed out. "I want to get it in the record. I want the record of this case to show that the district attorney made a certain suggestion in regard to the testimony of this witness, and that this witness proceeded to act upon that direction."

"I think on that theory, you are entitled to have it in the record," the judge said. "The witness will answer the question."

"Well," Noxie said, shifting his position once more, "the district attorney told me that I didn't need to say anything about that. He said that of course if I was asked it would be a different matter, that I'd have to tell the truth, but he didn't want me to volunteer any information along those lines, and that he didn't intend to ask me questions about it."

"And did he tell you particularly not to volunteer that theory?"

"Well, yes."

"Unless you were asked about it specifically and in so many words?"

"Well, something to that effect."

"And did he suggest that you refrain from bringing those photographs showing the peculiar wound of entrance to court with you?"

"Well, he said there was no use in getting them mixed up with the other photographs."

Mason smiled. "Didn't want you to get them confused. Is that right?"

"Yes."

"So that in case you pulled out a photograph of the test bullet and inadvertently pulled out at the same time one of these photographs showing the peculiar wound of entrance, I wouldn't happen to get a glimpse of that entrance wound."

"Well . . . I don't know what he had in mind. He simply said that he didn't think there was any use in bringing those photographs to court because I might get them confused."

"And more than that, he asked you specifically *not* to bring them to court, didn't he?"

"Well, yes."

Mason said, "I think that's all."

"That's all," Hamilton Burger snapped.

"Just one moment," Mason said, "if the Court please. It occurs to me there are one or two more questions I would like to ask Dr. Stirling on cross-examination. I see that he hasn't left the court. I would like to have him return to the stand so that I may ask him those questions. I realize, of course, that this is somewhat out of order; but I think under the circumstances the Court will bear with me."

"Very well," the Court said. "Dr. Stirling, will you return to the stand for one or two questions, please? That's right. You have already been sworn, Doctor. This is additional cross-examination by Perry Mason. Very well, Counselor, proceed with your questions."

Mason said with a smile, "Doctor, you didn't mention anything about this peculiar wound of entrance."

"I wasn't asked," the doctor snapped testily.

"That's right. I didn't ask you about it because I hadn't

been permitted to see the body prior to the time the post-mortem was performed, and of course after the post-mortem was performed an incision had then been made along the line of the neck in order to recover the bullet and the peculiar nature of the wound of entrance was not apparent. Therefore I was hardly in a position to ask you about it.''

"Well, I answered all your questions.''

"You did indeed, Doctor. You didn't misrepresent a thing.''

"Thank you,'' the doctor said with some acidity.

"But,'' Mason said, "on the other hand, you carefully avoided volunteering any information on this subject. Now then, Doctor, I am wondering if the District Attorney, Hamilton Burger, told *you* not to mention anything about the wound of entrance.''

"Your Honor, I object to this. It is improper cross-examination,'' Burger said. "It is personally embarrassing to me. It is casting an aspersion upon my professional integrity, and it seems to me to be entirely out of place. The Court would hardly permit *me* to inquire as to conversations which took place between the attorney for the defense and his witnesses.''

"I don't know why not,'' Mason said. "In the event I instructed a witness to suppress any fact and the witness so suppressed that fact . . .''

"No fact has been suppressed,'' the district attorney shouted angrily.

Mason said, "If the Court please, in the event I asked a witness for the defense to suppress certain facts, I would certainly think that the district attorney would be entitled to bring out that conversation on cross-examination, not for the purpose of showing any lack of integrity on my part but merely for the purpose of showing the bias of a witness who would suppress certain facts at the request of counsel for either side.''

"I didn't request anyone to suppress anything,'' Hamilton Burger said.

"Certainly not. I am talking about what would happen if I asked the witness to suppress something,'' Mason said, smiling. "But I do want to establish on the record that the bias of this witness was such that when a *suggestion* was made by the district attorney that it would be *advisable* not to comment on this wound of entrance the witness acquiesced and was thereafter very careful to mention nothing about the wound of entrance."

"I think the question as it is asked is proper," Judge Maxwell ruled. "The district attorney of course has the opportunity on redirect examination to clarify the situation in any way that is compatible with the existing facts."

"What did the district attorney tell you about that, Doctor?" Mason asked.

Doctor Stirling said, "He simply told me that I didn't need to say anything about the wound of entrance unless I was asked."

"That wound impressed you as being unusual?"

"No, sir. It did not."

"Nothing unusual about it?"

"Certainly not. It was a very ordinary keyhole wound. You see them lots of times."

"Do you indeed, Doctor?"

"Yes, sir."

"Doctor, do you know what causes them?"

"It's caused by defective ammunition or defective rifling. It may be caused by half a dozen things."

"How many such keyhole wounds have you seen, Doctor?"

"Dozens of them."

"How many wounds of entrance do you suppose you have seen in the last two years, Doctor?"

"I would say several hundred."

"Now then, in those several hundred can you recall any other wound of entrance where there was this peculiar keyhole effect?"

"Yes, sir."

"All right. What was it?"

"It was a case involving the shooting of a Negro. I have forgotten his name. It occurred about—it was around two years ago."

"All right. We'll consider for the sake of the argument that that comes within the province of my question. Now, what other ones?"

"Well, I—you say within two years?"

"Yes."

"I can't remember any others within two years."

"Within four years?"

The doctor said, "I think there was one other—I can't remember."

"So when you say that you have seen dozens of them, that is somewhat of an exaggeration?"

"Well, perhaps it may have been. I don't know."

"But a wound of that nature is rather unusual?"

"Well, naturally it's distinctive."

"And it can be caused by a glancing bullet?"

"Yes. If you want it that way."

"It's not the way *I* want it, Doctor. I'm simply trying to find out the cause of this peculiar condition."

"It could be caused by a glancing bullet, but I don't see what difference that makes."

"It makes this difference," Mason said. "In one instance the fatal wound would indicate a person must have *deliberately* aimed at the decedent, whereas in the other instance the aim might just as deliberately have been at some other mark; but owing to a fortuitous circumstance, such as the glancing of a bullet, the bullet aimed in a different direction, still penetrated the body of the decedent."

"I'm not going to argue that with you," the doctor said.

Hamilton Burger said with a frosty smile, "Thank you, Doctor. I think that when counsel comes to argue *that* theory to the jury, he will find some very peculiar legal stumbling blocks which will prevent him from cheating justice with any such . . ."

"That will do," Judge Maxwell snapped. "The jurors will disregard any interchange of personalities between counsel. Are there any further questions of this witness?"

"No questions," Hamilton Burger said.

"I have no further questions, Your Honor," Mason said.

"Very well. The witness will be excused and at this time

191

the Court will take a ten-minute recess during which the jurors are admonished not to discuss the case among themselves, permit it to be discussed in their presence, or to form or express any opinion as to the guilt or innocence of the accused.''

Chapter 20

Detaching themselves from the crowd of spectators, Mason, Della Street, and Paul Drake went into a whispered huddle over their cigarettes in the crowded hallway.

Drake said, "Perry, you've always been the one to take the lead, the one to give me advice, and the one to be right. Now I'm going to reverse the role. I'm going to give you advice. This is the time to bail out."

"What do you mean?"

"You know what I mean. We're stuck. You're defending a guilty client, and the minute her guilt is ascertained you're left wide open to that suit by Ellen Cushing. Right now I think we can make some kind of a settlement and get out from under."

"You can't get out from under when you're representing a client," Mason said.

"Perry, she's guilty as hell."

"I still don't think she is."

"How do you account for that bullet having been found in the man's spinal cord?"

Mason drew thoughtfully on his cigarette. "I don't account for it, Paul—yet."

"And you never will," Drake said. "You know just as well as I do, Perry Mason, the way that composite photograph showed up, there is absolutely no chance on earth of faking the thing. That bullet was fired from that revolver."

Mason nodded thoughtfully. "Yes, it was fired from the revolver, all right."

Drake said, "All right. You're doing a swell job of cross-examining those witnesses. It looks right now as though you're holding your own. But after a while people will quit thinking about the courtroom gymnastics and get down to brass tacks. Here was the woman lying there asleep, according to her story, with the gun on the dresser. The telephone rings and her husband says he's in the bow of the boat. Now obviously he couldn't have been in the bow of the boat and still have talked to her over that telephone. So that's a lie right there."

"Perhaps a lie on the part of the husband."

"All right. A lie on the part of the husband," Drake said. "But try to sell that to the jury. It was the wife who saw that telephone up in the bow when Parker Benton was showing them around. She immediately decided that she could use that telephone in her business. She had her murder planned, all carefully arranged, and all she wanted was an opportunity to put it into effect."

Mason said impatiently, "Even if she is guilty, I can't quit."

"Perhaps you can't *quit*, but you can get out from under. The D.A. may be willing to let you plead to second-degree murder. Then we can settle with Ellen Cushing. You go on past this point and you'll be in a fight with everyone concerned. You won't be able to cop a plea. Ellen Cushing will go ahead with her suit for damages and we'll both be stuck."

Mason said nothing but smoked in silent concentration.

Drake went on, "According to her own story, she saw her husband, apparently struggling with someone. He fell overboard and she heard the sound of a shot. She looked down in the water, recognized him. He was moving. He called her name, then he was swept back by the current under the overhang of the ship.

"Now, you know just as well as I do, Perry, that with a bullet smashing into the spinal cord between the first and second cervical vertebrae, there'd be an instant paralysis. The man never moved from the minute that bullet hit him."

Della Street said, "Look, Paul, couldn't some murderer have been waiting in the water, some murderer who was a good swimmer?"

Drake was grinning now. "All right, Della. What gun did the murderer use in shooting him?"

"Why . . . Let me see . . ."

194

Drake grinned. "Let you see is right! The murderer must have used the gun that was *in the hand of the defendant*!"

Mason scowled thoughtfully.

"The unfortunate part of that theory from our standpoint," Drake said, "is that Marion Shelby was the only one who had the gun."

"After a while she gave it to Parker Benton and then Parker Benton gave it to the officers," Della Street interpolated.

"That was long after the murder," Drake said.

Della Street met Drake's eyes. "How do *you* know?" she asked.

Mason pinched out his cigarette, said, "Wait a minute, Della. I think you've got something there!"

Drake said sarcastically, "Go ahead and be a sap! You mean Shelby was hiding under the bow and . . ."

"Or under the stern," Mason said. "There's an overhang there."

"Nuts!" Drake exclaimed.

"Court!" a bailiff shouted.

Instantly spectators began crowding through the doors in a milling stream of humanity.

"Court . . . Jury . . . Counsel!" the bailiff shouted.

Mason whirled and walked rapidly toward the door of the courtroom. Drake, almost running to keep up, said, "Perry, don't be foolish. There isn't *any* theory you can take in front of a jury. Let's bail out while the bailing is good."

"I'll talk it over with you tonight."

"Tonight will be too late. They're going to put Ellen Cushing on the stand. If you antagonize her, she never will settle. For the love of Mike, Perry, handle her with gloves."

Mason pushed his way through the door of the courtroom, walked rapidly down the aisle, and took his place at the counsel table just as Judge Maxwell entered the courtroom, waited for silence, and then said, "The jury are all present, gentlemen. The defendant is in court. Mr. District Attorney, call your next witness."

"Ellen Bedson Cushing," the district attorney said, "who is now Ellen Cushing Lacey."

Ellen Cushing Lacey, chin up, eyes sparkling in anticipation of the battle of wits which was to come, took the witness stand. She had evidently spent considerable time in a beauty parlor and chosen her wearing apparel with great care. Even Mason was forced to admit to himself that she was a well proportioned, vivacious, fully matured woman who knew her way around and who was going to make a devastating impression on that jury.

She held up her right hand and was sworn. She seated herself in the chair on the witness stand, crossed her legs, made the conventional gesture of pulling her skirt down over her knees, fidgeted slightly as though to get herself established in a comfortable position, then looked at the district attorney and smiled.

The district attorney hurried through the preliminary questions, then began to bring out the relationship, the fact that Scott Shelby had an office in the same building, that he had first taken notice of the witness some six months earlier, that he had gradually taken more and more notice, that he had begun to throw little things her way, opportunities to make commissions, business tips, and then finally had come the matter of the oil lease.

"You bought that oil lease?" the district attorney asked.

She turned and faced the jury, said, "Frankly, I did."

"Why?"

She said, "I'm going to tell you the truth. I knew that there was a sale pending. I felt absolutely certain that the lease hadn't been taken into consideration by the purchaser and I thought there would be an opportunity to get a very good cash settlement."

"Did you tell Mr. Shelby that?"

"I did not."

"Why?"

She said, "I knew Mr. Shelby was a married man and I knew he was taking an interest in me. I knew there wasn't anything platonic about that interest, and I knew he was using the little things he was throwing my way as bait for a proposition that would be made afterwards. I didn't feel that I owed Mr. Shelby anything. He was a businessman and I was a businesswoman. I had to make my living and he had

196

to make his. He offered me this oil lease thinking it was absolutely valueless."

"And you bought it?"

"I bought it."

"What did you pay for it?"

She smiled archly and said, "The consideration was purely nominal. In fact, Mr. Shelby considered it as so much wastepaper. He told me that if I wanted to make the back payments to reinstate it I could have it."

"And what did you do?"

"I drew up an assignment and a declaration of trust, had Shelby sign it, then got a man to act as my agent, and in the name of Scott Shelby make a tender of five hundred dollars to Jane Keller."

"You were willing to gamble five hundred dollars . . . ?"

She smiled and said, "I didn't even have to gamble five hundred dollars. I knew very well that Jane Keller couldn't afford to take it. If she had taken the money, she would have laid herself wide open on that sale. I was playing it safe all the way along the line."

"Were you in love with Mr. Shelby?"

"I certainly was not."

"Was Mr. Shelby in love with you?"

"He was not. He was looking on me purely as a possible biological adventure. I was in love at the time."

"With your present husband?"

"Yes."

"Go on," the district attorney said. "Tell us what happened after that."

Mason shifted his eyes from the witness to study the faces of the jurors. There could be no doubt that this was making a tremendous impression, that anything she said was destined to dominate the whole case. She was attractive enough, lively enough, and sophisticated enough to appeal to these jurors. There were whimsical smiles on the faces of some of the older men on the jury, smiles that showed a sympathetic understanding and a certain admiration. Ellen Cushing Lacey wasn't avoiding the issue. She was putting the cards fairly on the table. She was a business woman, and a playboy had been trying to get himself in solid by giving her little tips, small commissions, an oil lease which he thought was absolutely worthless. Ellen had taken it all in her stride. She had kept her head, had played the game knowing exactly what was at stake and very coolly and calmly intending to win.

In a more brazen woman that would have been golddigging. In a less frank woman it would have been hypocrisy. In a woman who didn't have the witness's attractive personality it would have been selfish exploitation. But with Ellen Cushing Lacey's trim figure, her ready smile, her alert manner, her undoubted individuality, what she had done was, in the minds of the jurors, simply outwitting a man whose interest in her had been purely selfish. The man had baited traps and she had stolen the bait without getting caught. It was a game which both parties played with their eyes open and Ellen had won.

The jurors settled down in their chairs. Their eyes were tolerant, their lips smiling. They were going to enjoy this. Mason turned his attention back to the witness.

The district attorney went on suavely asking questions which gave the woman on the stand an opportunity to present herself in the best possible light to the jurors. She had the gift of relating conversations so that the characteristics of the other persons were vividly portrayed. The jurors began to get a clear picture of Scott Shelby, a man who had been twice married, divorced, and then remarried, a man who was restless, a man who was quite frankly on the prowl, who regarded his domestic life as a mere convenience which entailed no perceptible obligations on his part. Because he was a man, however, he had entertained a fatuous idea of his own intellectual superiority in business, and while he undertook to play the part of the rich benefactor he was enough of a four-flusher so that the benefactions which he showered upon the recipient of his attentions were the husks of the business world, things from which all possible profit had already been squeezed, and Scott Shelby relied upon his glib-tongued salesmanship to make them seem attractive to the person to whom he gave them.

198

Then Ellen Cushing Lacey went on to tell about how she had taken the oil lease, how she had discovered that obscure provision of the oil lease, and how she had injected that into the deal for the sale of the island, the interest that had been aroused, and Mr. Mason's call to Scott Shelby asking for an interview.

Then Scott Shelby had suddenly become a changed person. He had realized for the first time that the thing he had so generously offered to Ellen, in place of being merely an expired oil lease, was a property of great potential value. Then almost immediately he had begun to show himself in his true character. He had become greedy. He wanted to get the lease back. He had tried one excuse after another, but Ellen had been firm. At length they had settled on an understanding by which Ellen Cushing, the real estate agent, would appear in the matter only as a witness, at least at first, and negotiations looking to a compromise would be carried on by Scott Shelby, who would receive one quarter of whatever he was able to get.

Shelby had at this point been kicking himself for letting a very profitable transaction slip through his fingers, and once his pocketbook was touched he had dropped his mask of the genial benefactor. He was a combination of the thwarted wolf and the outwitted sharpshooter.

Hamilton Burger was shrewd enough to give the witness every opportunity to relate conversations which showed this drama unfolding before the jurors. Then he introduced in evidence the oil lease, the assignment, and the declaration of trust.

"The purpose of these documents?" the Court asked, glancing down at Mason as though anticipating an objection.

"The purpose is to show the motive on the part of the murderer."

"I don't see exactly how this connects a motive with the defendant," the Court said.

Hamilton Burger said, "If the Court please, it shows the reason for this gathering aboard the yacht."

"I'm willing to agree with you there, Counselor, but what I am interested in is just how these documents and the testimony of this witness show a definite motive on the part of the *defendant* in the present case.''

"Well, Your Honor," Hamilton Burger said, "I think that it explains the background in the light of that which is to come out later on in testimony. It will explain the statements made by the defendant. Perhaps I should have introduced the statement of the defendant at this time. I think it is pertinent to take into consideration the atmosphere aboard that yacht, the tension, the hatreds.''

"But why?"

"Because it was against this background that the defendant felt that the time was right to strike. She had evidently contemplated this murder for some time and was awaiting only a favorable opportunity. It is the purpose of this testimony to show that such an opportunity existed and the extent of that opportunity, an opportunity which was, so to speak, made to order, an opportunity which the defendant could not afford to pass up and which she did not. Moreover, Your Honor, there is no objection from the defense.''

Judge Maxwell looked over his glasses at Perry Mason. "There is no objection, Mr. Mason? Is that correct?''

"That is correct," Mason said. "Let's get the facts before the jury. Let's get the *entire* picture. *I* want the whole thing.''

Hamilton Burger smirked. "That's exactly what we want, Your Honor.''

"Very well," Judge Maxwell said crisply. "The documents will be received in evidence and marked as appropriate exhibits. Do you have many more questions of this witness, Mr. Burger? The Court notices that it's approaching the hour of the afternoon adjournment.''

"Just a few more questions, if the Court please, and then I will be finished.''

"Very well, go ahead.''

"Now you and counsel for the defense occupy adversary positions on a matter of considerable importance to you?''

Judge Maxwell glanced down at the district attorney. "What is the object of that question?" he asked.

"I merely want to show the bias of the witness.''

"You mean that the witness is biased in favor of the defense?"

"No, Your Honor. She might be biased against it."

"Then that is a matter for the defense itself to bring out."

"I know of no rule of law which says so, Your Honor," Hamilton Burger said. "It is a fact in the case. The bias of a witness is always an important factor which may be shown. I have been accused by indirection of suppressing some evidence in this case. I don't intend to suppress any more."

"The defense can bring out any matter of bias if it so chooses," Judge Maxwell said.

"Certainly it may, Your Honor, but I don't know that there is any rule of law which provides that the facts of the case which are in favor of the defense can only be brought out by the defense and those which are in favor of the prosecution be brought out only by the prosecution. If that is the ruling of the Court, then I want the jurors to understand that there can be no possible censure upon the district attorney's office because the prosecution waited for the defense to bring out these facts concerning the glancing bullet—that is, the *alleged* glancing of the bullet."

"The situation is somewhat different there," Judge Maxwell said. "I think it would hardly be expedient for counsel to raise that question at this time. In the one case the facts are known for the defense, which has the opportunity to bring them out if it desires. In the other case the facts were apparently in the exclusive control of the prosecution."

"But the defense nevertheless discovered them and brought them out."

"Due to skill on the part of the interrogator," Judge Maxwell snapped. "The present question is different. I don't think there is any distinct analogy."

"I contend that it is exactly the same in the eyes of the law."

Judge Maxwell looked down at Mason. "What is your position on this, Mr. Mason?"

"I haven't any, Your Honor."

"You mean you consent to the question?"

"No sir. I do not. I am simply willing to let the record speak for itself."

"Of course, if you raise no objection to the question, that is another matter."

"I am not objecting and I am not consenting, Your Honor. I believe that the control of the examination of the witness is in the discretion of the Court."

"But where no objection is made the Court is not called upon to make objections for one of the parties, subject, of course, to the fact that the proof must be kept within reasonable limits of relevancy."

Hamilton Burger said, "Your Honor, I would like to read to the Court an excerpt from *Jones on Evidence*, Second Edition, page one thousand and fifty, where the author says as follows: 'It is always competent to show that a witness is hostile to the party *against* whom he is called, that he has threatened revenge, or that a quarrel exists between them. A jury would scrutinize more closely and doubtingly the evidence of the hostile than that of an indifferent or a friendly witness . . .' "

"Exactly," Judge Maxwell said. "There can be no question of that. That is elemental law. The Court needs no authority on that point. This question is entirely different."

"If the Court will permit me to go on reading, I think that the authority covers this very question," Hamilton Burger said. "I read that portion of the law in order to make certain that there could be no confusion in the minds of my listeners as to that which was to follow, inasmuch as there is no confusion on the part of the author of the text. In other words, the author was careful to keep the two points segregated."

"Go ahead," Judge Maxwell said impatiently. "What follows?"

"There follows this statement," Hamilton Burger said, pausing to read impressively, " 'hence it is always competent to show the relations which exist between the witness and the party *against*, as well as the one *for whom* he is called.' "

Hamilton Burger sat down.

"Let me see that book," Judge Maxwell demanded.

Hamilton Burger took the law book forward to the bench. "An old edition, Your Honor, but one that is most suitable for carrying in court. I prefer it to the more voluminous . . ."

"No apology necessary," Judge Maxwell said. "*Jones on Evidence* is a standard authority. Let me read that. I . . . yes . . . there's a citation . . . two citations . . . very well, in the absence of objection on the part of the defense I will permit the evidence to be introduced."

Hamilton Burger smiled triumphantly. "Answer the question, Mrs. Lacey."

"I am suing Mr. Perry Mason and Mr. Paul Drake for two hundred and fifty thousand dollars for defamation of character because they claimed to the officers that I had had a man in my bedroom, that I was shielding Scott Shelby after his murder and that the man was not actually dead, whereas in fact I hadn't seen him for more than twelve hours prior to the time of his death."

"You may cross-examine," Burger said triumphantly.

"Ah, yes," Mason said. "On that last question, Mrs. Lacey, the '*accusation*' I believe was that because a wet blanket and a pair of men's shoes that were soaking wet with water had been found in your garage the officers should investigate to see if perhaps some man who had been in the water had not been riding in your automobile."

"Your Honor," Hamilton Burger said, "I object to that as not being proper cross-examination. Counsel can show bias if he wants to but this case certainly is no place to try the merits of the suit for defamation of character."

"I am not asking to try the case on the merits," Mason said. "I am merely asking the witness as to the grounds of the communication made to the officers and the nature of that communication. Obviously there cannot be as much resentment for a communication that was founded upon fact as for one which was made up of whole cloth."

"That is the danger of this thing," Judge Maxwell said irritably. "The inquiry has the tendency to go far afield. I have permitted, over my better judgment, counsel for the prosecution to prove that a witness testifying for the prosecution is biased *against* the defense. Now then, under cross-examination, counsel for the defense certainly should be entitled to go farther into the question of bias than if counsel for the defense had been the one to bring it out. In that case, if the witness had made an answer which had shown bias, there would have been no necessity for further questions; but in view of the fact that this was brought out on direct examination counsel for the defense now has the right to a most searching inquiry.''

"Exactly, Your Honor," Mason said. "Which was why I didn't object to the question which the prosecution asked, although I thought that it was rather irrelevant.''

"I still think it was irrelevant," the judge said. "But I have permitted it, and in view of the fact that it was permitted on direct examination I see no alternative but to give you every latitude on cross-examination. However, it is approaching the hour of the evening adjournment, gentlemen.''

"If the Court will bear with me just another five or ten minutes," Mason said, "I think perhaps we can conclude this phase of the examination.''

"Very well.''

"Can you answer that question?" Mason asked.

She said, "I don't know what you told the officers.''

"But you do allege in your complaint that you know.''

"That allegation is on information and belief," Hamilton Burger said.

"But the witness *does* know that there actually was a wet blanket, a soaking wet blanket, found in the garage.''

"She'd used it to carry ice in," Burger said irritably.

"Would you mind holding up your right hand?" Mason asked the district attorney.

"What do you mean?''

Mason smiled. "If you're going to testify in place of this witness, I'd like to have you sworn.''

There was a titter in the courtroom. Hamilton Burger's face turned red.

"Proceed, gentlemen," the Court said. "Counsel will refrain from personalities but on the other hand the witness will be permitted to answer questions without interpolation by counsel.''

"There was such a wet blanket in your garage?" Mason asked.

"Yes. I used it to wrap ice in," the witness said angrily.

"And a pair of men's shoes that were also soaking wet?"

"My husband's shoes," she said. "I guess a woman has the right to have her husband's shoes in her garage if she wants."

"He was your husband at that time?"

"No. We were married four days later."

"Exactly. But you do admit that a soaking wet blanket and a pair of men's shoes that were also soaking wet were found concealed in a corner of your garage the morning after the murder?"

The jurors were leaning forward now, their eyes sharp with interest and perhaps a faint trace of suspicion. Hamilton Burger, distinctly uncomfortable, shifted his position and the swivel chair squeaked a protest. As the witness hesitated, the district attorney half arose as though preparing to make an objection, but then subsided and settled back in his chair as he could think of no appropriate manner of coping with the situation which had developed.

The witness said angrily, "If you want to know the facts instead of making a lot of nasty insinuations, Mr. Mason, I'll tell you the facts."

"Go right ahead," Mason invited.

"Your Honor," Burger protested, "I think this is most improper."

"I don't," Judge Maxwell said. "The witness testifies to bias on direct examination. Counsel now on cross-examination is questioning a witness who is admittedly and concededly hostile, not only from an academic, technical standpoint, but from a most real one. Inasmuch as the cause of that hostility and bias was deliberately brought out by the prosecution on its direct examination, I see no reason for curtailing the defense in its cross-examination on that point."

"Thank you, Your Honor," Mason said. "I feel personally that I am entitled to have these facts brought out."

"I'm the one who is entitled to have them brought out," the witness said angrily. "I went on a picnic with the man I was going to marry. I went out shortly after noon of the day of that yacht trip and I stayed out until four or five o'clock that afternoon, and I have pictures here to prove it."

"Indeed?" Mason said, "I'd be interested in those pictures."

"If the Court please!" Burger protested.

"Oh, let's have the pictures. Let's get it over with," Judge Maxwell said impatiently. "You opened the door for all this, Mr. Burger, and I'm not going to slam it in the face of the witness on the one hand, or the counsel for the defense on the other; not after the manner in which you deliberately opened it. Go ahead. Let's get the whole story."

Mason gravely took the pictures which the witness handed him.

"You can see in those photographs," the witness said, "that my husband—the man shown in this picture—is standing on a raft. He got his feet wet getting on and off that raft. It was something that he made himself out of a board and some sticks. And here's the blanket with the ice on it. We carried the ice in a blanket and carried it over in the blanket to the place where we were having a picnic."

"Why in a blanket?" Mason asked.

"Did you ever try to carry ice in your bare hands, Mr. Mason?" the witness asked acidly.

There were smiles in the courtroom.

"And after your picnic?" Mason asked.

"After the picnic I was with my husband."

"For how long?"

"Until I had to go to the train to meet my mother. And my mother stayed with me the entire night."

Mason glanced at the clock. "I take it that the Court now wishes to adjourn until tomorrow morning?"

Judge Maxwell nodded. He was plainly angry with the district attorney for the manner in which he had introduced the bias of the witness in an attempt to arouse the sympathies of the jury and equally irritated at Perry Mason for the manner in which he had exploited that blunder on the part of the district attorney. He said, "Court is about to take a recess. Tomorrow is Saturday, and there will be no session of the Court until Monday morning at ten o'clock. The jury will remain in the custody of the sheriff and will not converse about this case, discuss it in any way among themselves, or permit others to discuss it in their presence. They will refrain from forming or expressing any opinion as to the guilt or innocence of the defendant until the case is finally submitted to them. Court is adjourned."

The judge got up and stalked angrily away into chambers.

Burger glowered across at Mason. "Satisfied, I trust?" he said sarcastically.

Mason grinned at him. "Go ahead and open doors and I'll stick my foot in them," he promised.

"You've got your foot in it now," Burger said angrily, started to say something else, then got up and stormed out of the courtroom.

Mason said to the deputy sheriff who had Marion Shelby in charge, "Just a minute before you take her back. I want to ask her a couple of questions."

The deputy sheriff nodded, withdrew a few paces.

Mason leaned forward, said in a low tone to Marion Shelby, "The answer to this may be very, very important. Are you absolutely certain that the man you saw fall overboard was your husband?"

"Absolutely."

"Did you see his features?"

"Not when he was falling, but after he was in the water."

"You are certain it was your husband?"

"Absolutely positive."

"There was enough light so that you could see plainly?"

"Yes."

"You heard his voice?"

"Yes."

207

"It was your husband's voice?"

"Yes."

"Now then, be very careful about this. Was your husband moving?"

"Yes. He was moving. He was struggling in the water in a peculiar way."

"Lying on his back or on his stomach?"

"Lying on his back."

"So you couldn't see the back of his neck?"

"No, only his face."

"And you're certain he was moving?"

"Of course he was moving. He was making fighting motions with his hands and legs, kicking and struggling, not the way a man would who was strong and healthy but as though he had been . . . as though he'd been hit on the head. I think that blow on the head really has something to do with it."

"And he was alone down there in the water? There was no one with him?"

"No one with him. No."

"But there was an overhang to the bow of the yacht. You couldn't see what was under the bow?"

"No, I guess not. My husband was swept underneath that overhang by the current and out of sight. I thought he was drifting down the starboard side. He seemed to be heading in that direction. But when I ran down that side—well, you know, he'd gone down the port side."

"And you had heard the sound of the shot *before* you reached the bow of the boat and looked down into the water?"

"Yes. That shot took place just after my husband fell or was dragged overboard."

"You think he may have been dragged overboard?"

"There was something very peculiar about the way he was standing and swaying back and forth. It was as though something was pulling him from down in the water, some force that he seemed to be struggling against. He was wrestling . . . wrestling with an invisible antagonist."

208

Mason said, "It might help your case a lot, Mrs. Shelby, if the facts of the matter were that your husband was *not* struggling when you saw him in the water after that shot was fired. Perhaps he was just lying limp but the current was moving his arms and legs so that it appeared there might have been some gentle motion."

"It wasn't a gentle motion. He was kicking. He was trying to fight."

Mason said, "You realize the obvious implications of having the fatal wound caused by a bullet fired from this gun?"

"Of course, I do."

"Well," Mason said, "think it over. You don't have to go on the stand yet."

"You want me to change my testimony, don't you, Mr. Mason?"

Mason said somewhat wearily, "I want you to tell the truth, that's all. But if you are lying, I warn you that the lie is very apt to send you to the death cell."

"I can't help it. I'm not going to change my story. I told the truth and I'm sticking with it. The truth is the truth, and that's all there is to it."

"If it's the truth, that's all there is to it," Mason said, and his voice showed that he was suddenly tired. "Now let's find out a little more about that gun. It's your husband's gun?"

"That's right."

"How long had he owned it?"

"I don't know. He'd had it ever since I knew him."

"Did he carry it?"

"He didn't, at first, but the last couple of months he'd been carrying it."

"Know why?"

"No."

"Some new enemy perhaps?"

"I don't know."

"Was he carrying it with him that last day—the twelfth?"

"Yes. It was in his hip pocket when he went to bed. He took it out of his pocket and put it on the top of the dresser."

Mason thought that over. "And he asked you to pick up the gun and bring it to him when he telephoned?"

"Yes."

"Then, since he'd been carrying it, there must have been someone he feared?"

"I guess so, yes. One other thing Mr. Mason, he'd shot the gun the day before . . . no, two days before."

Mason's eyes showed quick interest. "How do you know?"

"It was empty when he took it out of his pocket on the night of the tenth. He opened a drawer, took out a box of shells and reloaded it."

"The deuce he did! Did you ask for an explanation?"

"No. I never asked him for explanations. I'd got over that."

Mason frowned. "Suppose he was practicing?"

"I suppose that must have been it."

"All six chambers were empty?"

"Yes. He reloaded them all."

"Then he must have fired one more shot after that. There was one empty shell in the gun when you picked it up off the bedside stand."

"Yes—that is, I don't *know* there was an empty shell in there then. The police *say* there was an empty shell in the gun."

Mason thought it over. "I wish we knew more about your husband's life, his friends, his enemies."

"I'm sorry, Mr. Mason. I can't help you a bit. We had no social life at all. He was very secretive. I hardly know a thing about him . . . his business, his interests, his associates."

There was another period of thoughtful silence.

"How do things look, Mr. Mason?" she asked at last.

"I can't tell you yet," he said.

She laughed nervously. "That's because you don't want to tell me, isn't it?"

"They don't look any too good, I'll tell you that," Mason conceded.

210

She sighed. "Well, do the best you can, Mr. Mason. Good night."

"Good night," he said and picked up his brief case, leaving the courtroom without once glancing back.

Chapter 21

Mason paced back and forth across the carpeted floor of his private office, his thumbs hooked in the armholes of his vest, his head slightly bowed.

Della Street sat patiently at her desk, an open shorthand book in front of her. The page was about half covered with notes. She was holding her pencil waiting for any other instructions Mason might choose to give.

Paul Drake had assumed his favorite position in the big overstuffed leather chair, sitting sideways with his knees draped over one of the rounded leather arms, his back propped against the other.

From time to time Mason made comments, more to himself than to the others, never pausing in his steady methodical pacing.

"You'd better give up, Perry," Paul Drake said, "there's no use butting your head against a brick wall. There isn't any solution. This is once where even your agile mind can't pull a rabbit out of the hat. Marion Shelby is guilty."

"I'm working on a theory," Mason said. "It's so far just a weird theory, but . . ."

"I'll say it's weird," Drake interrupted. "Now you let me tell you something about practical jury psychology, Perry. Something you know but which you won't admit. You've forgotten it, lost sight of it. You let this woman keep quiet, and Hamilton Burger is going to cut you up into hamburger. The jury will be sore because they got a run-around. You put her on the witness stand, and he is going to make her and you the laughing stock of the city and he's going to get a conviction of first-degree murder."

Mason said, "I know. The way things are now I'm licked, but because this is Friday, I have a week end to . . ."

The telephone rang.

Mason frowned, then said to Della Street, "All right, Della. See who it is."

Della Street picked up the telephone, said, "Hello, yes . . . All right."

She said to Mason, "It's the matron at the jail. Marion Shelby says she has to talk to you. The matron is going to let her talk on the phone."

"All right," Mason said, and picked up the phone. "Yes?" he said patiently. "What is it?"

Marion Shelby had evidently been crying. She said, "Mr. Mason you're nice. You're splendid. You're just a marvelous man. You're good. I'm afraid perhaps you're too good for . . . for this kind of a case. I want to spare you any personal embarrassment. I'm . . . I . . . I am going to relieve you of all responsibility."

Mason said, "Are you trying to tell me that you don't want me to represent you any more?"

"That's right."

"You mean you're going into court by yourself?"

"No, I'm going to have another lawyer. One who . . . one who understands this sort of case. A lawyer Mr. Lawton Keller is getting for me. He's going to call on you. He'll . . . he's on his way up there now. He'll explain everything but I wanted you to know . . . to understand . . . you're relieved of responsibility. You understand, Mr. Mason? I need a lawyer who understands this sort of case."

"You mean I'm being fired. Is that it?" Mason asked grimly.

"Not exactly fired, but I want to have a substitution of attorneys. I want you to be out of this mess. You'll consent to it, won't you?"

"You're damn right I will!" Mason said and slammed up the phone.

"What is it?" Della Street asked anxiously.

Mason said, "She's fired me. Lawton Keller has called on her. He's persuaded her to get another lawyer, one who, to use her own words, 'understands this sort of case.' "

Della Street jumped up, ran to Mason and threw her arms around him, kicking her right foot back from the floor in her excitement. "Oh, Chief, I'm so glad. I'm so *darn* glad!"

Paul Drake grinned, "After all, Perry, it's a break."

"A break?" Mason said angrily. "It puts me in the most humiliating position I ever occupied. I get taken for a ride and then . . ."

"Take it easy, Perry, take it easy," Paul Drake said. "Look at the thing the way it should be looked at. You made a swell job cross-examining those witnesses. The facts in the case are all against you. The cards were completely stacked, but you made a swell job. You didn't intimate what your defense was to be, you simply went into court and did a darn good job of cross-examining the witnesses of the prosecution.

"Now then, this smart guy, this Keller, enters the picture. He's one of these masterminds, these know-it-alls from way back. He talks the sort of language that your client is accustomed to. It's a break. You're out of it. Now we can square things with Ellen Lacey and wipe the slate clean."

Mason flung out his hand in a gesture of disgust. "All right, the hell with it," he said. "Let's go eat."

"It's about time," Della Street said. "Gosh but I'm starved."

Mason walked over to the hat closet, put on his hat. He said, "We take the deposition of Ellen Lacey at this office tomorrow, Della. I have a stipulation from her lawyer—old Attica, the shyster!" Mason was just getting into his coat when knuckles pounded on the outside of the door.

"See who it is," Mason said to Della Street, "and tell them to come back next Christmas."

Della Street called through the door, "The office is closed."

"Let me in, this is Lawton Keller. I want to see Mr. Mason."

Mason paused, grinned at Paul Drake and said, "All right, this is going to be good. We may as well let the situation

214

have its last ironical touch of humor. Open the door and let him in, Della.''

Lawton Keller was quite evidently well pleased with himself. A cigar was pushed up from a corner of his mouth at an angle of self-satisfied smugness. He entered the room with the utmost assurance, nodded, removed his hat, said, ''Evening, everybody,'' walked over and sat down.

Mason, perched on the corner of his desk, said, ''It's got to be brief, Keller, because I'm going out.''

''It'll be brief, all right,'' Keller said. ''I am sort of interested in this whole business.''

''Yes, I understand.''

''You're a fine lawyer, Mason.''

''Thank you.''

''For a certain type of case, you can't be beat.''

''You can't believe how much I'm thrilled at hearing you say so,'' Mason observed.

''Now don't get sore, Mason. Keep your shirt on. This is a case that's different from the kind you're accustomed to handle. I've got a lawyer that's a friend of mine that knows these things up one side and down the other. He's been wringing his hands all day, talking about how the defense was being butchered up. He says you're a swell lawyer to defend an innocent guy but when it comes to . . . Well, you know, a case of this kind . . .''

''Who is this lawyer?'' Mason asked.

Keller said, ''It's Attica of the firm of Attica, Hoxie and Meade.''

Drake whistled.

''Know him?'' Keller asked Drake. ''He's a whiz.''

Drake said, ''He's a shyster. He's the lawyer who's representing Ellen Lacey in that suit against us.''

''Sure he is,'' Keller said. ''And look how clever he is. He gets his client swell publicity as . . .''

''He stinks,'' Mason said.

''Now keep your shirt on, Mr. Mason. I shouldn't have mentioned what he said about you butchering up the case, but anyway, I'm calling on you and appealing to your sense of decency and sportsmanship.''

"What do you want?" Mason asked.

"Now what happened was this," Lawton Keller said, taking the cigar out of his mouth and gesturing with it. "This Scott Shelby was pretty much of a chaser. He was fooling around quite a bit, making passes at everybody. Well, that's all right, you can't blame him for that. After all, a man is only human. But this guy was pretty much of a rat. He kinda tried to blackmail his way. You know, he'd get something on someone or get them under obligations to him and then he'd strut his stuff. Get me?"

"Go on," Mason said, "let's hear the rest of it."

"Well, on this night that they were on the yacht, his wife had just about got fed up with the whole business. She decided she was going to get a divorce, but you can't get a divorce without evidence and naturally a fellow doesn't drag his sweethearts into the family bedroom. So, she had to get up and go out looking for the evidence. Get me?"

"I get you," Mason said dryly.

"Well, she woke up, hubby was gone. She sensed he was out on a philandering expedition. She saw the gun that was lying on the dresser and without thinking, she picked that up . . ."

"Let me finish for you," Mason said ironically. "She ran out on deck, half crazed with jealousy and disappointment. She saw her shattered romance falling in pieces about her feet. The poor little woman was beside herself. She didn't stop to think that she wasn't properly clothed. She wasn't thinking of anything. She couldn't think in the sense that one intelligently correlates one's acts. She had wakened, found her husband was gone, and still in that sleep-dazed half-wakened state, was running along the yacht looking for him, thinking perhaps that something had happened to him."

"Now you've got it," Lawton Keller said, with a trace of respect in his voice. "That's *exactly* the situation. Hang it, you make it sound damn good!"

"And there in the bow of the boat she found her husband, in the close embrace of another woman. The other woman jumped up and ran, and as soon as she did so, the husband saw his wife, and, in an angry mood, reproached her, telling her that he didn't want to have her snooping around, and demanding roughly to know what the hell she meant by following him.''

Lawton Keller nodded approvingly.

"The poor little woman was distraught. She was beside herself. She still wasn't fully awake,'' Mason went on, dramatically, "she was numb with the disillusionment of it all. She started to cry and then her husband got rough, grabbed her by the shoulders and turned her around and kicked her, told her to get back down in the stateroom where she belonged and stay there. And then, the kick did something to her. It aroused her resentment. It wakened her thoroughly. She told him she wasn't going to stand for it. She was going to get a divorce. And then, when he suddenly realized that she meant what she said, angry and in a frenzy of rage, he grabbed her and tried to throw her overboard.

"She struggled with him, tried to scream to him not to do that, but he had her by the throat and was throttling her. Then, just when she was on the point of losing her balance, she twisted and turned and fell and dragged her husband down with her. And, her husband stumbled over a rope, lost his balance, pitched overboard, and as he started to fall he grabbed her arm, trying to hold to her. The hand of that arm had the revolver in it; and just as she wrenched the arm from his grasp, she heard an explosion. She never did realize that the explosion was that of the gun that was in her own hand. She thought it was someone else who had fired the shot. It wasn't until afterwards that she realized that the gun must have gone off, apparently of its own accord. Or, perhaps, the husband, clutching frantically, had grabbed the barrel of the gun and pulled it down so that the pressure of her finger against the trigger discharged it. And the proof of that is that the bullet struck against the smooth side of the trim yacht, and then, *on a glance*, struck the husband.

"The man killed himself, fired by his own rage, trapped by circumstances which would almost seem to have been set in motion by some higher power. It was not murder. It was not even self-defense. She didn't kill him, this poor, half-wakened woman. The heel killed himself!"

Lawton Keller's eyes were wide and awestruck. "Cripes," he said, "you're doing it even better than . . . *You* don't need to get out of this case!"

"The hell I don't," Mason told him angrily, "I need to get out of the case, and you need to get the hell out of this office, beginning now."

Mason came down off the desk, crossed over to Keller's chair with two swift strides, grabbed the man's coat collar and jerked him up out of the chair.

"Say," Keller demanded in surprise, "what the hell's got into you? Look, maybe we can do business after all. I was just interested in the little girl because . . ."

Della Street glanced questioningly at Mason.

Mason nodded.

Della Street opened the door.

Mason straightened his arm, leaned his weight against Keller and gave him the bum's rush out of the office.

The man fell flat as he hit the corridor. Mason dusted off his hands, stepped back in the room. Della Street, acting as though the whole thing had been carefully rehearsed, closed the door and locked it.

Perry Mason finished dusting his hands, said, "And I guess *that* calls for a drink."

He walked over and opened a locked drawer in a filing cabinet, pulled out a bottle of whisky and glasses.

Paul Drake was watching him with admiration. "Cripes, Perry, I never saw it done neater."

"You mean throwing a rat out of the office?" Mason asked uncorking a bottle.

"God no!" Drake said. "The old hokum about the ag-grieved wife. Why the hell don't you stay in the case and get her off, Perry?"

Mason quit pouring the whisky. "Do *you* want to go out in the corridor?" he asked pointedly.

Drake grinned. "Have it your own way, Perry," he said dryly. "Keep on pouring the drink. But, for a guy that the district attorney claims is always cutting corners, you certainly are a babe in the woods. Make mine a double one, and then I'm going to ring up Ellen Lacey's lawyer and see how much kale it's going to take to let me wriggle off the hook.''

Chapter 22

Saturday morning Mason entered his office with his hat tilted back on his head, the old, carefree, boyish grin twisting his lips.

"Hi Della, what's new?"

She said, "The deposition of Ellen Cushing Lacey is set for ten o'clock, you remember?"

"Uh huh."

"The court reporter will be here. There's a notary public on this floor, who's ready to come in and swear the witness any time we're ready."

"Heard anything from Paul Drake?"

"I'm afraid Paul had rather a bad night. He got hold of Attica on the phone, tried to sound the old shyster out about a figure for a compromise."

"Get anywhere?"

"Attica said the compromise figure would be two hundred and fifty thousand dollars, and slammed the phone up."

Mason frowned. "Naturally he would. You can see what a sweet spot he's in, now that he represents *both* Ellen Lacey in her suit and Marion Shelby in the murder case. He isn't going to let anything adverse happen. One will now back up the other. He'll go ahead with Ellen Lacey on Monday, making Scott Shelby out to be the biggest heel in the state.

"After all, Attica can now . . ."

The telephone rang. Della Street picked up the receiver, said, "It's Paul. He just came in."

Mason took the telephone, said, "Hi, Paul."

"Don't say 'high' to me. I was high last night. This morning I'm lower than an income tax exemption. I feel as though my plumbing had stopped up and somebody was running a pneumatic riveter inside my skull."

"That bad?" Mason asked.

"Worse."

Mason said, "Pursuant to stipulation we're taking the deposition of Ellen Lacey this morning at ten."

"That so?"

"You hadn't forgotten about that case had you?"

"Forgotten about it?" Drake exclaimed. "That was the trouble. I kept on drinking just *trying* to forget about it. And not getting anywhere."

Mason said, "Think about it some more, Paul. You have a couple of newspaper reporters who have been pretty friendly with you and given you some tips, haven't you?"

"Yes, why?"

"Nothing," Mason said, "only it occurs to me that this deposition of Ellen Cushing Lacey might be news. Some of the boys might like to get in on it."

Drake said, "By gosh, Perry. You're right at that! It's a swell tip. Gosh, I'm glad you called me about it. I'd never have thought about it."

"Well, give your friends a buzz," Mason said. "We have room for only a couple of people. Get two of the boys who have been giving you tips. This will be your chance to do them a good turn."

"Thanks, Perry. It starts at ten o'clock?"

"That's right."

"Okay, I'll give them a ring. It's short notice but I'll get them on the phone right away."

Mason hung up, was just turning to Della Street to say something when the door opened and Gertie, in the doorway, said, "Good morning, Mr. Mason. I didn't want to ring the phone because I knew you were talking on the other phone but Mr. Attica of the firm of Attica, Hoxie and Meade is here on that deposition."

"That's not until ten o'clock," Mason said.

"He said he came a few minutes early because he wanted to talk with you."

Mason said, "Send him in."

George Attica was a tall, somewhat stooped man with gray eyes that managed, somehow, to keep his thoughts pretty

221

well concealed. He was in his fifties, had gray hair, a deep voice which he had carefully cultivated so that he had the booming delivery of an old-fashioned spellbinder; but his mind was alert enough and there were few tricks of the profession that he didn't thoroughly understand.

He said, "I'm afraid I lost my temper with Mr. Paul Drake last night."

"Apologies are always in order," Mason told him. "Sit down."

Attica sat down, glanced at Della Street, cleared his throat significantly.

"It's okay," Mason said, "she stays."

Attica said, "I haven't much time but there are some things I wanted to discuss with you before my witness appeared."

"I don't know what they can be."

Attica said, "I am going to release Marion Shelby's *real* story to make the Sunday newspapers. It's an intensely dramatic story. A story that will tug at the heartstrings of every woman in the world."

"That's nice," Mason commented.

"That story," Attica said, "deals with the broad basic human factors of life, Mr. Mason, particularly as they concern a woman, a woman who is married and has given her all to the man who has promised to love and cherish her until death parts them."

"Does them part, I believe is the way you want to express it in front of a jury," Mason said.

Attica made a deprecatory motion with his hand. "Don't be like that, Mason. It really doesn't become you."

"I don't give a damn what becomes me and what doesn't," Mason said. "Thank heavens I've lived my life so I can do pretty much as I please."

"That's nice. That's a very interesting philosophy. Very interesting indeed, but I am talking now about a person to whom you have a certain moral responsibility."

"Do I?"

"I think so. She lied to you. I will admit that. You have every right to resent that falsehood. But, after all, she was young, she was inexperienced and she was frightened. She didn't realize that the truth was her best weapon, was her only weapon. She felt that the truth would absolutely condemn her, in place of which, the truth may actually save her life, or as I shall quote to the jury, 'The truth shall set you free.' ''

"Very interesting," Mason said. "There's no use wasting it on me. Why don't you save it for the jury?"

"Because," Attica went on, "there is going to be an enormous amount of publicity in connection with this. Before she tells her story it's just another murder case; but the minute she tells that story, it becomes something which is brought right home to every woman in the world. Women can look at their Sunday newspapers, glance across at their husbands, look at the security of the home about them and wonder if it really *is* a security, wonder just how firmly entrenched they are.''

"There, but for the Grace of God go I, eh?" Mason asked.
"Exactly."

"Nice stuff," Mason said. "You're collecting it. I'm not."

"Now, it occurs to me," Attica went on, "that here is an opportunity for you to enhance your prestige in connection with this case, Mr. Mason. If you'll let it appear that you deliberately had drawn the district attorney off balance by keeping this story bottled up so that you could spring it purposely as a surprise, after he had been forced to disclose the entire ramifications of the case he had against the defendant . . .''

Mason said, "Let's quit beating around the bush. You want me to back your story up. Is that it?"

"At least not deny it.''

Mason was thoughtful for a few moments. He said, "Attica, I don't see any way that I can deny any story you put out without betraying the confidence of a client, and I'm not going to do that. I'm not going to tell anyone what a client did or did not say to me. Those are my ethics.''

Attica's face beamed. "That is very, very satisfactory, Mr. Mason. Very satisfactory indeed. And now, since you've been so broad-minded on that, I think that I'm in a position to talk about a fair compromise of this case against you and

Mr. Drake. After all, it was purely a natural mistake. A very unfortunate matter. I think that for payment of a nominal consideration, my client would be willing to let the matter drop."

"How much?"

"Oh, well, the financial end of it is relatively unimportant. After all, it's a question of human emotions having been aroused and . . ."

"How much?"

"Well, Mr. Mason, frankly I think two hundred and fifty dollars would cover the out-of-pocket expenses. You see, inasmuch as I am attorney for Mrs. Lacey and inasmuch as her good name has now been vindicated, and inasmuch as the whole thing can be handled in such a way that it might look as though the filing of the suit was part of a shrewd move to draw the district attorney off balance. Well, you know how those things are. There's going to be an enormous amount of publicity in this case."

Mason said, "You wouldn't sell out one client in favor of another, would you?"

"Certainly not."

"You mean that Mrs. Lacey is willing to accept a settlement of two hundred and fifty dollars?"

"She hasn't said so, but I think she *would* say so if I advised her to."

"And you would so advise her?"

"Is there any reason why I shouldn't?"

"The best reason I can think of," Mason said, "is that I'm not going to pay her two hundred and fifty dollars. I'm not going to pay her a damn cent."

"Why, that's absurd!" Attica exclaimed. "I was being nice to you. The nuisance value of the case alone is far greater than two hundred and fifty dollars. Think of it, Mr. Mason, that would only be a hundred and twenty-five from you and a hundred and twenty-five from Mr. Drake."

Mason yawned, looked at his watch, said, "It's approximately ten o'clock. Is your client going to be here?"

"There won't be any need to go ahead with the deposition if the case is settled."

Mason said doggedly, "The case isn't going to be settled, not as far as I'm concerned."

"Why Mr. Mason, you absolutely astound me! Mr. Drake let me understand over the telephone last night that he personally would be willing to settle for somewhere in the vicinity of a thousand dollars."

"Let him settle if he wants to," Mason said.

"Suppose he should pay the entire financial consideration?"

Mason said, "The plaintiff can always dismiss the action if she wants to but, as far as I'm concerned, I'm not going to pay a cent, and I'm going to have it definitely understood that I didn't pay a cent. I can't make any statement to the press about what Marion Shelby did or did not tell me without betraying the confidence of a client. But I certainly can tell the truth about *this* case. It's ten o'clock, bring in your client."

"But Mr. Mason, surely you can't be bullheaded enough . . ."

"It's ten o'clock," Mason said. "Bring in your client."

Attica got to his feet, his face flushed. "All right, if you want it that way, that's the way it'll be. You'll find out that we don't *have* to cooperate with you, Mr. Perry Mason. As a matter of fact, it won't take but just a little gossip to tarnish your prestige very greatly over this case. There are many people even now who are thinking that the defense of Marion Shelby was badly botched—under the circumstances."

"Let them think," Mason said. "It's ten o'clock, bring in your client."

Attica turned to the door with dignity. "Where do you wish to take the deposition?"

"In the law library," Mason said.

"Very well, my client will be there."

Della Street glided from the room, returned in a few minutes and nodded to Mason. "Everything's all set."

"Drake there?"

"Not yet."

"Attica's client?"

225

"He's waiting for her. He expects her any minute. He told her to be here at ten o'clock."

"It's ten minutes past now."

"Yes I know. I don't think Attica expected there would be any necessity for her to be here."

"It isn't what he thinks that counts," Mason said, "it's what happens. Let me know as soon as she comes in and let me know as soon as Drake comes in."

Della Street nodded, stepped back into the law library and Mason could hear the sound of chairs being dragged over the floor as last minute preparations were made for the deposition.

It was ten-seventeen when Drake arrived with "two friends" who were not introduced but who unobtrusively sat back in a corner.

At ten-twenty Della Street entered Mason's office, said, "You don't suppose she's standing you up, do you?"

"There was a stipulation that she'd be here at ten o'clock," Mason said. "In the event she doesn't show up, I'm going to put it up to Attica to get her here no matter where she is."

"He's telephoning now. . . . What happened, Chief? You seem all perked up. Have you found out something?"

Mason opened the morning newspaper, pointed to the half page photograph in the pictorial section. "Seen that?" he asked. "It's a new one."

"Yes."

"Nice stuff," Mason said. "I've been asleep at the switch. Listen to this. Here's the caption. 'PHOTOGRAPH OF PICNIC TAKEN WITH KODAK SELF-TIMER WHICH WILL FIGURE IN QUARTER MILLION DOLLAR SLANDER SUIT—THIS SHOWS EL-LEN CUSHING, NOW MRS. ARTHUR LACEY, AND HER HUSBAND ON THE FAMOUS PICNIC WHICH IS INVOLVED IN A TWO HUN-DRED AND FIFTY THOUSAND DOLLAR SUIT FOR DEFAMATION OF CHARACTER, MR. PERRY MASON, THE NOTED ATTORNEY, AND PAUL DRAKE, THE DETECTIVE, BEING DEFENDANTS.' "

"What about it?" Della Street asked.

"Nice picture," Mason said. "Nice composition. The man standing on the raft. The girl opening various boxes, spreading out plates on the ground, and above all a piece of ice reposing on the blanket.''

"What about it, Chief?"

"Beautiful cloud effect," Mason said. "Just notice those beautiful billowy clouds. Lights and shadows. A darn fine picture. It might have been used for an advertisement for a film company. Clear, full of tone value."

"Chief, *what* are you getting at?"

Mason grinned and said, "Every cloud, Della, has a silver lining."

"I don't get you . . ."

The door opened. Gertie leaned forward with the door, holding the knob of the open door with one hand, the jamb with the other. She said, "Mrs. Lacey's here. Attica wanted me to tell you. He says if you want to see him first . . ."

Mason folded the newspaper, opened his knife, slit out the printed copy of the photograph, folded it and put it in his pocket.

"Tell Attica I definitely don't care to see him. Come on, Della, let's go."

Mason entered the law library. Ellen Cushing Lacey, wearing dark glasses, a dark hat, a trim dark blue suit, blue gloves and blue shoes, regarded the lawyer coldly. The white rims of the dark glasses gave her face a weird, owl-like look.

Attica said, "All right, all right. Let's get going. This is the time heretofore fixed by stipulation for the deposition of Ellen Cushing Lacey in the case of Cushing vs. Perry Mason and Paul Drake."

Mason said, "That's right. This deposition is being taken pursuant to the provisions of the Code of Civil Procedure by which I have the right to take the deposition of an adverse party and to cross-examine a party of record on the other side without being bound by the answers."

"Very well," Attica snapped. "Go ahead with your questions."

Mason drew up a chair and sat down, said, "Let the witness be sworn."

The notary public swore the witness, then quietly left the

office. "I'll return whenever the deposition is concluded," she said.

Mason glanced over at Paul Drake, at the faces of the two newspapermen who were making themselves as inconspicuous as possible.

Mason said, "Mrs. Lacey, you're suing Mr. Drake and myself for damages because of defamation of character."

"That's right."

"Growing out of the fact that you claim we told the officers something about the wet blanket and the pair of wet shoes?"

"That and the fact that you told them I was harboring Scott Shelby, that he wasn't dead at all, and that I had participated in a frame-up in order to make it look as though he had died, that I had had a man in my bedroom all night."

"Now you explained that wet blanket by saying that you used it to carry ice in."

"Yes. Do I have to go through that all over again?"

"Not necessarily, if you'll refer to the testimony which you gave in court yesterday and say that it is substantially correct."

"It is."

"I hand you herewith a newspaper clipping setting forth that story. I'll ask you to glance through it and see if it conforms to the facts of the case."

"I've already seen it. It does."

Mason said, "Just to save time I'd like to have this introduced in evidence."

"Very well," Attica said.

"It might be attached to the deposition," Mason said, and handed it to the court reporter, who was taking down the answers in shorthand. "Now then, Mrs. Lacey, you told me, I believe, about the fact that the man who is at present your husband proposed to you on this day that Scott Shelby was murdered?"

"Yes, sir."

"Proposed to you at about what time?"

"Around eleven-thirty in the morning."

"And what did you do?"

"I've already gone into that with you."

"Would you mind going into it again?"

"We decided to go on a picnic. We went out in the country where there was a lake. In case you have to know the *exact* location, it was a place that I had listed for sale, an estate of some four hundred acres, with a beautiful lake and some timber on it, an ideal place for a picnic. I had fallen in love with it the minute I had seen it. I didn't have money enough to buy it myself, but I was rather romantic about it. I had sat down on the shores of that lake and visualized that Arthur might propose to me there. And so I wanted my dream to come true."

"So you went down and picked up a lunch at the delicatessen store?"

"I put up some myself. Arthur went to the delicatessen store."

"Now this was on the day that Scott Shelby was murdered, Thursday the twelfth, I believe."

"That's right."

"And you didn't see Mr. Shelby from the time you left on that picnic?"

"No, sir. From eleven o'clock in the morning I didn't see him. I never saw him again alive. The next time I saw him, he was dead in the morgue and they called on me to identify the body."

"Exactly," Mason said. "You put up some sandwiches for the picnic?"

"I did."

"And Mr. Lacey went down to the delicatessen store to pick up some food?"

"He did."

"And you had some beer, and I believe halfway out it occurred to you that you didn't have any ice for the beer; so you got some ice and put it in a blanket so you could have the beer cold?"

"That's right. My heavens, do I have to keep going over and over all this?"

"And in the press today there is a picture showing you on that picnic. Who furnished them with that picture?"

"I did."

"It was one you took?"

"Yes. I had a shutter attachment that gave me time to get in the picture."

"That was taken on Thursday, the twelfth?"

"That's right. Thursday, the twelfth. That was the day Mr. Shelby was murdered by . . . Well, by someone."

"At what time was that picture taken?"

"Along in the afternoon, three or four o'clock, I guess."

"After you'd eaten lunch or before?"

"After we'd eaten lunch, of course."

"And what time did you get out there?"

"Oh, I don't know. I think we arrived about half past one or two o'clock."

"And had lunch when?"

"Almost immediately after we arrived."

"And the way the blanket in the garage got wet was because this ice was carried in it?"

"Yes. Again and again and again. *YES!!!*"

"And Mr. Lacey's shoes got wet because he was playing around on that raft?"

"*Yes!*"

"And what time did you come home from the picnic?"

"We stayed out there until five o'clock. I had to hurry to meet my mother."

"And as I understand it, Mr. Lacey went to the train with you to meet your mother?"

"He did and the train was late, so he couldn't wait."

"But he came early the next morning to cook breakfast so he could meet her then?"

"He did."

"He is, then, a good cook?"

"At one time he was a highly paid chef."

"Now when he found the train was late, he couldn't wait for your mother to arrive because he had an important appointment?"

"Mr. Mason, I've told you that over and over and over."

"But there was a friend at the station who drove you and your mother home?"

"Yes."

"Then Mr. Lacey must have taken your car?"

"He borrowed it, yes. We were good friends. He took it once in a while."

"Mrs. Lacey, why are you wearing those dark glasses? Are your eyes bothering you?"

"I like them."

"Are your eyes weak?"

"No."

"You have perfect vision?"

"Yes."

"There must be some reason for the dark glasses."

"The glare of light bothers me."

"But there's no glare in here."

"I like the style. I like the white rims."

"After all," Attica said sarcastically, "after having slandered this young woman you certainly aren't going to criticize her wearing apparel, are you? Those dark glasses are really an article of dress. They are the stylish things to wear. Sort of a Hollywood touch to them."

Mason said, "I was just wondering *why* she was wearing them."

"Well, now you know," Ellen Cushing snapped.

Mason said, "I want you to take a good look at this picture, Mrs. Lacey, and I don't want you to say afterwards that the dark glasses prevented you from seeing anything. Would you mind taking them off?"

"I can see the picture very clearly. I know it by heart."

"This picture shows the status of your picnic about four o'clock in the afternoon, some two or three hours after you had eaten lunch?"

"Yes. Not over an hour and a half later."

"And it also shows the ice on the blanket?"

"It does."

"Why did you buy that ice?"

"Because we had some beer and we wanted to chill the beer."

"You didn't chip pieces off the ice and put it in glasses?"

"No. We chilled the beer."

"How?"

231

"Why, we . . . we . . . we dug a little hole and put the ice in there and then put the beer in and . . . and . . ."

"And had the beer for lunch?"

She said hastily, "That's right."

"But this photograph shows the chunk of ice as about a twenty-five pound square of ice, *reposing on the blanket*!"

She suddenly bit her lip.

"Come, come," Mason said. "What happened to the ice?"

"Well, that was what was left after we cooled the beer."

"Then Mr. Lacey must have got *fifty* pounds of ice in order to chill the beer?"

"He wanted to have it good and cold."

"And what was the object of saving the rest of this ice?"

"Well, I don't know. We thought we might . . . thought we might need it. The beer had been chilled . . ."

"Then you must have lifted this ice back out of the hole you had dug for it, and put it *back on the blanket*."

"Well, what if we did?"

"Did you?"

"Yes. I guess that's what Art did."

"This lake is about two hundred yards from the remains of the old house?"

"Yes."

"You couldn't drive in to this lake? You had to walk in?"

"Yes. We walked for about two hundred yards, I guess. We're able to walk."

"And Mr. Lacey carried *fifty* pounds of ice?"

"It was in the blanket. He threw it over his shoulder."

"In the wet blanket. And he threw the fifty pounds of ice over his shoulder and carried the entire fifty pounds in there?"

"That's right. Yes."

"This looks like about a twenty-five pound piece of ice, that's left, Mrs. Lacey."

"Yes. It is."

"But you had purchased that ice along about eleven thirty or twelve o'clock. This was at four o'clock in the afternoon. It had been rather a hot day, hadn't it?"

"Yes. It was very hot."

"As I remember it," Mason said, "the twelfth was a very hot dry cloudless day with low humidity until along late in the afternoon when fog started coming in."

"I think it was in the evening that it turned foggy. We were just going to meet Mother when the fog settled down."

"Before, it had been a hot day?"

"Yes."

"A very hot day?"

"Yes."

"And yet this large piece of ice was left at four o'clock in the afternoon?" Mason asked incredulously.

"Well, I think Arthur bought a fifty pound piece and then this ice was left. My God, is it a crime to put beer on ice?"

"But you remember the day particularly, Thursday, the twelfth, as a dry, hot cloudless day?"

"Yes."

"Then," Mason said, suddenly whipping the photograph before her, "how do you account for these lovely fleece clouds which are shown so plainly in this photograph you yourself took, and which you have said accurately shows the condition of your picnic party at four o'clock in the afternoon?"

"I . . . I guess I was mistaken . . . I guess there must have been some clouds."

"Think again," Mason said. "The weather records show that Thursday, the twelfth, was very dry and cloudless."

She bit her lip, glanced at Attica.

"After all," Attica said, "these clouds don't mean anything."

"Why don't they?" Mason asked.

"Well," Attica said, "we don't know. The newspaper people might have put them in."

"They show very plainly on the photographs which this witness introduced in court yesterday afternoon."

Mason turned suddenly to the witness. "As a matter of fact, Miss Cushing, these pictures were *not* taken on Thursday, the twelfth. They were taken on Friday, the thirteenth. Weren't they?"

"No."

"After I had called on you with Paul Drake and *after* the officers had started their investigation and you started making up stories, you worked up a purely synthetic and romantic story of a proposal of marriage and a picnic. The picnic accounted for the wet blanket and the wet shoes. Then in order to see that there would be evidence of that picnic you and Mr. Lacey went up to the courthouse with Lieutenant Tragg, secured a declaration of intention to wed, made application for a license, went to Attica's office and filed suit, talked with Sergeant Dorset and then at about three-thirty dashed out to take some picnic pictures. Didn't you?"

"No."

"And," Mason went on, "you remember when you were talking with us Mr. Lacey mentioned about the lunch you had, that there was roast chicken and how tough it was?"

"It was tough."

"Did you eat the bones?"

"Certainly not."

"But, when I went out to the spot where you had had the picnic," Mason said, "and prowled around in the garbage, I didn't find any chicken bones at all. But I did find the remains of some macaroni and cheese, and some creamed tuna. Now, the delicatessen store where you claim you purchased these things tells me that on Friday it makes a specialty of creamed tuna, that it sells creamed tuna on Friday, but not at any other time."

"I don't know what delicatessen store he got it at."

Mason said, "Better think carefully, Mrs. Lacey, because this is very very important."

"I *am* thinking carefully!"

"And suppose I should introduce a witness from the delicatessen store who would identify Arthur Lacey as the man who purchased some things for a picnic luncheon on Friday, the thirteenth? Suppose I should introduce a man from the lumber yard who would say that Mr. Lacey picked out that board on Friday, the thirteenth? And suppose I should introduce a witness who saw you taking that board out in an automobile on Friday so that you could rig up a raft and . . ."

"Stop it!" she screamed. "Will you please stop it! My God, do you have to go prying into everything?"

Mason smiled. "I've given you an opportunity to tell the truth. You're testifying under oath, Mrs. Lacey. I'm going to conclude this deposition now. If you don't change your testimony before the deposition is concluded, and it turns out your testimony is false, you'll be guilty of perjury."

She was crying now.

Attica said, "After all, Mr. Mason, she's under quite a strain. Suppose we discontinue this deposition for a couple of hours, and she'll be feeling a little better by that time. Your questions have been rather . . . well, rather ruthless."

Mason said, "We're going to continue with this deposition right now. Look here, Mrs. Lacey, isn't it a fact that you made up this story about the picnic out of whole cloth and that after that you rushed out on Friday, the thirteenth, and staged this picnic and took the photographs on that date?"

She glanced helplessly at Attica.

"If you're feeling too upset to answer questions," Attica said, "you can simply refuse to answer on the ground that your health won't permit. I can't blame you for being upset, my dear."

"In that case," Mason said, "I'll close the deposition and stand on the answers that have already been made, and we'll see whether we can do something about it when it comes to a prosecution for perjury."

Mason turned to the witness and said, "Let's try telling the truth, for a change, Mrs. Lacey. When Mr. Drake, Lieutenant Tragg and I called on you on Friday, the thirteenth, you didn't know one thing about what had actually happened the night before, except that Scott Shelby was supposed to have been murdered. But when we talked, and more particularly when we showed you the wet blanket and the shoes in your garage, you suddenly realized what must have happened.

"Your boy friend was there, and he was in a spot. He isn't a fast thinker. You are. You loved him, but he had never

235

proposed marriage and never intended to do so. You saw your chance. You made up a story out of whole cloth to account for the wet blanket and the shoes, and you were clever enough to demand as a price of your cooperation that Mr. Lacey marry you.

"The proposal of marriage didn't take place in your office as you have said. It didn't take place the day before. It took place there in the apartment right under our noses. *You* were the one who made it. And you made it in such a way that Arthur Lacey either had to stand a rap for murder, or confirm your story, which included a proposal of marriage.

"That was why he was reticent at first, that was why he didn't chime in with corroborating details until he realized fully that you had given him his only chance to get out, and that the price of your cooperation was marriage.

"And you very neatly made him go through with that marriage because a wife can't be forced to testify against her husband, and you knew that and he knew it, so he went ahead and married you—*after* you'd gone out and taken these picnic pictures, which you did as soon as you got rid of Sergeant Dorset. Isn't that right?"

The witness made no answer.

Mason extended the tube of lead Della Street had picked up at the picnic grounds to Mrs. Lacey. "Did you ever see this before, Mrs. Lacey?"

"No."

Attica said, "What's a sinker got to do with all this business anyway?"

Mason said, "I don't think it's a sinker. You'll notice it's a lead tube two and nine-sixteenths inches in length and around sixty-one hundredths of an inch in diameter. In other words, as I remember my ballistics, that is just the size to fit the bore of a sixteen gauge shotgun. And now, if you will notice," Mason said, taking a .38 caliber shell from his pocket, "I will insert a .38 caliber shell in the inside of this lead ring or tube and you will see that it fits perfectly, settles right in snug up against the lead. Now with this device, Mrs. Lacey, you could fire a shell through a revolver into a tub of water, recover the bullet, crimp it back in a fresh shell whose

236

own bullet had been removed, place that shell in this adapter, put the adapter in a sixteen gauge shotgun, pull the trigger, and discharge a bullet which has no marking of rifling or barrel scratches other than those which were imparted to it by the .38 caliber pistol from which it had been originally fired. The bullet would have a tendency to wobble or keyhole and it wouldn't have the power or the penetration that a bullet would have which had been fired from a revolver barrel because the gases of combustion would slip on past the bullet in the barrel of the shotgun. But at short ranges it would nevertheless be fairly effective. Incidentally, if you're interested, Mr. Attica, you'll find, in the excellent work on *Forensic Chemistry and Scientific Criminal Investigation* by A. Lucas, a discussion of the Dickman murder case in which two different caliber bullets were shot from the same gun by the use of a paper wrapping or adapter. And Smith and Glaister, in their book entitled *Recent Advances in Forensic Medicine*, state that 'the projectile may be much smaller in caliber than the weapon and still have been fired from it; for example the 0.32 inch bullet may be fired from a 0.38 inch weapon if it is wrapped in sufficient paper to grip the barrel.' This probably occurred in the Dickman case in which the presence of bullets of two different calibers in the body of the victim led to the belief that two different weapons had been used.

"And just to make a good job of it," Mason went on, smiling at the embarrassed attorney, "you'll find that in the very recent book entitled *Homicide Investigation* by Le-Moine Snyder, the statement is made that anyone considering the examination of bullets must take into consideration the fact that there are adapters used for firing rifle bullets from a shotgun. And I think that will conclude my deposition, unless the witness cares to make some statement."

Attica said to his client, "This has been a great strain, my dear. Mr. Mason's examination has been *most* ruthless. But, if you have any explanation, you had better make it now."

She shook her head.

"It's quite apparent," Attica said, "that this witness is a sick woman."

"It's equally apparent," Mason snapped, "what made her sick."

"I am not going to let her continue with this deposition," Attica said. "That's all, my dear."

One of the newspaper reporters tipped over a chair as he jumped to his feet. Both of them made for the door in a run.

"Who are those people?" Attica asked, frowning at the two men.

"A couple of newspaper reporters I invited to be present," Mason said.

"Oh my God!" Attica exclaimed and slumped back into his chair.

Chapter 23

The sun on the river was warm and balmy. Deck awnings were spread out over the reclining chairs on Benton's yacht, but Della Street would have none of the shade. Attired in a playsuit, she had moved her chair out to the sunlight and was leaning back with her ankles crossed on the teakwood rail, soaking up the sunlight.

Mason, more comfortably settled in the shade was at ease in one of those reclining deck chairs which furnish support for the legs and are conducive to long hours of lazy tranquillity in the open air.

So completely relaxed was he that he didn't even bother to go to the rail when he heard the sound of a launch approaching the yacht. Not until Parker Benton came strolling along the deck with the Sunday newspapers under his arm, did Mason show any interest.

Benton said, "I had the launch go over to that little town for the newspapers, Mason. Thought you'd like to see them."

"Go ahead," Mason said. "I'll wait until you've finished with them. I don't want to deprive you of . . ."

"It's all right," Benton interrupted, "I bought half a dozen copies of each of the papers. You see, I'm going to keep a scrapbook."

Mason smiled, reached for the newspapers, said, "What have you found out about Shelby? He must have been aboard the yacht before."

Benton shook his head, said, "I'd been intending to tell you about that. But, you looked so comfortable that I thought I'd wait until I brought you the papers. When you told me last night that Shelby must have been aboard the yacht before, I felt absolutely confident you were mistaken; that the night of the twelfth was the first time he'd ever been aboard."

"The plans Shelby made showed more than a superficial familiarity with the yacht," Mason said positively. "Somewhere, somehow, he *must* have been aboard. The knowledge that there were *two* telephone systems and that he could trap his wife by telephoning from a cabin, the . . ."

Benton smilingly interrupted. "I'm afraid, for once, Mr. Mason, you overlooked something."

"What?"

"I don't think Shelby had ever been aboard the yacht but Lacey had. Remember that Lacey was working hand in glove with Shelby. Remember also, that Lacey was a professional cook. I find, on looking back over my records, that Arthur Lacey worked aboard as cook for a period of two weeks a year ago, filling in when my regular cook took his two weeks' vacation. Hang it, when I saw the pictures in the paper last night, I thought the man's face was familiar and yet I couldn't place it."

"Oh, oh," Mason said, "*that* accounts for it."

Benton went on, "One of the crew recognized him from his pictures and told me about it just a few minutes ago. Well, here are the papers. Are you comfortable? Like to have something to drink?"

Mason shook his head, said, "Thanks, Benton. All I need is a chance to soak up some of this fresh air and sunshine. The knowledge that there isn't any telephone within four miles and that I won't be interrupted by someone ringing me up to get me involved in another murder case makes for perfect repose."

Benton said, "To my mind, Mason, that's the charm of yachting—and the real lure of this island. Once I get aboard my yacht, I can completely isolate the outside world. Well, go ahead and relax. You certainly have earned it. If there's anything you want, just press the button for the steward."

Parker Benton, showing an understanding for the lawyer's mood, moved away.

"Want to look at the paper?" Mason asked Della Street.

She smiled languidly, shook her head.

Mason bestirred himself, stretched, yawned, unrolled the

Sunday newspapers, said, "I always like to see what they say about a case."

"Anything interesting?" Della Street asked after a few moments.

"I'm just starting in on this story by Drake's friend."

Della Street straightened, "I'd forgotten about that angle. Drake's friend being present at the deposition. What does he say, Chief? Want me to read it out loud?"

"You'll ruin your eyes," Mason told her. "You can't read in the bright sunlight. Stay where you are, Della. I'll read it to you."

Mason straightened out the paper, said, "There are a couple of preliminary paragraphs and then this:

" 'Never has Perry Mason, the master cross-examiner, put on a better exhibition of his skill than at the deposition of Ellen Cushing Lacey. Never has a witness been more confounded, nor her attorney more nonplused.

" 'There was every element of exciting drama in what had happened before, but what happened at that deposition made everything else seem dry as dust. And while one is handing out kudos, one must not overlook Ellen Lacey. Caught finally in a trap which had been set for her by a past master of courtroom strategy, she seemed very bewildered and helpless. But one must not forget that it was this same Ellen Lacey who whisked a murderer right out from under the veteran nose of Lieutenant Tragg with all the deft skill of a conjurer making a rabbit disappear.

" 'Realizing that the man whom she loved had quite apparently made an arrangement with Scott Shelby to aid in his disappearance, she invented a story out of whole cloth which completely fooled the officers. And she pulled this story right out of the thin air. Arthur Lacey, in place of being a jealous suitor, was in fact, a casual trifler with her affections. In place of being almost a stranger to Scott Shelby, he had actually been acquainted with the murdered man for months. It was to Arthur Lacey that Shelby turned when he wished to engineer a scheme by which he would "disappear" leaving his wife faced with a murder charge. It was Arthur Lacey whom Shelby hired to meet him on the river and row him ashore.

It was Arthur Lacey who had wrapped Shelby in a blanket. Arthur Lacey whom Shelby used as a dummy in liquidating his business affairs.

" 'The conspirators almost had their plans upset by the fog which had settled so thickly that Benton had not taken his yacht all the way to the island anchorage as had been intended, but had anchored a few hundred yards downstream. However, Lacey, an expert oarsman, had located the yacht and signaled Shelby that all was ready.

" 'Shelby had already arranged to frame his wife by leaving her with a story to tell which would sound utterly impossible. He had already trapped her into such a position she was about to be accused of having tried to poison him. He had placed arsenic in his own food, even putting a small amount in her food, and then had called a doctor, taking great care to detail such typical symptoms that the doctor would not only give proper treatment, but would strongly urge a report to the police.

" 'So on this fatal night, everything was in readiness. There was only one hitch. There were too many people aboard the yacht and there were no vacant staterooms. Oddly enough, it was the midnight restlessness of Perry Mason that furnished the conspirators their opportunity. The lawyer dressed and went on deck, which gave Shelby the opportunity he wanted. Sneaking into the unlocked stateroom, he telephoned his wife, then rushed to the bow of the boat, where he had already doubled a length of rope so that he could "fall" down into the water, yet fire a gun at the proper time.

" 'The plan worked without a hitch. There was only one thing on which the shrewd Shelby had slipped up. He had juggled his accounts around so no one could tell just what he had and just what he didn't have. He had salted away large sums of cash which he had in a money belt around his middle. He fired the gun, saw that he had caused a general alarm, and then swam down the port side of the yacht, kicking at the hull as he went by. Then he dove, swam under water, came to the surface, floated, and the current washed him right down to where his accomplice was sitting waiting in an

242

anchored rowboat, a small flashlight furnishing a guiding beacon for the swimmer.

" 'As police reconstruct what happened after that, Shelby climbed into the rowboat. Lacey wrapped him in a blanket, rowed him ashore. There he made certain that Shelby had the money in the well filled money belt. All of this time Shelby was chuckling. He had staged a perfect disappearance. His wife was even then being questioned with growing suspicion. Shelby was free to escape his liabilities, to go to a far city and start a new life.

" 'But then the one thing on which Shelby hadn't counted confronted him. Lacey had plans of his own. Since Shelby had so conveniently arranged his own murder, Lacey saw no reason for passing up an opportunity to enrich himself by some forty thousand dollars, which it now seems was the amount that Shelby was carrying in his money belt.

" 'Some days earlier, Lacey had fired a bullet into the water from the .38 with which Mrs. Shelby was to be framed. He had recovered this bullet and put it in another shell. He had previously experimented with his 'adapter' by which he could fire a .38 caliber cartridge from a sixteen gauge shotgun . . . Shelby became suspicious. Lacey tapped him over the head with an oar, shot him in the neck with the bullet he had so carefully saved for just this occasion, then calmly picked the body up in his arms, waded out to where the boat was floating in some eighteen inches of water, deposited the body, sculled out to midstream, dumped the body overboard, and returned to Ellen Cushing's car, which he had 'borrowed' for his 'important appointment.'

" 'He made one mistake after that. He returned the car to the garage. The wet blanket had been thrown on the cushions of the back seat. He intended to dispose of that later. He had taken the precaution of carrying along a change of trousers and dry shoes. He carried his wet trousers up to his apartment with him, but the shoes and blanket he concealed in a corner of the garage, intending to return for them the next morning.

" 'He had committed the perfect crime—thanks to the cooperation of his victim . . . And then, on the next day,

Friday the thirteenth, came retribution. For a moment it must have seemed to Lacey that all was lost, and then the quick wit of Ellen Cushing offered him a way out—at a price.

" 'The interesting thing about the crime is that Lieutenant Tragg actually had the culprit in his hands, actually had the evidence which, properly construed, would have sent the man to the death chamber—and he let himself be talked out of it. For this he is taking a bit of quiet ribbing from his associates in the Homicide detail, a bit of kidding which is relished all the more because it is the first time that his associates have been able to get anything on the capable Lieutenant.' "

Mason looked up at Della Street, grinned. "Imagine how Tragg feels this morning. Remember what he called to me when he drove away from Ellen Cushing's apartment, 'Goodby—Sherlock!' "

Della nodded, smiled, "I'm charitable this morning. I couldn't even feel peeved at Sergeant Dorset."

Mason started browsing through the pages until he came to the classified real estate. He ran down the column dealing with suburban properties, said suddenly, "Right here it is, Della. Listen to this. 'Four hundred acres, marvelous country estate within sixty minutes of the heart of the city, completely isolated, timber, lake fed by spring. Rural relaxation within commuting distance of your city business. Priced for a quick sale at twenty thousand dollars. Ellen Cushing Lacey, real estate.' "

Mason put down the paper. "Della, how about it? We could buy the property in your name."

"Would you," she asked archly, "put the sale through Ellen Cushing Lacey?"

Mason smiled. "I'm afraid that this is a deal on which Mrs. Lacey is going to lose her five per cent commission. When you stop to think how small a time margin there was between our two picnics that Friday! They must have left not over an hour before we arrived. And I wonder just how deep in all this George Attica is. He may have been the one who advised them to rush out with a camera, get some picnic pictures, plant some food refuse and then dash back. Then, of course, he used Lawton Keller as his tool to get Marion

Shelby to fire me. That property has become a spot that's filled with pleasant associations for us, Della. Let's buy it. We could have it for a little hideaway. I could put up a bungalow out under those trees back from the lake. Perhaps some day . . ."

Mason stopped to regard the horizon with dreamy eyes.

Della Street smiled. "Go ahead, Chief," she said. "Even if you are just day dreaming, it's a swell idea."

About the Author

Erle Stanley Gardner is the king of American mystery fiction. A criminal lawyer, he filled his mystery masterpieces with intricate, fascinating, ever-twisting plots. Challenging, clever, and full of surprises, these are whodunits in the best tradition. During his lifetime, Erle Stanley Gardner wrote 146 books, 85 of which feature Perry Mason.

SHREWD and SUSPENSEFUL...
MYSTICAL and MYSTERIOUS

*from the number one
mystery writer of all time*

THE PERRY MASON MYSTERIES

by

ERLE STANLEY GARDNER

TA-165